TEC

COUNTING

TO

INFINITY

OTHER JAKE DIAMOND BOOKS BY J. L. ABRAMO

Catching Water in a Net
Clutching at Straws

J. L. Abramo

COUNTING

TO

INFINITY

THOMAS DUNNE BOOKS

ST. MARTIN'S MINOTAUR

New York

THOMAS DUNNE BOOKS.
An imprint of St. Martin's Press.

COUNTING TO INFINITY. Copyright © 2004 by Joseph L. Abramo, Inc. All rights reserved. Printed in the United States of America. No part of this book may be used or reproduced in any manner whatsoever without written permission except in the case of brief quotations embodied in critical articles or reviews. For information, address St. Martin's Press, 175 Fifth Avenue, New York, N.Y. 10010.

Library of Congress Cataloging-in-Publication Data

Abramo, J. L.
    Counting to infinity / J. L. Abramo.—1st ed.
        p. cm.
    ISBN 0-312-32650-5
    EAN 978-0312-32650-0
        1. Diamond, Jake (Fictitious character)—Fiction. 2. Private investigators—California—San Francisco—Fiction. 3. San Francisco (Calif.)—Fiction. I. Title.

PS3601.B73C68 2004
813'.6—dc22

2004041819

First Edition: August 2004

10 9 8 7 6 5 4 3 2 1

For Charlotte and Fred

As a general rule, people, even
the wicked, are much more naive and
simple-hearted than we suppose.
As we ourselves are, too.
—FYODOR DOSTOYEVSKY,
THE BROTHERS KARAMAZOV

Cast of Characters

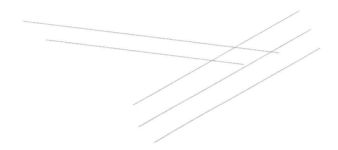

Part One

FLYING

One

THE SCENT OF DEEP-FRIED CALAMARI floated in through my office window like an invitation to triple-bypass surgery. I could almost have tasted the squid if not for the Camel nonfilter dangling from my lip. I was working the Sunday *Examiner* crossword, grasping for a four-letter word for Egyptian goddess. I was sure Darlene would know it, but I was being stubborn. It was well after noon on a Sunday and not a single telephone call. I had vowed that I would hold off ordering lunch until my desk telephone rang at least once. The last time I'd tried that, I hadn't eaten for two days.

When Darlene called out my name from the front room my heart sank.

"Use the telephone," I called back, "while we have one."

The phone rang. The blinking button indicated that it was Darlene. I wanted to call in my food order to Angelo at Molinari's Salumeria two floors below *before* picking up the interoffice line. I got a grip on myself.

"Yes, Darlene," I said.

"Get out here, Jake, before this gorilla trips over his own shoelaces and blows my head off."

The urgency in her voice was convincing.

I pulled open my desk drawer to fetch my .38 police special. I figured it wouldn't take much more than two hours to locate it beneath all of the accumulated debris. Near-empty cigarette packages,

3

partial bottles of antacid, books of matches from every dive in San Francisco, long-expired fast-food restaurant discount coupons.

I closed the drawer.

Truth was, I hadn't fired the .38 in so long it would more than likely have exploded in my hand.

Assuming it even held bullets.

"I'm on my way," I said into the phone receiver.

The line was dead.

"Jake, I'm losing my nerve," Darlene shouted.

"I'm coming," I called, turning up the volume. I clawed my way out of my desk chair. The springs were so rusted that it sat at a perpetual forty-five-degree angle.

"With your hands above your head, Diamond."

The guy had a voice like a wood chipper.

I walked through the connecting door and threw my arms into the air. Darlene sat at her desk with her hands together, fingers interlocked, like a kid in Sunday school. The gorilla with the sawmill voice pointed his arm in my direction and I was looking down the barrel of a handgun so long that it could have been used for a tent pole.

Darlene let out an involuntary sigh when she found herself out of the crosshairs.

"Sit," he growled, indicating the client chair with his free hand.

"You picked the wrong place to come waving that cannon around," I said.

"Why is that?" he asked.

Good question.

I sat.

"You okay?" I asked Darlene.

"Ask me tomorrow," she said.

"So," I said, turning to our first customer of the week at the office of Diamond Investigation, "how can we help you?"

It was then I noticed his free hand wasn't exactly free. He was rolling a pair of metal balls the size of large marbles in his left paw. Either he was brushing up on an audition piece for *The Caine Mutiny Court-Martial,* or we were in really deep shit.

"It's this babe here that you'll be helping, Diamond," he grumbled.

"Did you say 'babe'?" Darlene hissed.

"Easy, Darlene, I'm sure that our guest meant it only in the most general way. Please forgive my rudeness," I said, turning back to the ape, "I haven't thanked you for dropping in or asked your name."

"Here's the deal, Diamond," he snarled. "You come with me to talk with the Boss and nothing gruesome happens to the dame. You try anything funny before we get there and she'll be seeing me again, and she'll like me a lot less the next time."

"I doubt that's possible," said Darlene.

I would have told her to keep quiet but the look on her face scared me more than the barrel of the .44 grazing my chin.

"Oh, it's possible. Extremely possible," he promised.

It was definitely a good time to intervene.

"Sure, pal, let's go see the Boss. Where to?"

"Chicago."

"Put it out of your mind, Kong. It's the middle of winter. There's no football, no baseball, and the wind-chill factor is minus infinity. I wouldn't go to northern Illinois in February if my life depended on it."

"Are you sure?" he said, pulling back the hammer of the sidearm.

"Is the pan-style pizza as good as they say it is?" I said, catching myself checking his shoelaces. "I'm going to need a heavier jacket."

"I've got just the thing down in the car," he said. "Let's go."

I began to rise slowly from the chair, placing my hand on the corner of the desk for balance.

"Darlene," I said, "what's a four-letter word for Egyptian goddess?"

"Isis," she answered.

"Well, kick the dog," I said, trying to make it sound like "Well, I'll be darned."

"What?"

"I said, 'Well, kick the dog.'"

"Oh, Jake."

"Darlene."

She kicked the dog. Tug McGraw yelped and jumped straight up, lifting the desk off the floor. The desk slammed back down, the primate shifted the large gun toward Darlene's feet, and I grabbed the three-hole punch from the desktop and clocked him. He went down to his knees, the .44 squirted out of his hand and landed on the desk, and I snatched it up by the barrel and whacked him across the head again. He went flat on the floor. The two metal balls spilled out of his hand and rolled across the room.

I turned the gun around and pointed it his way.

He wasn't stirring.

Darlene was busy apologizing to the mutt.

"Darlene, do you think you can find something to tie him up with?"

"I'm sorry, boy, Jake made me do it," she was saying, stroking the confused canine's neck with one hand while she reached into her desk drawer with the other.

"Darlene, please."

"Try these," she said, handing me two pairs of handcuffs.

I didn't ask.

I dragged the body over to the wall radiator, cuffed his arms to a leg of the cast-iron eyesore, and cuffed his feet together around another iron leg for good measure.

I rifled through his pockets until I found the wallet.

Then I sat down in the client chair and tried breathing again.

"Should I call 911?" Darlene asked, finally satisfied that she was forgiven, the dog having planted a half-liter gob of drool on her left cheek.

"Give me a minute," I said, placing the gun down and going through the wallet. "Here we go. Ralph T. Battle. This driver's license photo looks like an illustration in a Jane Goodall book. Twenty-seven forty-one Central Avenue, Cicero, Illinois."

"He moved, Jake."

"How could you possibly know that?"

"I just saw him move."

I looked over to Battle, who was slowly coming awake. Even as big as he was, I was convinced that he couldn't budge the radiator.

Well, fairly convinced.

I picked up the gun.

I watched as Battle began to wriggle, then began struggling against his restraints.

"You're going to pay for this, Diamond," he croaked.

Battle was quickly using up his store of well-worn phrases.

I decided to pull out a few of my own.

"Look, Ralph, *here's* the deal. If your boss wants to speak with me, all you had to do was ask nice. How about we start over. The Boss doesn't have to know that we were anything but civil to each other. Let me give him a quick jingle and ask him what he needs."

"Fuck you."

"Glad you got that off your chest, Ralph. I'm not going to Chicago anytime before June. I'm not going to think about how you threatened my associate, because it makes my trigger finger itch. But if you ever refer to her as a babe or a dame again, I'll let her shoot you. And if you don't give me a phone number for your employer in thirty seconds, I'm going to show you what assholes San Francisco cops can be."

"And you won't tell Mr. Lansdale that you got the drop on me?"

Unbelievable.

I had once asked Jimmy Pigeon what he thought was the most surprising thing about private investigation work. He had answered without hesitation: *When you try something stupid and it works.*

"Not a word, Ralph, honest."

Battle spit out the ten-digit number.

"I'm tempted to call collect, Ralph."

"Give me a break, Diamond."

"Fuck you," I said.

I dialed the number. After three rings it was picked up. It was a woman's voice. She sounded like a babe.

"Mr. Lansdale, please."

"May I ask who is calling?"

"Go ahead," I said.

"Huh?" she said.

"Just joking," I said, wasting a few more words. "Tell him it's Jake Diamond."

"Hold just a sec, Jake," she said, stretching my name into two syllables.

I held.

Ralph squirmed.

Darlene fidgeted.

Tug McGraw disappeared back to his stronghold beneath the desk.

"Is that calamari frying?" Ralph said.

"Jesus," Darlene said.

"Mr. Diamond," the tenor voice on the Chicago end of the line said, "it's good of you to call."

"Mr. Battle put it so nicely I could hardly resist. Unfortunately, I'll have to pass on the invite to the Windy City. I've given up air travel for Lent."

"How about I come to see you?" Lansdale asked.

"These telephones are a pretty neat invention, Mr. Lansdale," I said. "Seems like a pity not to take full advantage of the technology."

I was already getting tired of hearing myself speak.

"I need to talk with you face-to-face, Mr. Diamond. I'll be happy to come to you if it's necessary. Or perhaps you might consider giving up bungee jumping instead, just until Easter of course, and hop a jet. I'll make it worth your while."

Battle was distracting me with his attempts to tear the radiator out of the wall.

All I could think of was getting him as far away from Darlene as possible, as soon as conceivable.

I decided that Chicago would have to do.

"All right, Mr. Lansdale. I'll come up there. I'll meet you in the airport, we'll chat, and I'll hop the next jet back."

"I was really hoping to take you to dinner, Jake."

"And I appreciate it, but I'm really pressed for time. I have bingo tonight. Could you give me a little clue as to what this is about?"

"Have Ralph call me when he knows your ETA, and I'll see you at O'Hare."

"Speaking of Ralph, you can do me a favor. Tell him what a good egg you think I am and how you would like my journey to be a pleasurable experience."

Battle stopped yanking at the radiator and was hanging on my every word.

"Ralph didn't inconvenience you in any way, did he, Jake?" Lansdale asked, as if he didn't know.

If he kept calling me Jake I was going to shoot myself in the foot.

"Not a bit, Mr. Lansdale," I said.

"Let me speak to him."

"Sure."

I put the gun down on the desk and walked over to hold the receiver to Battle's ear, closing my eyes and silently praying that he wouldn't bite my hand off. He greeted Lansdale with reverence and then listened. He knocked his head against the phone to let me know he was through. I returned the phone to Darlene's desk and asked her if she had a key for the handcuffs.

Sadly, she did.

"Okay, Ralph. I'm going to set you free. You're going to wait for me in the hall and then we can mosey over to Chicago."

After getting back up on his simian legs, Battle reached down to scoop the metal balls off the floor and immediately began working them.

"How about the gun?" he asked.

Darlene sat at her desk, playing with the .44, making us both edgy.

"You won't be needing it, Ralph. I'll donate it to the Museum of Heavy Artillery," I said. "How did you ever get it past airport security in the first place?"

"I didn't carry it with me," he said. "I purchased it after I arrived, at San Francisco International."

"You bought a firearm at the airport?"

"You can find anything at the airport if you know where to look."

"Great, maybe when we get there you can find me a decent cup of coffee for less than four bucks," I said. "Wait in the hall, Ralph."

Ralph wasn't happy, but Lansdale had surely reminded him that he wasn't getting paid to be happy. He walked out into the hall.

"Wow, I never knew you were so tough, Jake," Darlene said when he was out.

"Aw, shucks. It was nothing. Or are you being sarcastic?"

"Absolutely. You're a lunatic. How can you even think about taking a trip with that goon?"

"Thinking has nothing to do with it. Listen, I don't want to keep Ralph waiting. I don't figure him for a high patience threshold.

Find out everything you can about this Lansdale. See if the phone number does any tricks. Give Sonny a call to see what he can do. If all else fails, throw the name at Tony Carlucci. And for heaven's sake, put that gun down."

"If you're not back by midnight I'm calling out the National Guard."

"You do that, pal. Shit, I blew lunch waiting for that damn phone to ring."

"You want a PowerBar?"

"No thanks. I'll grab a Cinnabon at SFI. Does that mutt do anything but sleep?"

"Hardly a thing, unless you kick him real good."

"Wish me luck," I said.

"You need a shrink, Jake," Darlene said.

I could hear Ralph grinding his teeth on the other side of the door.

The mere thought of nearly four hours sitting beside Battle in a closed airplane had *my* teeth chattering.

I stepped into the hall to join him in a two-part harmony.

T W O

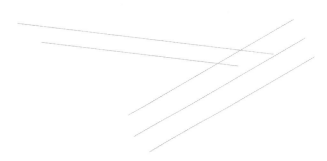

IT'S A SAFE BET THAT somewhere in the world someone is wondering whether you can find a cozy, handsomely appointed meeting room within the confines of Chicago's international airport.

The answer is yes.

I never gave it much thought myself, but there it was. Down a short hallway off Concourse A, looking like the set of an Alistair Cooke PBS series. Complete with a fully stocked bar, Persian rugs, framed reproductions, a huge-screen television showing *Lou Dobbs Moneyline* with the sound muted, leather armchairs, and a working fireplace.

"Make yourself at home," Lansdale said, once Battle had ushered me in.

If the place had been a little closer to the Pacific Ocean, I would have been searching around for a change-of-address form.

I settled into one of the two armchairs.

Between the chairs stood a glass-topped table holding a silver tray covered with tiny sandwiches, crackers, and a mound of foie gras that cost some poor fowl a lot more than an arm and a leg. The bread was ink-jet black, the crusts had been cut off, and the beef spilling from the corners was so rare it made tartare look overdone. The crackers were multigrained, ten or eleven at least. They had the appearance of untanned shoe leather. The chopped liver looked as appetizing as corned beef hash. Granted I wasn't very hungry, and I'd had my fill of goose for the day. The cinnamon roll that I inhaled while dashing to make takeoff was like eating a down comforter.

Lansdale had moved to the bar and was busy determining how much noise he could make clinking ice cubes together.

Battle had placed himself squarely in front of the only door and had taken on the demeanor of a San Quentin prison guard preparing for a breakout. He was clicking his metal balls in tune to Lansdale's ice cube number.

I was way out of my element.

"How do you take your Dickel, Jake?" Lansdale called from across the room.

All was not lost.

The man had done his homework.

I was about to say *Shaken not stirred,* but Battle was giving me a glare that said one more wisecrack and I'd be added to the pâté.

"Straight up," I said.

Lansdale walked over and handed me a glass.

He reached out for a handshake.

"Jonathan Maximilian Lansdale," he said, giving my mitt a healthy squeeze. "Good to finally meet you."

"Likewise, Mr. Lansdale," I said.

It was all I could muster up.

"Call me Max," he said, snatching a cracker as he sat.

I caught a look from Ralph Battle that said *Don't you dare.*

I was tired and bored, so I wanted to get the small talk out of the way as quickly as possible.

"How did you manage the digs, Max, on such short notice?"

"Let's just say that I have friends in high places, Jake."

I guessed he wasn't talking about the air traffic control tower.

"So, what can I do for you?" I asked, moving right along.

"I'm looking for a man," he said.

"I don't really know the town, Max," I said. "I'd be lucky if I could find the Sears Tower."

"I have reason to believe that the man is in San Francisco."

"Why didn't you say so when I had you on the phone? I could have brought you the white pages."

"Mr. Diamond, you're very clever, but we're wasting time. And you have a bingo game to get to. Can you concentrate, or do you need Ralph to help you to focus?"

"Mr. Lansdale, I came up here to get Ralph out of San Francisco because the zoo is already heavily overpopulated. I'm prepared to hear you out, but don't threaten me. I happen to be a favorite of the Carlucci family."

"John and Tony?" he said.

"Precisely."

"Johnny Boy is locked up in Quentin for the next lifetime or two and his brother Tony is a pimp. You're going to do more than hear me out, Mr. Diamond."

Oops.

I couldn't tell if he was bluffing, but I knew that I was. And Lansdale was right, we were wasting time.

I decided on the better-safe-than-sorry approach.

"I'm all ears," I said.

It went something like this.

Eight years earlier, two men walked into the law office of Lansdale and Sons on South Wacker in downtown Chicago. While one babysat the receptionist, the second entered the private office of Randolph Lansdale, Max Lansdale's law partner and older brother.

A few minutes later he was back out and the two men left as quickly as they had come in. The receptionist buzzed the elder Lansdale and got no response. She then entered the office and found Randolph Lansdale slumped in his chair with a bullet hole in his right temple. The woman's screams brought Max Lansdale in from the adjoining room.

"I think you can imagine what a horrible discovery it was," said Lansdale.

It was difficult to imagine.

I tried to imagine my own brother, Abe, with a bullet hole between the eyes, but it didn't work. It clashed too much with his thick, black-framed Sergeant Bilko eyeglasses.

I thought about Jimmy Pigeon's murder. At the time I had

spent all my energies trying to discover who killed Jimmy and not a moment trying to imagine how his lifeless body had looked. And I wasn't about to try conjuring it up now.

I did my best to empathize with Lansdale.

"I can imagine," I said.

"Randolph had just returned from a business and sightseeing trip to Los Angeles a few days earlier. The pictures he took while he was away were still in his camera. I had the roll of film developed, and our receptionist identified the man who murdered my brother from one of the photos."

"Pardon the interruption, Mr. Lansdale," I said, "but if I'm following correctly, this happened six years ago and is perhaps tied to your brother's visit to LA. I'm not quite sure how you expect I can help you."

"I'm coming around to it, Jake," Lansdale said, shooting a glance over to Battle. "Do you think you can bear with me a while longer?"

I stole a look at Battle also.

"Absolutely," I said.

"I hired a well-regarded private investigator from the Los Angeles area," he continued. "His report came back in less than a week. The man in the photograph was Harrison Chandler, and Harrison Chandler was no longer among the living."

"Good news," I said, more like a question.

"Not exactly. I remained very interested in identifying the second man. All I could discover was that it could possibly have been someone known as Joe Clams, out of San Francisco, who ran around with Chandler. I've been trying to locate such a person since the day my brother died, with no success. And I went through a lot of men and women in your business to get nowhere."

The reference to San Francisco helped me to relate, but not enough to understand even vaguely what the hell *I* was doing in Chicago.

I chose not to mention it.

"No other names came up for the second man?" I asked.

"None. Clams was it," he answered.

Joe Clams. I could see where the phone book I'd offered to bring along might not have done Lansdale much good.

"Okay," I said, "I'm with you."

"Two days ago I heard from one of the many investigators I've dealt with during the past eight years, Stan Riddle—perhaps you know him?"

I knew Riddle all right, from back in the days working with Jimmy Pigeon in Santa Monica. The guy played at being a private investigator as if it were a movie role with a script written by Nora Ephron.

"And Riddle recommended you call on me?"

"No," Lansdale said. "May I continue?"

"Please do," I said.

"Riddle told me that he had spotted Harrison Chandler at Venice Beach, very much alive. So I'm hoping that you can help me locate Chandler, and with him this Joe Clams character," said Lansdale. "And that, Mr. Diamond, is the reason I have invited you here."

Voilà.

Nearly six hours since Ralph Battle had stormed into my office and I finally discovered what Jonathan Maximilian Lansdale was after.

The problem was that I still had no idea *why me*.

And the big problem was that I had no idea how to ask.

"Now, you are probably wondering why I chose you, Jake," Lansdale said.

"I'm curious, yes," I said.

I waited for his response, knowing it might solve one little uncertainty and absolutely positive it would fall far short of getting me off the hook.

"If you recall," said Lansdale, "I mentioned that an investigator whom I hired out of Los Angeles reported to me that Harrison Chandler was deceased."

I wasn't sure if it was a question, so I kept waiting.

"The man was apparently mistaken or he purposely lied to me. Since that man himself has since passed away, and since it is my understanding that you were a close associate and confidant, I feel that you deserve to inherit the responsibility that he failed so terribly to honor."

I really didn't have to ask, but sometimes when you wish hard enough the thing that you know is true might simply be a bad dream.

"It was Jimmy Pigeon," I said.

"Yes, it was," said Lansdale.

I placed my drinking glass on the table.

I slowly rose from my chair.

"I can't help you, Mr. Lansdale," I said, "and I really do need to be getting back to San Francisco."

"Sit down, Mr. Diamond," he said calmly. "You're not going anywhere quite yet, and you will help me."

"I can't help you," I repeated.

I began to turn toward the door when a cannonball, which had to be Ralph Battle's fist, struck me in the back between the shoulder blades and knocked me straight down to the floor. My right elbow hit the edge of the food tray, flipping it end over end into the air.

The pâté did a fine job of turning a Norman Rockwell on the wall behind Lansdale into a Jackson Pollock.

I tried to rise, but my neck was wedged between the Persian rug and Ralph Battle's shoe.

"Sorry about that, Mr. Diamond," Lansdale said from somewhere above me. "I believe that Ralph is still upset about what happened back at your office."

I guess Battle kept no secrets from the Boss after all.

"If you'll promise to listen politely for a short while longer, I'll explain why I'm so convinced that you will feel compelled to work with me on this. I can ask Ralph to allow you to resume your seat, I can freshen up your drink, and we can have you out of here and back to San Francisco in no time."

I was forced to speak out of the corner of my mouth. A piece of horsehide that tried to pass as a food snack was poking me in the eye. I wanted to tell Lansdale to drop dead. I wanted to tell Battle that if he didn't get his Florsheim wingtip oxford off me I would bludgeon him to death with a wheat cracker. I wanted to ask them what the fuck they thought they were going to do if I said no. I realized that that was exactly what Lansdale was itching to tell me.

"I'll listen," I managed to squeak out.

"Now, isn't this a lot better?" Lansdale said when I was once

16

again seated across from him with a fresh bourbon in my hand.

"Let's get on with it, Mr. Lansdale, sir," I said in my most polite voice.

I took a long drink. It was a tremendous challenge due to a severe limitation of neck motor ability.

"If you agree to assist me, and do a conscientious job, I will reward you handsomely. If you decline my offer, or approach the assignment with less than due diligence, I will make your life a living hell."

Lansdale didn't mince words. He was a man with a mission. I was waiting for the part about how the tape would self-destruct in thirty seconds.

I tried to guess what Lansdale felt it would take to turn my life upside down. "What exactly are you threatening, Mr. Lansdale?" I asked, as much as I didn't want to hear it.

"I am threatening the well-being of Darlene Roman and Sally French," he answered.

My well-loved associate.

And my ex-wife, current steady date.

Lansdale had it pretty effectively covered.

All I could think about was how much I wished he would die, instantly.

"Can you tell me something about the purpose of your brother's visit to Los Angeles just before he died?" I asked, fighting to keep the tremble in my chest out of my voice. "The business end of the trip. I believe that I can guess about the sightseeing part."

I was trying to avoid any talk of Disneyland.

"You ask good questions, Mr. Diamond."

"It's my forte. If you want someone who can't ask a good question, get Larry King."

"I really can't say much concerning the nature of Randolph's business," Lansdale said. "And Jake, I really wouldn't bother about it if I were you."

I was being shoved hard against a locked door and being warned not to look for the key. I guess it just wasn't my day.

My next two good questions would have been:

Why do you think your brother had a photo of his assassin in the camera?

Do you still have the photograph?

Intuition told me that I already knew how Lansdale would answer.

"I'll do my best to locate Harrison Chandler, Mr. Lansdale," I said.

"And Joe Clams."

"Yes. May I go now?"

"Certainly, Jake. Here is a little something to get you started," Lansdale said, pulling out a wad of cash from his pocket and peeling off ten C-notes.

As much as I could use the cash, Lansdale was the last person in the world I wanted to be retained by.

"I would prefer billing you, Mr. Lansdale, if that's okay."

"Whatever," he said. "Can I have Ralph escort you to your plane?"

"No, thank you, I'll manage. No offense to Mr. Battle."

"Fine, then. I look forward to hearing from you, Jake. Have a good evening."

"You do the same," I said, taking the long way around Ralph Battle and heading for the exit.

"And, Jake."

"Yes, Mr. Lansdale?" I said, without turning or slowing my pace.

"Thank you so much for dropping by."

"Don't mention it," I said.

And then I was in the corridor and rushing to the concourse and then racing to the gate.

Twenty minutes later I was in my seat on the jet, rolling down the runway for takeoff.

When the flight attendant kindly asked if I was okay, I realized that my hands were shaking.

I was back in my apartment on Fillmore Street just before midnight and gave Darlene a ring, telling her to call off the National Guard and insisting that she would have to wait until morning for details.

"Don't you want to hear what I learned about Max Lansdale?" Darlene asked.

"In the morning," I answered.

As tired as I was, I was afraid to go to bed.

I realized that the stabbing pain I felt in my entire upper body was nothing compared to how it was going to feel after sleeping on it.

So I did what I usually did when I was too tired, too wired, or too scared to go to sleep.

I took my cigarettes, the ashtray, the bottle of bourbon, and the paperback novel I was currently reading into the bedroom.

I thought about calling my mother, calling Sally, calling Joey Russo, calling Lieutenant Lopez of the SFPD. But I knew after calling Darlene that I wasn't prepared to talk to anyone about the mountain of trouble I was in.

I might have been able to talk it out with my dear friend, former employer, and mentor.

But Jimmy Pigeon was not available.

Three

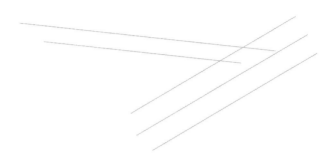

I SLEPT LATE.

I could hardly move.

The place between my shoulder blades where Battle had pounded me felt like a railroad tunnel. My neck felt as if it had been used for a doormat. Come to think of it, it had been. But that didn't explain the paralysis in my legs. I hadn't felt as reluctant to get out of bed since the morning of my SAT exams.

I found the alarm clock on the floor beside the bed. It took me forever to pull it up by the cord and check the time. It was well past 10 a.m.

I wondered why Darlene hadn't called eight or nine times already to ask when I thought I might be dropping in to work, until I found the telephone receiver off the hook. I reeled it in and managed to place it in its cradle. The phone rang immediately.

"Give me an hour, Darlene," I said, before the handset dropped out of my hand and bounced off the end table.

I braved it over to the bathroom and looked into the mirror. I needed a shave badly. It would be tricky with no head movement, even if I could somehow work my arm up high enough.

I decided to come back to it and staggered into the shower. It was basically a quick rinse because I couldn't hang on to the bar of soap. It was impossible to towel dry my hair, let alone get a comb up there. I struggled into a suit, vest no jacket, didn't consider a necktie, slipped into an overcoat, and hobbled down to the street.

I ruled against attempting to drive and tried hailing a cab. Four taxis flew by without slowing. I couldn't blame the drivers; I was a very scary sight. The guy that finally picked me up had no excuse not to stop, since he looked considerably worse than I did.

"What's with the Fred Munster impersonation, Jake?" said Darlene when I walked into the office at eleven.

Bless her little heart.

"Tell me about Lansdale," I said, painfully lowering myself into the client chair.

"He's big trouble," Darlene said.

"Tell me something I don't know, Darlene."

"Your vest wasn't made to be reversible."

Fifteen minutes later Darlene had my coat off, the vest turned right side out, and my shirt rebuttoned so the bottoms of the tail would meet, and had me back in the chair with Tug McGraw's sleeping pillow propped behind my back.

The dog wasn't happy.

"I did a little research on the Internet last night," Darlene began. "I'll explain how the Internet works some other time."

And she told me all she had learned about Max Lansdale.

Max's father was Simon Lansdale, who for nearly fifty years had been one of the most respected and feared members of the Chicago legal community. Respected by those who for a very hefty sum were cleared of criminal charges, whether innocent or guilty, by way of his courtroom acumen and his influence on the street. Feared by those who, when careers hinged upon winning high-profile cases, found themselves up against the lawyer who didn't know how to lose.

Simon was only twenty-one years old, and still in law school at the University of Chicago, when a summer apprenticeship had him sitting at the defense table during the Al Capone tax evasion trial in 1931. Simon Lansdale was young enough to be spared the displeasure that Capone violently displayed toward his counsel after the prison sentencing.

At the same time, Lansdale was mature enough to understand that he was in the right place at the right moment.

Simon completed his law studies with one eye in his textbooks and the other on the realignment of Chicago's power structure, political and otherwise.

Simon Lansdale had ambition.

Legend had it that a case forcing him to work late in the office of one of the city's largest law firms in late July of 1934 caused Simon Lansdale to miss an appointment to join John Dillinger for a movie at the Biograph Theater.

By 1940, at the age of thirty, Lansdale had opened his own shop, Lansdale and Sons. It would be six years before he would slow down enough to find time to stand at an altar, let alone think about male children and their prospective vocations.

When Simon Lansdale finally decided it was time to start a family, he thought mostly in terms of alliances when shopping for a bride. After due consideration as to the direction of Chicago's future, Simon courted and then married a niece of Sam Giancana. Giancana had started in the Capone organization running guns as a teen, and with Scarface in prison, Sammy "Momo" Giancana was systematically working his way to the top.

And Simon Lansdale liked heights.

"Take a look at this," Darlene said. "I took it off one of the Web sites."

She handed me a page with a photo she had run off her computer printer.

"Is that Joe Kennedy?" I asked.

"Chicago. Summer of 1960. Drumming up support for his son's bid for the presidency. The gentleman standing shoulder to shoulder with Kennedy wearing a matching smile was Simon Lansdale."

If I had to describe Simon Lansdale in two words they would have to be *dapper* and *confident*.

"Sam Giancana was shot to death in 1975. One bullet in the head and five in the mouth while in bed. Simon Lansdale took it as an omen, a strong suggestion to put distance between himself and his most unsavory clients. By that time, Jonathan and Randolph Lansdale were working for their father in the law firm," Darlene said. "Simon decided he would prefer a less dangerous work environment for his sons to inherit."

"Very considerate," I said.

"Simon cleaned up his act. He did such a good job of making the law practice totally legitimate that he succeeded in dying peacefully in his sleep at the ripe old age of eighty-five. Randolph, by virtue of being the oldest son, took over as chief mouthpiece for the firm. At least until three months later, when he stopped a bullet with his head."

"And you got all this off the Internet?"

"There was much more. I gave you the Cliff's Notes version."

"Any mention of someone named Harrison Chandler?" I asked.

"Not that I recall, but I can go back and look for it."

"What made you say earlier that Max Lansdale was big trouble?"

"You mean other than the way you look?" Darlene said. "I borrowed the turn of phrase from Tony Carlucci."

"Carlucci said that Lansdale was big trouble?"

"High praise coming from Tony, don't you think?" she said.

"Did Tony say anything else?"

"He said that if you wanted more you could visit him at the restaurant."

Terrific.

"Meanwhile, I couldn't reach Sonny," Darlene reported. "Joey, Angela, Sonny, and Connie are doing two weeks at the Russos' condo in St. Martin. They left yesterday morning, won't be back until Sunday after next."

"How do you know?" I asked.

I certainly didn't know.

"I called Joey's place and Vinnie Strings answered the telephone. At first I thought I had misdialed, but then I remembered that I went through a session with a hypnotist to purge Vinnie's phone number from my consciousness. He's house-sitting. Joey offered him five hundred dollars and all the food he could eat if he could succeed in keeping Angela's basil plants alive."

"That's the first good news I've heard in twenty-four hours," I said. "At least Strings won't be able to follow me down to Los Angeles."

"What's in LA?" Darlene asked.

"I need to talk to a private dick named Stan Riddle."

"I thought you hated the term 'private dick,' Jake."

"Unfortunately, sometimes it's appropriate."

"How about taking me along," said Darlene. "You could use some help walking."

I thought about Lansdale's threats. Maybe keeping Darlene close wasn't a bad idea. I couldn't bring myself to tell her about the danger she could be in just for being someone I cared about. Not to mention that I had no idea about how in the world I was going to broach the subject with Sally French.

I decided to put it on hold until I caught up with Stan Riddle.

For the time being, I took Darlene up on her offer to join me.

After all, it wasn't as if the office telephone was ringing off the hook.

"Sure, why not," I said. "I'll give Willie Dogtail a call and see if he can put us up at his house on the beach. Riddle works out of Santa Monica; maybe we can avoid Los Angeles entirely."

"I might want to run into the city and surprise Lenny. He's down there for a Gatorade commercial."

L. L. Bruno was Darlene's boyfriend, an offensive lineman for the 49ers.

"Great, we can drive down in the Impala," I said. "I have a few calls to make, maybe some people to see. Do you mind leaving tonight? We can be down there in the morning."

"Fine with me," Darlene said. "Do you hear that, boy? We're going on a road trip with Uncle Jake."

Tug McGraw peeked out from under the desk. As usual I had forgotten that the dog existed.

I gave them both a goofy smile, painfully lifted myself out of the chair, and baby-stepped my way to my cubbyhole in back to try reaching Willie Dogtail.

Willie Dogtail was a full-blooded Sioux, a friend from the old days with Jimmy Pigeon in Southern California. Willie made his living selling authentic Native American artifacts, which his mother and her sisters wove or molded or painted or carved and shipped down to him from South Dakota. Willie Dogtail took hospitality very seriously. His door was always open.

Willie answered his phone on the fifth ring. He was out of breath.

"Dogtail's Inn," he said, "no reservation needed."

"Willie, it's Jake Diamond."

"Hey, compadre, how's your tomahawk hanging?" Willie wheezed.

"Been out jogging on the beach, Willie?"

"Are you kidding, Jake. You know I don't run unless someone's chasing me. I was out back working on the cinder-block addition," he said. "What's up? I haven't had any smoke signals from you in ages."

"Darlene and I are heading down your way for a day or two; I was hoping you could put us up."

"You shacking up with your trusty assistant, Jake?"

"Don't be ridiculous."

"I was trying to be envious," Willie said, "and you know you don't have to ask, Jake. Mi tepee, su tepee. Sorry I'll miss you, though, unless you're calling from Ventura."

"Oh?"

"I'm out of here in an hour, heading down to see my little señorita in Guadalajara," Willie said. "You remember where I keep the house key?"

"In the front-door lock?"

"Make yourself at home, Kemosabe. There's some choice buffalo jerky in the cabinet above the stove, next to what's left of the bottle of Dickel from your last visit."

"Thanks, Willie."

"De nada, Wyatt. Give me a little more warning next time and I'll throw a bash. What's the occasion, anyhow?"

"I have to see a guy named Stan Riddle," I answered. "Happen to know him?"

"To my dismay, pardner. He's real well known in these here parts for leaving messes around for all us luckless pedestrians to step in. I'd ask why in the name of Sitting Bull you'd want to get anywhere near the clown except I'm running late."

I thought of asking Willie if he knew anything about Harrison Chandler but decided to let him go.

"Okay, Willie, I'll let you go. Thanks again."

"You bet. Later, paleface."

I spent the remainder of the afternoon on the phone, either pacing the room as much as the cord would allow or sitting on the edge of my desk. I knew that if I sat down in my chair it would take a come-along to hoist me out of it.

Tom Romano was a fellow San Francisco private investigator who had been in the business a lot longer than I had. I had met Romano three years earlier at a Holiday Inn cocktail lounge. I'd been hired by a woman who suspected her spouse of infidelity, and I'd followed her husband to the hotel. He entered the lounge, walked over to a booth, and greeted the redhead sitting there with a lusty kiss. I took a seat at the bar and watched as they worked on their gin and tonics.

As I nursed my own drink, I noticed a bearded guy at the bar who seemed to be as interested in the couple in the booth as I was. And I soon realized he was more than a little interested in me also. When the couple finally rose to leave the booth, the beard and I were so busy observing each other that we almost missed their exit.

I turned away from him, made a theatrical event out of lighting a cigarette, and watched from the corner of my eye as he took off after the couple. I crushed the Camel into an ashtray and headed out to the hotel lobby.

I caught sight of the couple getting into an elevator and then saw the beard at the check-in counter slipping the clerk some cash. Then he walked straight over to me.

"Room 1416," he said. "You owe me ten bucks."

"Excuse me?"

"Tom Romano, TomRom Detective Agency. I'm following the redhead. She's married to the poor sap who hired me. I'm guessing that you're here on behalf of her boyfriend's wife. The room number cost me twenty, I figure you owe me ten."

He put out his hand; I went for my wallet.

"Forget the dough," he said, grinning; "professional courtesy."

"Jake Diamond," I said, accepting the handshake.

"Didn't you work with Jimmy Pigeon down in Santa Monica?"

"Yes I did."

"Good to meet you. I was a big Jimmy Pigeon fan," Romano said. "How about I let you buy me a scotch and soda."

"Sure."

"I'll meet you at the bar," he said. "I need to call my client and tell him where his wife is. You might want to call and break the news to your client. We can have a drink and wait to see the fireworks when they both show up here. Then we can remind each other about how much we hate domestic-treason cases."

Tom and I had been buddies ever since.

After my call to Willie Dogtail, I gave Romano a ring. As I waited for his assistant to get him to the phone, I tried to stretch my aching neck. I slowly leaned my head back and moved my chin in small clockwise circles. The sound it made was like popcorn in a microwave.

"Jake," Tom said, "hope you're not calling to cancel Thursday night."

Tom, Ira Fennessy, and I played pinochle on the first and third Thursday every month. Fennessy was another PI. The game was like group therapy.

"Thursday looks good," I said. "I should be back from Los Angeles well before the first hand."

"What's in LA?"

"I need to see Stan Riddle."

"Jake, not for anything," Tom said, "but if you're that hard up for things to do, you might want to consider taking up needlepoint."

"Does the name Harrison Chandler mean anything to you, Tom?" I asked.

"Sure. He was a legend in the business."

"The PI business?"

"There must be thousands of private investigators who have worked LA, but aside from fictional characters there were only two who were worthy of respect. One was Jimmy Pigeon. The other was Harry Chandler," Tom said. "I can't believe you never heard tell of him; Jimmy and Harry were like a mutual admiration society."

"It must have been before my time with Jimmy," I said. "I understand Chandler checked out eight years ago or so. Do you know the details?"

"Not really. It was sketchy. Something to do with a case that Harry was working and a woman he wasn't supposed to be seeing. Someone planted a bomb in Harry's place in Westwood, killed them both."

"Chandler and the woman?"

"Boom."

"Who was she?"

"Couldn't tell you. All we heard up here was that Harry had met her in Chicago and that maybe someone wasn't too happy to find her in Los Angeles with Chandler. I'm guessing Jimmy may have known more about it," Tom said, "but not much help there. What's Stan Riddle got to do with it?"

"Riddle's been claiming that Harrison Chandler is alive," I said.

"Not a chance. Who is he trying to sell that fairy tale to?"

"A scary attorney named Lansdale. And Lansdale hired me to check it out."

"Don't know the name, and I know every mouthpiece in Northern California."

"This nightmare is in Chicago," I said.

"Chicago," Tom said. "Coincidence?"

"I don't believe in them, Tom, any more than you do."

"Why take the case, Jake?"

"At the moment I don't have much of a choice," I said, "and I could use a favor."

"Sure, Jake, ask away."

"Could you keep an eye on Sally while I'm down south?"

"Is this Midwest fuck threatening to hurt Sally?"

"He mentioned it, and I don't know if the man is as dangerous as he seems to think he is. I'd feel better if someone was paying attention."

"No problem, Jake, I've got you covered. Anything else I can do, don't hesitate."

"Thanks, Tom. I'll call when I get back."

"Jake."

"Yeah."

"You might want to look up Ray Boyle while you're down there."

"Ray and I don't exactly get along, Tom. I work hard at avoiding him."

Ray Boyle was an LAPD homicide detective who had often referred to me in terms usually reserved for a discussion of hemorrhoids.

"You may want to make an exception this time. Boyle was the primary investigator on the bombing incident that I mentioned earlier."

"Thanks for the tip, Tom. Maybe I will. Talk to you in a few days."

The thought of having to deal with Ray Boyle had the tiny vertebrae in my neck popping again.

On the up side, it made a chat with Lieutenant Laura Lopez of the San Francisco Police Department a bit less undesirable.

On top of that, I wanted to put off calling Vinnie Strings for as long as humanly possible, and I thought that a reasonable amount of walking could help work out some of the kinks in my upper extremities.

So I decided to take a stroll to visit Lopez.

"When was the last time you ate something?" Darlene asked as I passed through the front room.

"I don't know if I could chew. I'm off to see the lieutenant."

"Why don't you pick up a couple of smoothies from the Juice Barn on your way back?" Darlene suggested. "Make mine a banana-kiwi."

"Do they do a sausage and pepper?"

Tug McGraw peeked out from under the desk, his ears straight up, looking at Darlene as if he were listening for an affirmative.

As much as the mutt ignored me, when it came to certain subjects we shared a strange, unambiguous understanding.

Darlene stayed out of it.

McGraw looked to me, I gave him a shrug that cost me no small amount of pain, and I headed out for the Vallejo Street Police Station.

F o u r

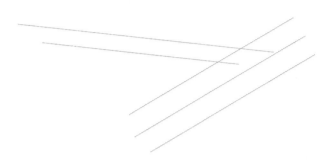

D ARLENE HAD REMINDED ME OF how hungry I was. When I made it down to the street I was in front of the door to Molinari's Salumeria and couldn't come up with an excuse not to go in. There were plenty of excuses; I just couldn't come up with one in time.

"What happened to you yesterday, Jake?" Angelo Verdi asked, in the way of a greeting. "I saved an order of calamari for you all day. I wound up having to take it home with me for dinner."

I decided to try jumping right past it. Maybe he would forget he asked. I needed something of sustenance that I could digest with minimum effort.

"What do you have for soup today, Angelo?" I asked.

"I've got a beautiful chicken soup, Jake. Huge chunks of white meat, crisp celery, crunchy carrots, and al dente orzo."

"Think you could strain out the big stuff and give me a cup of the liquid?"

"I could do that, Jake. But you'll be forcing me to go to the confessional on Sunday to atone for the sin."

"I'm having trouble chewing and swallowing, Angelo. I'll give you a note for Father Conti."

Angelo did the deed with a mesh strainer, filling a large to-go coffee cup with hot chicken broth.

"Angelo," I said, not thinking, "ever hear of a guy called Joe Clams?"

"There was a guy they called Joey Crab, had the newsstand down on Stockton and Fallon. Joey lost one of his paws in Korea and the VA fixed him up with one of those mechanical hands, worked like a vise grip. He got loaded on Thunderbird one night and spray-painted the thing red. Looked like an Alaskan king claw."

I thanked him for the soup and wondered if I would ever learn.

I was told that I would find Lieutenant Lopez in her office on the second floor. Her door was open but I had to tap on the glass a few times to get her to look up from the book she was reading.

"Is that the latest Oprah selection?" I asked.

Lopez held the book up just long enough for me to read the cover: *Deadly Choices: Forensic Psychology in an Age without Conscience.*

"Catchy title," I said.

"What do you want, Diamond?" she said.

"Can I come in?"

"I haven't decided yet."

"I'm here to lodge a complaint," I said.

"The Complaint Department is back down near the street entrance," said Lopez. "You can't miss it. It'll be on your right just before you leave the building."

"I was hoping to bypass the normal channels and take advantage of my ties within the department."

"Speaking of ties, who dressed you this morning?" she said. "Come in and sit so we can get this over with."

I went in and sat.

I sipped the soup.

"What's the gripe?" she asked. "Someone stiff you for the 'plus expenses'?"

"An ape named Ralph Battle barged into my office waving a forty-four and threatening Darlene harm."

"And?"

"I took the gun away," I said. "I'm afraid that I may have hurt his feelings and that he might be looking for satisfaction. I wanted to get it on record so if he bothers us again I won't have to hold for forty minutes when I call 911."

"Was the gun licensed?"

"Battle claimed he picked it up at the airport when he got in from Chicago."

"A lot of that going around," Lopez said. "Did you bring it along?"

"I didn't want to walk up Columbus Avenue with the barrel sticking out of my pocket."

"Don't forget to turn it in. This guy came all the way from Chicago to pester you? What's with that?" Lopez asked without missing a beat.

"I don't know."

"You're a riot, Diamond. You come in here, interrupt my quiet time, give me half a story, and I'm supposed to be able to assist you in some way? Tell you what. I'll set up a special unit and have them stake out the airport, the bus terminal, and Union Station. Now, why don't you run along so I can get started on it."

"Ever hear of a big-shot lawyer in Chicago named Max Lansdale?"

"Okay, now we're getting somewhere," she said. "Never heard of him; why do you ask?"

"How about Joe Clams?"

"Didn't he run a newsstand over on Stockton?"

"Have a nice day, Lieutenant," I said, getting up to leave.

"It may be too late," she said. "Are you going to tell me what this is all about?"

"I just wanted to make you aware of Battle, should he return and endanger the tranquillity of your peaceful precinct."

"Thanks for being such a model citizen, Diamond. Keep in touch."

With that she went back to her reading and I left the office and the building.

I knew the lieutenant well enough to feel confident that although Lopez wasn't planning a dragnet for Ralph Battle, I had stirred her curiosity. Which, truth be told, was all I had expected. The next time I came to Lopez with questions about Max Lansdale or Joe Clams, she'd have more information.

I would wait until that time came before I began agonizing over how I would get her to spill it.

I picked up a smoothie to take back to the office for Darlene.

"Get anything out of Lopez?" Darlene asked.

"Only a reminder that she's a lot smarter than I am."

I went to my desk to call Vinnie Strings.

"Jake, am I glad you called," said Strings, sounding, as usual, as if it were the end of the world. "It's the basil plants. I can't remember if Angela said four cups of water every day at three, or three cups at four."

"Why don't you play it safe and alternate day to day, Vinnie," I suggested.

"Jeez, why didn't I think of that?" he said.

I could list a million reasons.

"Do me a favor, Vin."

"Absolutely."

"Check the oil in the Chevy, top it off if needed. There's Quaker State 10-40 in the trunk."

"Sure, Jake. Going somewhere?"

"LA. Want to come along?"

Okay, so I'm not perfect. Who is?

"Damn. I'd love to go with you; I'm stuck here with these fucking plants."

"I understand, Vin."

"Is there something else I could do?"

Vinnie Stradivarius lived for any opportunity to help. He wasn't very good at it, but he really tried.

"There may be one or two things you can do for me while I'm gone, Vin. Let's talk when I come for the car."

"Okay, Jake," he said.

"I'll be over around seven."

"Jake."

"Yeah."

"Should I do the four cups today, or the three?"

I looked at my watch. It was ten past four.

"Do three today, Vin," I said, "and don't forget to check the oil."

I went through my desk drawer and located the .38. I opened the chamber and found it was loaded. I emptied the gun and pulled the trigger a few times. It did what it was supposed to do. I reloaded and slipped the revolver into my jacket pocket.

"How about I pick you up at eight," I said to Darlene when I came out to her desk. "We'll grab a bite while I talk with Tony Carlucci."

"Think I'll pass on Carlucci's, Jake. There's really nothing on the menu that I can eat. And I don't want to inhibit you or Tony from being totally candid. You can call me at home when you're leaving and we'll be ready to go when you get there."

"You're serious about Tug McGraw coming along? You know Vinnie could look after him for a day or two."

"Don't be callous, Jake. The poor dog would have about as much chance surviving two days with Vinnie as those poor basil plants do."

"I'll call when I'm leaving Carlucci's," I said. "What did you do with Battle's gun?"

"I locked it in the safe."

I took the Powell streetcar to Market and the bus up Market to Fillmore, then walked the two blocks to my apartment.

I was feeling a lot more limber than I had in the morning. I managed to do a much better job showering, was able to shave and to get my clothes on right side out. I threw what I thought I might need for two days into a small travel bag.

I had an hour or so to kill before driving the Toyota over to pick up the Chevy from Joey Russo's garage and deal with Vinnie.

I killed the time with a strong pot of espresso and the paperback copy of *The Brothers Karamozov* that I was working on. Whenever I need to feel better about my own circumstances, a Russian novel always does the trick.

"What can I do?" Vinnie asked.

He was sitting on the Russo porch when I pulled up front in the Toyota, and he spit out the question before I was out of the car.

I followed him into the house and let him talk me into a Miller Lite.

"Jimmy Pigeon ever talk about a PI named Chandler?" I asked.

"Sure. I met Harry a few times. He worked a couple of jobs with Jimmy in the old days, before Jimmy moved to Santa Monica. Chandler was LAPD before he went private."

"Oh?"

"Harry was working a grand theft auto case. It led him to a chop shop out on Broadway near the LA River that was doing thirty to forty high-end vehicles a month. While he was staking out the place, Harry spotted a city politico dropping in to visit. He took it to his captain, asking for a go-ahead to raid the shop. Next morning, Harry was placed on suspension. Story was they found cocaine from a recent drug bust in Harry's locker. When the troops finally hit the chop shop all they found were stripped Beemers, Benzes, and Jags and not a single soul to talk about Mr. City Councilman. The evidence from Harry's locker mysteriously disappeared and he was reinstated, but when Harry went in to retrieve his gun and shield he broke the captain's nose, and then he quit the force. And a year later the very same councilman was photographed by PI Chandler in a motel room playing doctor with a high school cheerleader. Sort of put a damper on the guy's mayoral campaign."

"Chandler sounds like someone Jimmy would run with," I said. "How did he take it when Chandler was killed?"

"You knew Jimmy, Jake. He always took everything in stride."

"Any chance that Chandler is alive, Vinnie?"

"Where did you get that idea?"

"I heard that Stan Riddle was selling it."

"Riddle is a joke."

"Maybe so, but somehow my name managed to get included in the punch line. I'm headed down to check it out. While I'm gone, maybe you could sit in the office for a few hours the next day or two and check calls."

"Sure."

"The name Joe Clams mean anything to you?"

"Nope."

"Ask around."

"Will do."

"Did you check the oil in the Impala?"

"Sure did. I added a quart and filled the window-washer reservoir."

It was the first answer Vinnie gave that didn't sound to me as if it had been briefly stuck in his throat. It wasn't like Vinnie to hold out on me, so I decided that for the time being I would believe that I was hearing things.

"Thanks for the beer. Don't kill the plants. I'll call you when I get back," I said.

I went out the back door, pulled the Impala out of the garage, and backed out of the alley to the street.

Vinnie waved at me from the front porch as I left. He was wearing what looked to me like a three-dollar-bill smile.

Or maybe I was just seeing things.

Any other time, Vinnie's behavior would have been distracting, if not impossible to ignore. But when you're on your way to a sit-down with Tony Carlucci, it's easy to forget what happened a minute ago.

I took a table in the rear of the dining room and ordered a Dickel and a plate of ziti with eggplant. I asked the waiter to tell the chef to seriously overcook the pasta.

Tony Carlucci didn't show up at the table until the plates were cleared and the espresso was poured. Tony had strong feelings about interrupting people while they ate. And much stronger feelings about being interrupted himself.

"How was the ziti, Jake?" he asked, slipping into the chair across from me. "It looked a little mushy coming out of the kitchen."

"Tell me what you know about Lansdale," I said.

"His mother is a Giancana."

"So?"

"So he has a lot of leeway," Carlucci said.

"Is he untouchable?"

"What do you mean?"

"I mean is he protected?" I asked. "For instance, if he referred to you as a pimp could he get away with it?"

"The fuck called me a pimp?"

"It's a theoretical, Tony. This fuck is squeezing me and I need an idea about how difficult it would be to get him off my back."

"Let's put it this way, Diamond," Tony said. "The guy has connections, but his protection isn't carte blanche. If a good case could be made, whoever may be looking after him could be persuaded to turn their backs for a minute or two. It's tricky, but my brother John might be able to help out."

"If?"

"If this fuck Lansdale ever referred to Johnny Boy as a pimp."

Johnny Boy Carlucci was doing twenty to life at San Quentin.

But his influence out in the street, particularly by way of his younger brother Tony, was undiminished.

"I'll let you know," I said. "Thanks, Tony."

"Don't mention it, Diamond," Carlucci said, "and I mean that literally."

I drove over to Buena Vista to pick up Darlene and the mutt.

We drove straight through, reaching Willie Dogtail's place just after 5 a.m.

Dogtail's beach house was not much more than a shack. A very valuable shack. It had a Santa Monica mailing address but was actually in Ocean Park, on a squiggle of a street called Sea Colony Drive. The house had been a gift from an uncle from the Narragansett tribe who did extremely well running a casino in Connecticut.

An area of dense growth separated the house from the ocean. The view from Willie's back door reminded me of pictures I'd seen of the Mekong Delta. A heavy long-sleeved shirt was required to negotiate the twenty yards to the beach if you didn't care to have your arms amputated by thorny branches. Coming through Willie's private jungle at night always had me expecting to stumble upon a corpse or two. That being said, it was a magnificent location.

I had done most of the driving from San Francisco so that I wouldn't have the responsibility of entertaining the dog. Darlene was much better at that. At one point I could have sworn that they were taking turns counting out-of-state license plates.

When we got into the house all I wanted to do was nap.

"Mind if I take the car into LA, Jake?" Darlene asked. "I could get there in time to surprise Lenny with a wake-up kiss."

"Sure. Give him one for me."

"Mind if I leave McGraw here?" she asked.

"As long as he doesn't try to get in bed with me," I answered.

"What time do you need the car back to go see Riddle?"

"Take your time, I'll use Dogtail's truck if you're not back."

I crawled into Willie's bed after determining that he had made it up with clean sheets. I tried reading a little Dostoyevsky but was out cold before I turned a page.

When I woke up four hours later the dog was lying pressed up against me with his chin on my knee.

I threw some fresh water into one of his bowls and some soy chow into the other. Unfortunately for the canine, Darlene's eating habits were contagious.

I took a shower. I thought about trying to unclog Willie's shower massage but didn't know where he kept his blowtorch.

I thought about coffee but remembered that Dogtail didn't own a coffeemaker. He cooked his Folgers camp-style in a saucepan on the gas burner.

Stan Riddle's office was in downtown Santa Monica. I decided that I would drop in unannounced.

I found the keys to Willie's truck in the ignition. It was a 1954 Ford with a camper top that looked like Mickey Rooney's log cabin. It was so full of junk that I would have to let the dog ride up front with me. Instead, I let him stay to guard the house.

The receptionist at Riddle's office looked as if she'd stepped off the cover of *Monster Movie* magazine. If she'd been standing in a group photo with the Alice Cooper Band, you would have had trouble picking her out. She batted her eyelashes while she told me that I had just missed Stan. I felt as if I were in a wind tunnel.

"You can catch him at the Broadway Bar and Grill on the Third Street Promenade," she said. "A great place for lunch if you like a fifties theme."

Terrific.

Stan Riddle and the Five Satins. I could hardly wait.

"I don't much care for it myself," she added.

It didn't surprise me.

I thanked her for her candor, left the truck in front of the place, and walked the three blocks over to Third.

F i v e

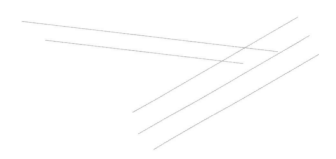

I FOUND STAN RIDDLE SITTING at the bar, leaning into a plate sporting a thick slice of meat loaf and a mound of mashed potatoes smothered in brown gravy. The jukebox was pounding out "Moody River" by Pat Boone. A movie poster from *The Wild One* hung on the wall behind the bar. I slipped onto the stool next to Riddle.

"How's the grub, Stan?" I said.

He looked up at me, swiped a smear of gravy off his chin with a cloth napkin, and swallowed.

"Do I know you?" he asked.

"This won't take that long," I said. "What's this I hear about Harrison Chandler being alive?"

"Where did you hear that?"

"Max Lansdale. He says he got it from you."

"You're Jake Diamond."

"Guilty. Tell me about Chandler."

"I was down at Venice Beach. There's a Chinaman down there sells me herbs for my allergies. I spotted a young lady in a bikini on Rollerblades that I couldn't tear my eyes from and I literally walked into Harry Chandler. I said something stupid like 'Holy cow, I thought you were dead.' He said 'Hold that thought' and he walked away."

"You're certain it was Chandler?" I asked.

"As certain as one can be in this illusory day and age."

"Save the philosophy, Riddle. What made you run to the phone to call Chicago?"

"Money, Diamond. Lansdale has been paying investigators all over creation for any tip on what happened to Harry Chandler. No reason why I shouldn't take a piece of the action."

"Why is he shelling out cash looking for someone who's supposed to be dead?"

"I wondered the same myself," Riddle said. "Maybe Lansdale knew something that the general public didn't know. But it's idle curiosity; it doesn't really concern me if I can make a buck or two, and I have no idea why Max Lansdale is so interested in Harry Chandler to begin with."

"Lansdale claims that Harry killed his brother," I said.

"For what reason?"

"He wouldn't say."

"Was this before or after the bomb went off?"

"What do you mean?"

"I thought you said that this wouldn't take long. My mashed potatoes are turning to stone."

"Look, Stan. I'm in the middle of a very unpleasant situation because you ogled some skater in Venice. Forget the potatoes for a minute and help me out a little before I put your face in the meat loaf."

"When did you get to be such a tough guy, Diamond?" Riddle asked.

"The Brando poster inspired me. Tell me what you're thinking so I can get out of this fucking place before someone plays 'Earth Angel' on the Wurlitzer."

"Okay," Riddle said, pushing the plate of food away. "Let's say, for argument's sake, that Harry Chandler didn't die in the explosion. Let's go on to suggest that that's a pretty good bet, being that I saw Chandler in Venice. And, going a step further, let's grant that Chandler snuffed Max Lansdale's brother. All I was asking, just before you went Mickey Spillane on me, was did Harry pop Lansdale's brother before or after the bombing at Harry's place?"

Good question.

"What do you think?" I asked.

Stupid question.

"As little as possible," Riddle said. "Look, Diamond, like I told you, I'm not much interested. I just do my job, provide information, and leave it to the client to sort out the details. I'm a pragmatist; I leave theory to greater minds. If I somehow put you in a bind because I was doing my job, it certainly wasn't my intention."

"And it doesn't matter who you're doing the job for?"

"Why shouldn't I take Lansdale's money? He's dishing it out to everyone else. He's obviously enlisted your services or you wouldn't be down here ruining my lunch."

"I don't have a choice," I said, thinking about Darlene and Sally.

"We always have a choice, Diamond. Look, I'm not entirely insensitive," Riddle said. "If I can help you out, I will. I had the greatest respect for Jimmy Pigeon. Just don't ask me to guess what goes on in other people's minds. It's a losing proposition."

"What about the woman?" I asked.

"It was a string bikini and she had a body like Cindy Crawford."

"I mean the woman in the room with Chandler when the bomb went off."

"I never learned who she was, Diamond," Riddle said, "and as far as I know, no one has seen her since."

I'd run out of questions.

Stan Riddle took full advantage of the lull in the conversation to hop off his stool.

"Don't bother thanking me, Diamond," he said. "If there's something I can do, you know where to find me." And with that he was quickly to the door and gone.

For a moment I considered ordering food, but "Mr. Sandman" by the Chordettes chased me away. I watched Riddle walk into his office building as I got back to Willie's pickup. I decided to go back to the house to see how the dog was doing.

After that, like it or not, I was going to have to pay a visit to Parker Center to have a word or two with Ray Boyle.

When I made it back to Dogtail's place, the Impala was in front. I looked around inside the house; Darlene and the pooch were gone. I was guessing they had negotiated the path to the beach. I threw on one of Willie's heavy sweatshirts to do the same.

Darlene was sitting at the edge of the water; the mutt was playing tag with the waves.

"Back so soon?" I asked. "Didn't you find Bruno?"

"Oh, I found him," Darlene said.

"Was he surprised?"

"Oh, he was surprised. Almost as much as the pom-pom girl I found in bed with him. The door to his hotel room was unlocked so I slipped in. The patent leather boots in the hall outside the door should have been a dead giveaway, but you know how I'm a glutton for punishment."

"I'm sorry, Darlene," I said.

"Promise me, Jake," she said, "if you ever see me go anywhere near an athlete or a musician again you'll slap me silly. From now on it's exclusively doctors and financial advisers for this kid."

"What makes you think they're any more faithful?"

"I don't," she said, "but at least I would be learning more than how to heat up a Hungry Man TV dinner or play the opening chords of 'Stairway to Heaven'."

"Are you going to be okay, pal?"

"Sure. I've got a dog and a bicycle. What did you learn from Riddle?"

"That I need to see Boyle," I said.

"Are you in a hurry?" Darlene asked.

"Not particularly."

"Did you eat?"

"What do you think?"

"Would you take me out to lunch?"

"It would be a pleasure," I said.

I gave her a hand to her feet and walked her back to the house with the dog at our heels.

Later that afternoon, Darlene said she needed to do some therapeutic shopping. I let her use the convertible. With the .38 stuffed in the glove box of the truck, behind Willie's eight-track tapes, I drove to Parker Center. Ray Boyle was in his office on the third floor. He was on the telephone. When he noticed me standing outside his door he gave me a look that said exactly how glad he was that I had dropped by and waved me in as if I'd come to spray for termites.

"Have a seat, Diamond," he said, pointing at the chair beside his desk. "I'll be a minute. Don't touch anything."

A minute later, Boyle put down the phone. He was shaking his head the way my father used to when I brought home a poor report card. "Know a PI named Stan Riddle?"

"Sort of," I said. "In fact I saw him a few hours ago."

"So I understand." He gestured to the phone. "That was the Santa Monica Police Department. Courtesy call. Seems that Riddle was shot to death in his office this afternoon."

"You can't be serious."

"I'm very serious. His secretary found him when she came back from having her nails done. She mentioned that you'd been by looking for him," Boyle said, "so if you're here to turn yourself in, you came to the wrong place. It's out of my jurisdiction."

"You know better than that, Ray."

"Perhaps I do. But you'd better start talking so I can try to convince the SMPD. They haven't closed a case in so long they'll carve your name onto the bullet that killed Riddle."

"I went to see him about Harrison Chandler," I said.

"Let's take a walk, Jake," Boyle said.

Ray and I sat in a booth at a diner across from Parker Center. Boyle was recapping all that I'd told him, claiming that it helped him to get it straight.

"Stan Riddle bumps into Harry Chandler at Venice Beach, gives Lansdale a call, and Lansdale sends a goon to escort you to Chicago. Lansdale chooses you, he says, because you were so tight with Jimmy Pigeon. Sends you back to locate Chandler, and this Joe Clams, or else," Boyle said. "Or else what?"

"Or else Darlene and Sally get hurt, if I don't ship them off to Timbuktu. And you know them both well enough to agree that neither would budge. I decided to play along until a better idea comes along, so I came down to see Riddle. Riddle sticks by his story about running into Chandler. Tom Romano told me that you were at the scene where Chandler is alleged to have exploded, so I came to see you. I'm guessing that Lansdale sent his goon, Ralph

Battle, to stop Riddle's clock, but I can't help wondering why. Lansdale put me onto Riddle in the first place. If Lansdale didn't want me to talk with Riddle he wouldn't have dropped Stan's name, or he would have gotten to Riddle *before* I did."

"What does that tell you?" Boyle asked.

"That Lansdale wanted me to talk to Riddle?"

"At least once," Boyle said.

"I need some help here, Ray. Lansdale scares the shit out of me. If you know something about Harrison Chandler, give me a hand."

"I know plenty about him," Boyle said. "Harry Chandler was my partner before he was bounced off the force. I wanted to follow him out the door when they fucked him over, but he talked me out of it. Harry said I needed to stay inside to bring the captain down while he worked at toppling the city councilman. A year later the captain took early retirement and the councilman moved to Arizona."

"Is Chandler dead or alive, Ray?"

"Harry was hired by Max Lansdale to investigate Lansdale's brother. Randolph Lansdale was taking regular trips to Los Angeles and Max was curious. Their father had been tied in with the Chicago mob for almost forty years. The old man supposedly cut himself loose after Sam Giancana was killed, but Max seemed to think that there was some kind of holdover from the old days and that his brother was still playing ball with the Italians. Harry made a few trips to Chicago to meet with Max Lansdale, and that's when he met Carla."

"Carla?"

"Carla Rosario. She was a lawyer with Lansdale and Sons. Harry and Carla clicked at first sight. Harry took her to dinner the evening they first met at Lansdale's office, and they spent the weekend together at her Chicago apartment. Harry kept an eye on Max's brother for a while. He found that Randolph Lansdale's trips to Los Angeles had to do with some legal research he was doing, and was in no way connected to any crime syndicate. Harry reported his findings to Max Lansdale, which effectively ended their business arrangement. Meanwhile, Harry was spending more and more time with Carla. He would go to Chicago or she would come to LA."

"Okay," I said.

"Turns out that Randolph Lansdale was in love with Carla. He was much older, but a very charming bachelor. They dated nearly a year, and Lansdale apparently had marriage in mind. Then Harry came along. Carla tried to ease out of her relationship with Randolph, all the time insisting that it wasn't about another man. Lansdale was unrelenting. Finally she had to admit that she had met someone she cared more for, and Randolph Lansdale fired her on the spot. With nothing holding her in Chicago, she picked up and moved to LA. She found a job in a law firm here and settled into an apartment out near Cal State. And spent most of her free time with Harry Chandler."

The waitress walked over and refilled our coffee cups. Boyle took a few sips before continuing.

"A few weeks later, Harry gets a call from Max Lansdale. Lansdale tells Harry that his brother Randolph is acting irrational, ranting about Carla this and Carla that. Crazy talk about making plans for the wedding, will Max be his best man, who they should invite from their mother's side of the family, and so on. Max says he found photos in his brother's desk, of Harry and Carla outside of Harry's apartment. Max says that his brother has still been making trips to LA and Max believes that Randolph has been stalking Carla. He says that he's worried about his brother; he's been trying to get Randolph to seek professional help. Max says he wanted Harry to be aware of the situation. The next day, Harry and Carla traveled up to Monterey for the weekend. Carla was afraid to stay alone at her place, so they went over to Harry's apartment when they got back. Harry was in the shower when the telephone rang. The bomb was planted underneath the bed. It was rigged to explode when the receiver of the telephone on the bedside table was lifted. Carla answered the call. She was killed instantly. The bathroom door tore loose and knocked Harry into the tiled shower wall. Harry was in the hospital for two days."

Boyle paused for a moment that felt to me like a week and a day.

"Ray, please."

"Chandler called Chicago and discovered that Randolph Lansdale had been in LA that weekend. He walked out of the hospital, flew to Chicago, and Randolph turned up dead."

"Who was the second man? Who is Joe Clams?"

"He was Carla's brother. That's all I can tell you about him," Boyle said. "Let me finish. After Lansdale was killed and Harry was implicated there was a hefty price put on Harry's head. Randolph's mother was a Giancana and she demanded a vendetta. We had to kill Harry Chandler ourselves: me, Jimmy Pigeon, and Joe Clams."

"What are you talking about?"

"We staged a shoot-out between Harry Chandler and the LAPD. Myself and a couple of Harry's old friends in the department. Chandler was killed trying to get away; Jimmy Pigeon witnessed the showdown and reported it to Max Lansdale. We used the body of a John Doe we'd found under the freeway near the Coliseum a week before. We sent Harry up to San Francisco, he laid low for a few days, and then Clams got him out of the country. There was a lot of heat for a couple of years, but it eventually died down. At least until recently, when Max Lansdale suddenly became interested in Harry again."

"Because Stan Riddle saw Harry in Venice."

"Word had it that Lansdale started asking about Harry again months ago, long before he got the call from Riddle," Boyle said. "On top of that, Stan Riddle never saw Harry Chandler in Venice. Harry hasn't been anywhere near California for years, and I know that for a fact."

"So why did Riddle call Max Lansdale to say he'd spotted Chandler?"

"To make a few bucks I would guess, or maybe it was Lansdale's idea to begin with."

"Lansdale somehow knew that Harry was alive."

"Seems like a possibility."

"How?"

"I don't know. I'll look into it, Jake. I'll try to find out if this guy Ralph Battle or anyone connected to Max Lansdale was anywhere near Riddle's office when he was shot. And I'll clear you with the Santa Monica police," Ray said. "I can't promise you more than that. I'll do everything I can do to help. I can't force the Chicago PD to cooperate, but I will reach out to them."

"Where is Chandler now, Ray?"

"I can't tell you that, Jake. I'm sorry."

"You're going to be a lot sorrier if something happens to Darlene or Sally, Ray," I said, "that much I know about you. Get in touch with Chandler and tell him that he's put me in deep trouble and if he gives a shit he'd better think of something fast."

"I'll do that, Jake," Boyle said. "What are you going to do?"

"I really don't fucking know, Ray," I said, and I walked out of the diner.

When I made it back to the beach house I could see that Darlene wasn't any more interested in staying down south than I was. And the dog couldn't seem to find a spot half as comfortable as his haven beneath Darlene's desk.

I left a short thank-you note for Willie Dogtail, wrapped around a twenty-dollar bill for truck fuel.

And we ran back home to San Francisco.

S i x

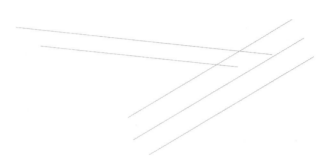

THE FOLLOWING MORNING DARLENE and I were sitting at her desk drinking coffee out of matching mugs with the inscription "Oswald Acted Alone," a gift from Vinnie Strings on my last birthday. Tug McGraw was safe and cozy underneath the desk. It was Wednesday, and since Sunday afternoon I had been to Chicago and back and to Los Angeles and back. I was getting ready to travel again, and I was clueing Darlene in.

"Why in heaven's name would you want to go back to Chicago, Jake?" Darlene asked.

"Wanting has nothing to do with it. Lansdale somehow gets a notion that Harry Chandler might be alive, so Max puts me onto Riddle, who is supposed to have bumped into Chandler on the beach. The thing is, according to Boyle, Stan Riddle never saw Chandler. So either Riddle made the story up himself, to make a buck, or Lansdale put Riddle up to fabricating a Chandler sighting."

"Why would Lansdale do that?"

"To make me believe there was some real evidence that Chandler was alive and then watch to see what I would do. Lansdale has an idea that Chandler is alive, he thinks that I know something about it, so he uses Riddle to put me in motion to possibly lead him to Chandler. Then Lansdale eliminates Riddle before Stan can change his story. But it's a bluff, except where poor Riddle is concerned. If I know nothing about Chandler, it doesn't matter if Riddle said he saw Harry a thousand times. Or Elvis, for that matter. Trouble is, Lansdale is so convinced I do know something, he won't believe me when I insist that I don't."

"And remind me again," Darlene asked, "why does Lansdale think you know something about Chandler?"

"Lansdale believes Pigeon knew a lot about Chandler, and with Jimmy gone, Lansdale thinks I'm his best bet."

"And Ray Boyle can't help you?"

"Ray says he can't. He confirms that Chandler is alive, but won't say where. And there's the rub. Now I actually do know something about Chandler's mortality," I said, "but not a thing that will help to get Lansdale off my back."

"Why not just call Lansdale's bluff, tell him that you know nothing and that he can go fuck himself if he doesn't buy it?"

"He won't believe me."

"So? What's he going to do, sue you?"

And then it was time to tell Darlene that she was part of the equation.

"Good of you to finally get around to telling me that my life was in danger, Jake."

"I was hoping to avoid worrying you."

"That's sweet of you, Jake. But not too politically correct. Some of us girls actually like to know when we're on someone's expendable list, just to be prepared. I can do a pretty good job watching out for myself when I know that there's something to watch out for. I would strongly recommend you get the news to Sally as soon as possible. I'm pretty sure she'd be interested."

"You're right, and I will."

"So," said Darlene, "getting back to the original question, what do you hope to achieve by going back to Chicago?"

"I *will* call Lansdale's bluff, just for grins. I'll tell him that I haven't heard anything to convince me that Harry Chandler is alive, including Riddle's story," I said. "When that doesn't work, I'll do my best to assure Lansdale that I'm giving the matter of locating Harry Chandler and Joe Clams my undivided attention and pray that it satisfies Max enough to give us some breathing room. Maybe Ray Boyle will get hold of Chandler and good old Harry will come galloping to the rescue. In the meanwhile, if I can't get to Chandler, maybe I can find Joe Clams. Boyle told me that Carla Rosario was Joe Clams's sister. I'll do some snooping around."

"How long will that take, Jake?"

"I have no idea, Darlene. Maybe I'll get lucky, I'll go visit Max Lansdale and he won't remember who I am or he'll tell me it was all a joke. I can't simply ignore it; I can't sit here waiting for the phone to ring or for Ralph Battle to pop back in."

"You're going to need help, Jake."

"I can't think of anyone who's available right at the moment, unless you think that taking Vinnie along is a good idea."

"Are you kidding?"

"Yes, Darlene."

"I wish Joey Russo wasn't down in the Islands. You know that if you called him he'd come running. I'm sure Vinnie knows how to get in touch with Joey, in the event of a basil-plant emergency."

"I'll be all right, Darlene. Just keep on your toes while I'm gone. I've got Tom Romano keeping an eye out for Sally; if you want I can ask him to look in on you."

"That's okay; I have my trusty guard dog."

"Funny. Make sure you have Tom's number handy just in case."

"When are you leaving?"

"I'll fly into Chicago later today, get a car and a motel, and get started first thing in the morning."

"And you'll see Sally before you go?"

"Yes. I will. Thanks," I said. "And now I have a few phone calls to make."

I picked up the coffee mug and went back to my desk to check in with Tom Romano, make airline arrangements, and find out if Sally French was free for lunch.

"That was quick, Jake," said Tom Romano when I rang him up at his office. "How did it go down in LA?"

"Not very well for me, a lot worse for Riddle. He told me what he was supposed to tell me and then someone, I'm guessing Lansdale, shut him up for good."

"Dead?"

"Extremely."

"Did you get with Boyle?"

"It's a long story, Tom. And if I took the time to tell you everything I know, then there would be two of us holding a lot of worthless information."

"Gotcha. So what can I do for you?"

"The names Joe Clams or Rosario mean anything to you?"

"Chicago?"

"What makes you say that?"

"There was a Louie Clams I've heard tell of, came up in the Capone organization, or at least what became of it after Frank Nitti killed himself. I don't know where the nickname Clams came from, just that he butted heads with the Giancanas a few times and then disappeared. No one knew if he left crime, left Chicago, or left the planet," Romano said. "This was way back in the fifties, like ancient history."

"Any real name to go with the alias?" I asked.

"Not that I can recall."

"Could it have been Rosario?"

"Could have been anything. I've got a friend in Chicago, Eddie Hand. He does what we do for a living, if you can call this living. Eddie is a student of Chicago history. If you gave him a call, he might be able to fill in the blanks."

"He wouldn't mind?"

"Not at all," Tom said. "Eddie loves to talk."

"Sure. Let me have his number, maybe I'll look him up when I get up there."

"You're going back to Chicago?"

"Unfortunately."

"Want me to keep keeping an eye on Sally?" Romano asked.

"I'd appreciate it, Tom. And I know it's a lot to ask, but maybe you could do the same for Darlene. After what happened to Stan Riddle, I'm not feeling any better about there being goons like Ralph Battle on the loose."

"No problem, Jake. I have enough time and extra help to watch out for the women. Just watch your own back. Let me know if I can do anything else."

I thanked Tom and called to reserve a seat on a late-afternoon flight to O'Hare.

Then I called Sally to ask if she could meet me at Black Cat for lunch.

Black Cat had gone through a number of reincarnations during its three years nestled between the strip joints on Broadway.

The latest was as a French bistro, a little touch of Paris not far from my office in North Beach. Sally said she could meet me at one, so I walked over fifteen minutes early to try to grab a table in back.

Sally was wearing white, and watching her glide across the black-and-white-tiled floor was mesmerizing. She gave me a peck on the cheek before taking her seat and got right down to brass tacks.

"What's the occasion, pal?" she said.

"Wine?" I asked.

"Only when all else fails."

The waiter brought menus and I ordered two glasses of chardonnay.

We decided to share the crab stew, with sides of pommes frites with garlic aioli and broccoli rabe.

Between spoonfuls I told her about Max Lansdale's threats.

"That's not happy news," Sally said. "Is this guy seriously dangerous?"

"Recent events in Santa Monica would indicate so."

Sally French's biggest complaint about my work, once she got past the stage of considering it life-wasting, which was unfortunately after our two-year marriage ended in divorce, was the danger involved. I continually assured her that what I did wasn't all that risky.

Having to tell Sally that she might be in peril was no fun.

"I'm off to Chicago in a few hours to see if I can somehow straighten it out," I said. "In the meanwhile I've asked Tom Romano to keep an eye on you. Don't worry about Tom; you won't even know he's watching."

"That's a comforting thought."

"You have no idea how sorry I am about this, Sally," I said.

"I have some idea," she said. "I'd have a better idea if you would order the crème brûlée."

"If I throw in the orange profiteroles with caramel ice cream and fudge sauce," I said, "can I get a ride to the airport?"

Seven

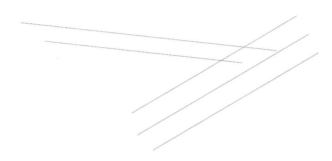

I LANDED AT O'HARE JUST BEFORE EIGHT and walked toward the terminal exit. I had taken only as much as I could carry on, actually the same bag I had packed for the trip down to Santa Monica that I had never dipped into. All I had added to my wardrobe was the knee-length Harris Tweed, which I had dug out of the back of my closet. The heavy wool coat had been referred to, depending on the San Francisco neighborhood where I sported it, as everything from a lovely piece of vintage outerwear to a horse blanket. To me it was simply my father's topcoat.

When I reached the unsafe side of the security area, a tall, handsome fifty-something character straight out of a James T. Farrell novel walked directly to me and asked if I was Jake Diamond. Either the man recognized me from a B film I'd done in my short Hollywood career, or he was there to meet me.

Since he wasn't holding out a pen and paper for an autograph, and since he didn't fit the physical profile of someone that Max Lansdale might send to welcome me back to Chicago if Ralph Battle was occupied breaking someone's thumbs, I confessed.

"Lucky guess?" I said.

"Eddie Hand," he said, reaching out an arm. "Do you have anything to pick up at the luggage claim?"

"This is it," I said, accepting the handshake.

"Good man," he said. "Let's beat it out of this place."

I nearly had to skip to keep up with him.

I followed Hand out to a gold 1986 Pontiac Bonneville coupe in the short-term parking area and climbed into the passenger seat.

"Where to?" I said, though I thought he should have been asking.

He threw the turbo-glide transmission into drive.

"I have a spare bedroom in my house that you can use while you're up here," Eddie said. "I insist."

Eddie's small stucco two-story house was on Seminary Avenue between West Eddy and West Cornelia streets in north Chicago, less than two blocks south of Wrigley Field. I followed him up the stone steps and into the front room.

"Yours is the bedroom on the left," he said, indicating the stairs. "Drop your bag up there, lose the coat, and I'll fix a couple of drinks. George Dickel on ice sound okay?"

"Perfect," I said.

Tom Romano had come through for me in a big way.

"I've got some homemade lentil soup heating up on the stove," Eddie said when I came back down. He handed me a drink and invited me to sit on one of two overstuffed armchairs in the living room and took the other. "While we wait, I hear that you're interested in the life and times of Louie Clams."

The story went like this.

Louis Vongoli grew up in Cicero, just east of Chicago, where members of the Capone crime family had located to avoid the law of the big city, where Chicago mayor Big Bill Thompson and later Mayor Anton Cermak waged war against organized crime, not to stop it, but to gain control of its rewards.

After Capone was imprisoned, Frank Nitti took control of the Chicago mob. Although Nitti kept an office on North LaSalle in downtown Chicago, he made his home in Riverside just east of Cicero. In December 1932, Chicago detective Henry Lang, a member of Mayor Chermak's "Special Squad," attempted to assassinate Nitti at the North LaSalle office. Nitti took six bullets but he survived. Testimony later revealed that the hit was ordered by Mayor Cermak in an attempt to take over the entire syndicate that Capone and Nitti had built.

Cicero and Riverside became safe havens for Nitti and his men, while Cermak and his partners stepped up their assault on the Italians with all the resources of the Chicago Police Department.

In February 1933, while Cermak sat in an open car with President-elect Franklin Delano Roosevelt during a parade in Miami, a gunman fired five shots at the limousine, hitting four people and the mayor. Although the incident was reported as an attempt on the life of Roosevelt, the fact that the shooter was an Italian immigrant named Giuseppe Zangara suggested the possibility that Cermak had been the target. Cermak died three weeks later, and Zangara was electrocuted just thirteen days after Cermak's death.

Giovanni Vongoli worked in the train yards in Cicero. Vongoli was killed in an accident while unloading cargo in 1934. Giovanni's only son, Louis, was fourteen years old.

To help support his widowed mother, Louis ran errands, shined shoes, washed windows, swept bars and restaurants, and sold newspapers on the streets of Cicero.

Louie also began a life of petty crime, from stealing coal from the train yards to heat their small apartment to stealing food from restaurant kitchens accessed from back alleys.

One day Louie was nabbed by one of Frank Nitti's men after grabbing a large porterhouse from the kitchen of a mob-operated steakhouse. Louie was given two choices: have his legs broken and his mother thrown out on the street, or pick up and deliver numbers bets. So at fifteen, Louie began running numbers. Since *vongoli* is the Italian word for clams, Louie soon had an official nickname.

"The soup should be hot enough," Eddie said. "Let's move into the kitchen."

At the kitchen table, Eddie and I ate soup and drank bourbon. Eddie took breaks between mouthfuls to continue.

"In 1943 Frank Nitti was facing a prison sentence. Nitti had been imprisoned before, for tax evasion, and swore he would never be locked up again. He committed suicide. With the disorganization that Nitti's death caused, Louie Clams took the opportunity to go out on his own."

"By the late forties, Louie had built a very profitable numbers racket in Cicero with a small group of handpicked cohorts. At the same moment, the Giancana family was also taking advantage of the world war and Nitti's demise and establishing a stronghold in

Chicago. It was only a matter of time until they turned a greedy eye to all of the money that was being made in Cicero. Louie Clams tried to resist a takeover, but wasn't strong enough. When one of Louie's men killed a favorite of Sam Giancana's, word came down that Louie Clams was marked for death and that his family was in danger.

"Louie Clams took his wife and his small son and fled to California, changing his name before settling in San Francisco."

"Changing his name to what?" I asked.

"I couldn't tell you," Eddie answered.

"But Carla Rosario was his daughter."

"Carla was born after the family left Cicero. Rosario was her mother's maiden name. She took it when she came to Chicago for law school. I doubt that anyone made the connection until after she was killed, when the name Joe Clams came up in the case of Randolph Lansdale's murder. How about some coffee?" Eddie asked, carrying the empty bowls to the sink. "I have some good Italian espresso."

"Sounds perfect," I said.

Eddie started a flame under the pot of coffee on the stove top. He uncovered a large tin of anisette toast and carried it over to the table. If I hadn't known better, I would have sworn that my mother had shipped it over.

"It will be very difficult if not impossible to find Joe Clams, Jake, unless he wants to be found. The name he grew up with has been a secret for fifty years. I understand you came to try to buy more time from Max Lansdale, but I'm afraid that no amount of time will be time enough. And Max Lansdale is not a patient man, and he's pretty well connected."

"I thought his old man severed those connections."

"He more or less did, but apparently Max Lansdale was approached around the time of his father's death and he has been involved ever since," Eddie said, pouring the coffee into demitasse cups.

"But I was told that Max hired Harry Chandler to find out if his brother Randolph was picking up where his father had left off."

"Randolph was like a carbon copy of his father, and totally devoted to the old man. If Simon Lansdale told Randolph to stay clear of the Italians, Randolph wouldn't have dreamed of going against his father's wishes," Eddie said. "Max Lansdale, on the other hand, was less interested in the position his father had risen to and more fascinated by the means that his father had used to get there to begin with."

"Then Max hiring Chandler to investigate his brother doesn't make sense."

"Not to me, but this is the first time I've heard it," Eddie said, "and a PI from LA, like Chandler, wouldn't see the contradiction."

"But why would Max Lansdale throw suspicion on his brother in the first place? Why open up a can of worms?"

"Good question. Here's another. I was watching a movie the other night and one of the characters brought up an interesting point. You've seen *King Kong*, right?"

"A hundred times."

"The islanders built a tall wall around their village to keep Kong out. So why did they put a door in the thing large enough for the ape to walk through?"

"I'll have to think about that one," I said.

"You must be very tired," said Eddie Hand. "I know I am. I have an idea or two about how to approach Lansdale; we can pick this up in the morning. There are clean towels in the linen closet outside the bathroom. Go on up and get some sleep."

"Thanks for everything, Eddie," I said. "Your generosity is overwhelming."

"Tom Romano assured me that you'd do the same."

"Anytime," I said, and started for the stairs.

"Sleep well," Eddie said.

"I don't know about that—I'll probably be up all night thinking about Fay Wray."

Eight

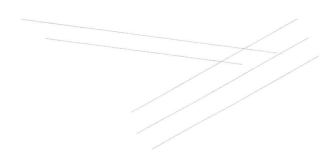

THE FOLLOWING MORNING, EDDIE and I walked over to the Salt and Pepper Diner on North Clark, a block from Eddie's house and that much closer to Wrigley Field. We sat at the counter. I was working on a very decent bacon and Swiss omelet and Eddie was tearing toast into small squares and mixing the pieces into his bowl of soft-boiled eggs.

"How do you like living so close to the stadium?" I asked.

"Love it. I grew up in that house. My father was head ground-skeeper at Wrigley. I've got a basement full of autographed base-balls; my Ernie Bankses would flood the market. We used to play Little League on a grass field on North Wilton, and we could hear the fans at Wrigley singing 'The Star-Spangled Banner' before their game."

"What do you know about the Randolph Lansdale shooting?" I asked him after we'd polished off the food.

"The basics," Eddie said. "Chandler, the PI from LA, was identified from a photo. The Chicago PD reached out to LA and Chandler was killed in a shoot-out with the LAPD."

"Did that close the Lansdale murder case up here?" I asked.

"For all practical purposes. Of course there was no trial or conviction, and all they had was a photograph and testimony from Lansdale's brother and the receptionist, but it seemed to be enough to move the Chicago cops on to other cases. I'm sure that there's still a file somewhere in the bowels of the department, and it should be public domain if you wanted to check it out. Have you thought about how you're going to approach Max Lansdale?"

"Some," I said, "but you mentioned that you had an idea or two of your own and I'm wide open."

"Okay. I'm going to make assumptions based on talking with Tom Romano," Eddie said. "First, I'm guessing you're more concerned about the safety of your women friends than you are about your own safety."

"That would be correct," I said.

"At the same time, you wouldn't mind getting your head off the chopping block. At least for a while."

"I'd like that."

"Third," said Eddie, "you're probably thinking that it wouldn't hurt to know a little more of what Lansdale isn't telling you."

"You're batting a thousand."

"And you'd be a lot more comfortable, for lack of a better word, if you could chat with Lansdale without Ralph Battle hovering over your shoulder."

"Absolutely."

"Well, then," Eddie said, "let's start from there. It's eight thirty. We have about ninety minutes before we need to be in front of Lansdale's office building."

So, over more coffee and great homemade apple pie, we spent the next hour or so working up a strategy.

The office of Lansdale and Sons was located on the 300 block of South Wacker, in the shadow of the Sears Tower. Eddie Hand had been watching the building for two days, since first getting a call from Tom Romano just before Darlene and I left for Santa Monica. Eddie drove us downtown in his Pontiac. I gazed out at Lake Michigan and could think of only two words to describe the lake.

Very cold.

"The last two mornings at exactly ten," Eddie said, "Battle has come out of the building to pick up bagels at the shop across the street. If it's not a daily ritual, it's going to put a serious kink into our well-laid plans."

"No kidding," was all I could come up with.

Eddie pulled into a Standing Only parking spot in front of the deli at seven minutes before ten. He pulled an official-looking parking permit from the glove box and put it on the dashboard.

"Stand over there, in the vestibule of the Payless shoe store," Eddie said, pointing across Wacker. "When Battle comes out and starts across, get into the building. How much time do you think you'll need with Lansdale?"

"Can you give me fifteen minutes?"

"I'll give it my best shot."

"How are you going to delay Battle?"

"Let me worry about that," Eddie said; "get over to the shoe store."

It was two minutes after ten when Battle appeared, a very long two minutes. As curious as I was as to how Eddie was going to handle his end, I tore my attention away from Battle and quickly ducked into the office building.

I checked the building directory and took the elevator to the twelfth floor.

I was greeted in Lansdale's office with a stunning smile from a woman who would have looked much more at home in front of lights and cameras than behind the large reception desk. Her teeth alone could have sold millions of tubes of Crest.

"May I help you?" she asked, with a voice that I recognized from my call to Lansdale from San Francisco. Her voice alone could have sold anything.

"I'm here to see Max. I'll just go on in," I said, and headed quickly to the door behind her before she could finish her protest.

"Ah, Jake," Max Lansdale said when I walked in, not seeming all that surprised to see me, "it's too bad I just sent Ralph out for bagels. If I'd known you were coming, I would have asked him to bring you one."

I plunged into my speech before I forgot the gist of it.

"Mr. Lansdale. I saw Stan Riddle while he was still able to talk, and he admitted that he had never actually bumped into Harrison Chandler. Riddle said he fabricated the story to separate you from a buck or two. Which means that I have no leads yet as to the whereabouts of Chandler, nor do I have confirmation that the man is alive. But the course of events has piqued my curiosity, so I'll continue the investigation."

I took a short pause for emphasis.

"However, the ground rules will have to change or you can go fuck yourself."

"My goodness, Jake, you are a constant amazement. I'm so disappointed that Ralph is missing part of this."

"I'm banking on Ralph missing all of it, and there's not much time," I said. "Hold the editorial and let me finish."

"By all means, Jake, continue."

"I'll take you on as a client under my standard terms. Save your threats. Get over your big bully act, it doesn't suit you. And leave the women out of it entirely, it's a sign of weakness. Pick on someone your own size. Threatening the ladies won't inspire me to work any harder, it only pisses me off. Give me some time and I guarantee that I'll locate Chandler, if he's alive. Fuck with my friends and I guarantee you'll never find him."

"How can you be so sure, Jake? There are plenty of other private investigators out there."

"Sure, and you've used almost all of them the past eight years and found nothing. I'm the only one who has a chance of flushing Chandler out if he's alive, and you know it or you wouldn't have gone through all this trouble to coerce my help."

"I'll grant you a little time, Diamond, and I'll back off your girlfriends if it upsets you so much. But I would still like more than simply a money-back guarantee. I promise that if I'm dissatisfied, Ralph Battle's face will be the last thing you ever see."

"Fair enough," I said. "Give Ralph my best."

I walked out of Lansdale's office. The cover-girl receptionist, Jill Ballard if the nameplate on her desk was any indication, showed her teeth again. I stopped at her side for a few very quick questions.

"This must be a wonderful job, Ms. Ballard," I said lamely. "How long have you been working for the firm?"

"Six years, Mr. . . . ?"

"Jake Diamond. So you were around when Mr. Lansdale's brother was killed. It must have been horrible."

"Actually I missed that scene by a few days, thank God."

"Oh?"

"The woman who was here before me left her job right after the shooting. I couldn't blame her."

"Do you know her name?"

"I never met her. I do know her name was Katherine Carson, and she was called Kit."

"Kit Carson?"

"Scout's honor," she said.

"I don't suppose you know where she went?"

"Sorry, no clue," she said. Her phone rang. Ballard answered with the stock greeting, listened for a moment, set the receiver down. "Eddie says it's time to go, Jake," she told me.

I thanked her, hurried out into the hall, and made it into the stairwell just as Ralph Battle arrived. I ran down to the floor below and caught the elevator down to the lobby. Eddie had the car idling out front and I hopped into the passenger seat.

"How'd it go?" he asked as he pulled away from the building.

"Either I bought some time, or a down payment on a bucket of cement."

I quickly summarized my short talk with Lansdale.

"Did you get anything out of Lansdale that was helpful?" Eddie asked.

"I didn't ask anything straight out." I said. "I didn't want to push it too far or make him doubt my single-mindedness. But I did learn a few things. I'm not sure if Lansdale believed me when I told him that Riddle admitted lying about running into Chandler, but I could tell that Lansdale knew, one way or another, that Riddle had never seen Harry Chandler. And Lansdale didn't appear very surprised about Riddle's death. I did my best to draw Lansdale's attention away from Darlene and Sally and at me. I appealed to his dignity, but that assumes he has dignity. I really don't understand why Lansdale is so convinced that I'm his best chance at locating Chandler and Joe Clams, but since you and I agreed that it's our only playing card at the moment, I reinforced the idea."

"Well, I'd say you made the best of fifteen minutes."

"I did manage to squeeze in a few words with his receptionist. It seems that the woman that had the job before her, who was in the office when Lansdale's brother was killed and identified

Harrison Chandler from a photo, left immediately after the shooting. I wouldn't mind talking with her, but finding her might be tricky."

"I've got a friend in the Chicago PD, tools of the trade," said Eddie. "Maybe he can help. We can at least get a look at the file on the Randolph Lansdale murder case. When we get to the police station, let me do all the talking."

"With pleasure," I said.

We headed out State Street to Central Station.

We found Detective Lieutenant Daniel Washington behind his desk in the corner of the Homicide squad room on the second floor. Eddie Hand and Dan Washington had grown up together in the same neighborhood on Chicago's North Side. After they did a few minutes of catching up, we got down to business.

"I remember the Lansdale case well," Dan said. "I did the initial interviews. The receptionist described the two men, and the next day she identified Harrison Chandler from a photograph. We got the search for Chandler to the LAPD, and before I could get out there we received word that Chandler had been killed. I did go out to San Francisco for a few days, to work with the SFPD trying to locate the second man, but nothing came of it. We were almost certain that the second man was Louie Vongoli's son, but that and four bucks will get you a hot dog at Comiskey."

"Any idea where I could find the Carson woman?" I asked.

"Not offhand," Washington said. "I tried to reach her shortly after the shooting. Nothing official, the case was more or less closed, but just to find out how the woman was doing. She had naturally been very disturbed about the incident, and I usually follow up, see if counseling might be recommended. She was gone, from the office and from her place in town. No forwarding address. It made me curious for a while, but not enough to take time away from the more immediate issues that come up every day. I haven't thought about it since. Any particular reason you're interested in finding her?"

"Nothing I could put a finger on," I said. "Just seemed odd that she disappeared."

"I can look into it, if I can find time," said Washington.

"I'll do the same, Jake," Eddie added.

"Thanks, I really appreciate your help," I said. "Do you think it would be possible to see the photograph that was used to identify Harrison Chandler as one of the men Carson saw in the office that day?"

"Sure," Washington said. "I'll call down and have it scanned for you. I'll get you a hard copy and also put it on a disk so you can re-size it if necessary."

Washington called down to the Records Department and ordered the copies.

"Anything else we need, Jake?" Eddie asked.

"Can't think of anything—I probably will the minute we get into the car. Thanks again, Lieutenant."

"Thank Eddie," Washington said. "For a box seat to the Cubs opener I will help anyone Eddie brings in. Give me a call if you think of something else. I'll let Eddie know if I find anything on Katherine Carson."

Eddie led me down to the Records Department and less than five minutes later we walked out of the police station with an eight-by-ten color copy of the photograph and a floppy disk.

"Well," I said, looking at the photo when we were back in the Bonneville, "it may not help, but at least now I know what Harry Chandler looks like. I don't recognize the building behind him, not that I know downtown Los Angeles all that well."

"Let me have a look at that," Eddie said. "That's the Chicago Sun-Times Building, Jake; what made you assume it was taken in Los Angeles?"

"I don't know. Probably something that Max Lansdale said when I first talked with him at the airport on Monday. I can't re-member."

"It'll come back to you," Eddie said. "Let's get back to my place. We can put the photograph up on my computer and take a closer look. See if there's anything there that helps jog your memory."

"Jesus, I'm in my early forties and I'm already forgetting things from three days ago."

"Wait until you reach fifty," Eddie said. "You'll need a map to find your way home. Come to think of it, would you mind grab-bing the Chicago city map from the glove box?"

"You're kidding, right?"

"Kidding about what?" Eddie asked.

Ten minutes later, Eddie had found his way back home, and we were looking at the photograph on Eddie's twenty-five-inch computer monitor.

Harry Chandler was standing in front of the newspaper building with his back to the entrance.

"I would guess this was taken in August, possibly September, judging from what the people on the street are wearing," Eddie said.

"Does Chandler look to you like he's waiting for someone?" I asked.

"Hold on, I can zoom in on his face," Eddie said. "It looks to me as if he's reacting to something behind him. What do you think?"

"A sound?"

"Maybe, let's see what's back there."

"Look at this guy," I said. "He seems to have just come out of the building, and is moving toward where Chandler is standing."

"I recognize that guy," Eddie said, zooming in on the man's face. "Jesus, that's Phil Cochran. It had to be no later than late September 1995."

"Why's that?" I asked. "And who the hell is Phil Cochran?"

"Cochran was a crime reporter for the *Sun-Times*. In late summer of '95 he wrote a piece theorizing that Simon Lansdale might not have died of natural causes. It created a commotion, to put it mildly. The newspaper got all sorts of grief for running the thing, and when Cochran couldn't back up any sources to even suggest the possibility, he was canned outright. No appeals. The pressure was coming from everywhere, all the way up to the mayor's office."

"Do you think there was anything to it?" I asked.

"Hard to say. Phil was famous for stirring things up and wasn't above substituting wild speculation for news."

"The story that I heard had Chandler working for Max Lansdale, trying to find out if Randolph was still tied up with the Italians. What if Max was really looking for some kind of hint that his brother killed the old man to take over the helm?"

"Go on," said Eddie.

"So Chandler snoops around and maybe teams up with this Cochran character for background. Maybe they stumble across something, no matter how weak, and Cochran jumps the gun with a story, shooting for a Pulitzer. What happened to Cochran?"

"No one knows," said Eddie. "He got drunk for a few weeks after he was fired and then he disappeared."

"And a few months later someone puts a bomb under Chandler's bed in LA."

"Slow down, Jake, you're beginning to sound like a reckless newspaperman."

"Do you think that Cochran is still alive somewhere?"

"Haven't given it much thought in a very long time, and very recently you've had me wondering about whether or not Kit Carson is still with us. Not to mention Chandler himself. I don't know, Jake. This whole business is beginning to look like some kind of mortality study, and we don't even know if anyone, dead or alive, can do anything to help you out from under Lansdale's thumb. I'd even venture to speculate that the more you find out, the deeper in shit you're going to be."

"Good point," I said. "So what do I do?"

"I say you go back to California and try to get your friend Lieutenant Boyle to roll over. I'll see what I can do to discover the fate of Phil Cochran and Katherine Carson, with help from Dan Washington, but I think that finding Harry Chandler is your best bet. Particularly since that's what Max Lansdale is paying you to do."

"If you're suggesting I not get personally involved, Eddie, I think it's a little late for that," I said.

"I'm only suggesting that the shortest distance between two points is a straight line," Eddie said, "and the line between Boyle and Chandler seems like the best route right now. How about some lunch? What's your fancy?"

"How's that Chicago-style pizza I've heard tell of?"

"Well, all I can say about it is that it's better here in Chicago than in most places. Myself, I'd prefer a slice from any corner joint in Brooklyn."

"You've been to Brooklyn?"

"Sure. My father took me to see the Cubs play at Ebbets Field a few times. More recently, I was there working on a joint case with the NYPD, Brooklyn Homicide Squad. They were looking into a

Chicago drug dealer as a possible suspect in a shooting out there. Sometimes it's easier for them to call in a private operator than to try working out the logistics with the local cops."

"Why do you think that Max Lansdale called in a PI from LA to scout his brother? There are probably plenty of able investigators here, if you're any indication."

"That's very kind of you to say, and you're correct, there are plenty of good investigators here. But I thought you said that Lansdale answered that—something about his brother taking mysterious trips to LA."

"That's it."

"What's it?" asked Eddie. "I'm not *that* good."

"Lansdale said that the receptionist identified Harry from a photograph from his brother's camera, implying that it was taken the previous weekend, when he claims Randolph was in Los Angeles. The same weekend that the bomb went off at Chandler's place. That's why I thought the picture used to ID Harry was taken in LA and was surprised that it was this one, taken here in Chicago."

"Do you have a camera, Jake? Have you ever had a roll of film going for months before you shoot it all and get it developed?"

"Granted, but why would Randolph be shooting pictures of Chandler in Chicago in September? Months before he knew about what happened when Harry met Carla?"

"Maybe he suspected, back then, that Chandler was romancing his flame."

"Or suspected that Max had a PI on his case. Didn't you say something about lunch?"

I suppose I expected Chicago-style pizza to be very thick, that a leftover slice could be used for a step exerciser. In fact, the deep-dish concoction looked more like the pan it was baked in. The crust was a thin circle with high sides, creating a large crusty bowl into which the ingredients were poured. First in was the cheese, followed by the Italian sausage, which Eddie claimed was a must, red bell peppers, and portobello mushrooms. Finally, tomato sauce covered the works. We sat at a pizza parlor not far from Eddie's place and the ballpark. Eddie assured me that the pie was as good as any you could find in the city, that it was shipped in dry ice to customers all over the country.

"I could have one delivered to me in San Francisco?"

"Sure, if you don't mind paying forty bucks."

"For forty dollars, the thing had better do my laundry when it gets there."

As we ate, I was thinking out loud about all I thought I had learned from talking with Max Lansdale, Tom Romano, the late Stan Riddle, and Ray Boyle. I tried throwing it all into a mental cauldron, mixing it well, and sampling the results. Eddie listened, all the while alternating between roles as the staunch supporter and the devil's advocate. In the end we arrived at the same conclusion. Go through the motions of trying to locate Chandler and Clams, for Lansdale's benefit, until I found a way to get loose of it. Start by trying Ray Boyle again, since he was the only person I'd spoken with who seemed to have a line to Chandler and seemed pretty certain that Harry was alive. If somehow I actually came face-to-face with Chandler, I could ask him to clear up a few things, if I even cared by then. Or simply beg him to do something to get Lansdale out of my life.

So, it looked like it was time to start building up my frequent-flier miles again. Back at Eddie's place, I gave my cousin Bobby a call in Westwood and asked if he would pick me up at LAX and put me up at his apartment for the night.

Eddie gave me a warm send-off at O'Hare. As luck, or dumb luck, would have it, I had just enough time to get to Parker Center before Boyle went off duty.

Part Two

FALLING

Nine

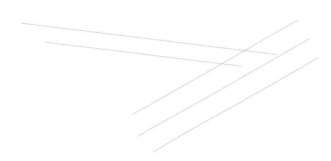

BOBBY DROPPED ME OFF in front of Parker Center a few minutes before seven that evening. I knew from experience that Ray Boyle rarely got out of the building before eight. I promised my cousin that I would buy him dinner after I was done with Ray, unless the lieutenant had me arrested.

It was Thursday. I had been to Chicago twice and now two times to LA in four days and all I seemed to have accomplished was to get myself in deeper. On the upside, I hadn't rested in one place long enough for jet lag to catch up with me.

I found Ray in his office, just as I had two days earlier. The difference was that instead of finding Boyle talking on the telephone, I walked in just as he hurled the phone into the blackboard against the far wall.

"Jesus!" he said, well above a roar, "If they can put a man on the fucking moon, why can't they keep a goddamn rapist off the street for more than three hours?"

Or, as Darlene might have said on the same subject, if they can put a man on the moon, why not put them all there?

"Ray, we need to talk," I said, watching him closely for any sign that might suggest he wasn't through throwing heavy objects.

"I'm in no mood, Diamond. Make a fucking appointment."

"I'm not leaving until you tell me what's really going on between Harry Chandler and Max Lansdale. And save the bullshit. You may need it later on to explain destroying perfectly good office equipment."

"Did I detect a little hint of a threat in your tone, Diamond?"

"I'm dead serious, Ray."

"Boy, Diamond, you must be fucking insane. You're standing in a building that at this moment has the largest population of police per square inch in all of California, if not the world, and you come barging in uninvited thinking that you can throw your weight around? I said I'm not in the fucking mood. Do yourself a favor, leave me alone. Take two fucking Valiums and call me in the morning."

"Fuck you, Boyle."

"Don't bother. I'm sure that the animal they just released will grab me in some alley and beat you to it."

"C'mon, Ray. Don't take it out on me. Throw the fucking stapler or something. But calm down and give me a little time. I need help, and I have nowhere else to turn. I'm sure you'll believe it when I tell you that there are many places I would rather be than here watching you have a tantrum."

"I need a fucking drink," he said.

"Fine, I'll buy you a drink."

"I'm sick of it, Jake."

"Well, Ray, it's a dirty job but somebody's got to do it. Will you help me?"

"I don't know if I can," Boyle said.

"Will you at least try?"

"I need a fucking drink."

"Fine, let's get out of here. I'll buy you a drink."

I had to jog to keep up with him.

Out of the building, down the street, and into a local saloon.

I didn't catch the name of the joint, only the neon shamrock over the front door. The barkeep had a scotch poured for Boyle before we made it up to the bar.

I asked for a shot of Dickel on ice and got that all-too-familiar look of mystification from the bartender. I asked him to make it a Jack Daniel's. I spilled a good portion of the drink trotting after Boyle as he moved rapidly to a booth in the rear.

I slid into the bench seat opposite him. He knocked down the scotch in one gulp and before the empty glass hit the table the barman had another round set down in front of us.

After dispensing with his second drink, Boyle cooled down enough to take a stab at dispensing with me.

"Make it fast, Diamond. If I'm in this drinking hole much longer you'll have to carry me out with a backhoe," he said, waving to the bartender for a refill.

"Why did Randolph Lansdale put a hit on Chandler?" I asked, wasting no time. "Was it because of Carla Rosario or was it something else? Something that Harry Chandler had discovered about Lansdale?"

"I told you what I know, Jake. My understanding was that when Lansdale knew that he couldn't have Carla, he made sure that no one would. If there was something else on Lansdale's mind, I never heard about it."

"Tell me where I can find Chandler, Ray. I want out of this thing."

"I can't do that, Jake," Boyle said, "but I did get word to Chandler, and he agreed to meet with you. He'll come up to San Francisco; he'll pick the time and place. You'll have to hold out for a week at most."

"A week. Jesus, Ray, where's the guy coming from? Fucking Siberia?"

"Might as well be," Boyle said, draining his third scotch, "and that's all I can say. Get back home and wait until you hear from him."

"And if I don't?"

"If you don't get the fuck back to San Francisco?"

"If I don't hear from Chandler."

"You will. He knows who you are, knows you were tight with Jimmy Pigeon, and he wants to do the right thing," Ray said. "And if that's not enough, Harry owes me and he gave his word of honor that he wouldn't let you dangle."

"His word of honor. What is he, a fucking Boy Scout?"

"His word is solid, Jake. I'm doing all I can. Stay out of trouble for a few days and then you can put it all behind you."

"If I don't hear from Chandler by the middle of next week I'm coming back down here, Ray, as much as I hate this place," I said. "And I'm coming straight to you."

"If you're trying to frighten me, Diamond, save it for when I'm sober. I'm too stupid at the moment to be afraid of anything, and I've got to get out of here."

Boyle rose from his seat, threw a twenty-dollar bill on the table, and turned toward the exit.

"Ray," I called as he moved away.

"Hold that thought," he said, and he was gone.

I called my cousin Bobby from a pay phone at the bar entrance and asked him to meet me at a steak house we both knew a few blocks from Parker Center. After dinner we sat up for a few hours at his apartment in Westwood while he filled me in on the new movie he was set to start work on the following week, but the air travel was finally catching up with me, so I soon stretched out on Bobby's sofa, and he went off to his bedroom to sleep. I managed to get through a few pages of the Dostoyevsky novel before I was out cold.

The next morning, Friday, I took an early flight back to San Francisco. Darlene picked me up at the airport. It didn't take long for me to fill her in. I didn't have much filler. Darlene claimed that a few calls had come in during my absence. Possible new cases. She said that she had the rough details waiting on my desk for consideration.

"Could take your mind off this Lansdale business."

"Maybe," was all the response I could manage.

I sat at my desk in my back office looking over Darlene's notes. Three cases.

A store owner who suspected that his new manager was skimming off sales.

A mother who was afraid that her teenage daughter's boyfriend was a drug dealer.

A defense attorney who wanted evidence to demonstrate, if only to himself, that his client wasn't guilty of circulating child pornography.

I was so distracted, the best I could do to decide which if any of the cases I would as much as follow up on was going to require tossing a coin or two.

Mostly, I was looking at the telephone waiting for Harrison Chandler to make it ring.

When the telephone did ring I nearly swallowed my cigarette.

"It's Ted Harrison, Jake," said Darlene. "His client goes on trial Monday for distributing child porn and he's frantic."

I pushed the blinking button on the phone console.

"Mr. Harrison," I said, "Jake Diamond."

"Mr. Diamond, I need some help, fast. My client is innocent."

Tell me about it, I thought.

"Tell me about it," I said.

"Sal Fuller runs a small mail-order business, ships mostly Northern California. Seeds."

"Seeds?"

"Plant seeds, flowers, vegetables, that sort of thing."

"Okay."

"A package sent from his warehouse was delivered to the wrong address. The woman who received it opened the package. There were photographs. Disgusting photographs. She called the police."

"Wasn't she afraid of the penalty for opening someone else's mail?"

"I suppose that opening the package was one thing, but the nature of the pictures was another. She claimed that the package arrived damaged and she spotted the contents. In any event, the authorities were less interested in mail tampering than in who was doing the mailing."

"How about who was doing the buying?" I asked.

"They questioned the man who was supposed to have received the package. His lawyer worked out an immunity deal if he would explain how he ordered the material. He claimed that he ordered from a site on the Internet, and paid by cash through a post office box."

"Did the police stake out the box?" I asked. "Find out who picked up the payment?"

"The story hit the *Chronicle* and no one has showed up at the PO box since. All the police had to go on was that the package originated from Sal's Seeds, and my client was arrested and charged."

"What's Sal's story?" I asked.

"Sal Fuller is a model citizen, Mr. Diamond, a family man. But all of the testimonials that I could drum up are not going to make a jury ignore the fact that the package was shipped from Sal's warehouse."

"If your client is innocent, it had to be someone who had access to his shipping facility; does Mr. Fuller have a suspect?"

"No. But I do."

"Oh?"

"Fuller has a son, seventeen years old. The boy works for his father on weekends, in shipping. I've suggested to Fuller that his son might be responsible, but he refuses to consider it."

"Or Fuller has considered it, and decided to protect his kid," I said. "I really don't see how I can help you, Mr. Harrison. I think you'll just have to do your best to make your case on the man's good reputation. There's not much more you can do. Wherever the chips fall, in the end it's between the father and son."

"What if I leaked my suspicions about the boy to the police?"

"You have to decide what's in the best interest of your client. I don't envy you and I wouldn't dream of advising you."

"And what if the boy is involved in something that is hurting these young children in the photographs?"

"I'm guessing that if the kid is the culprit he's simply buying the photographs from somewhere else and reselling at a profit. He's probably too naive to really understand the implications of the source. If it were something else the kid was peddling, he'd probably be up for a Junior Achievement award. Maybe that's the solution. Maybe you can find out where he was getting the material and get both father *and* son off the hook."

"Could you help me do that, Mr. Diamond?"

"The kid is a minor, Mr. Harrison. I can't touch it. Tell you what you might do. Give Lieutenant Laura Lopez a call at the SFPD, Vallejo Street. Lopez works with teenagers. Feel her out. Give her the rough details, without naming names. Convince her that you're interested in helping the boy without ruining his life. You can trust Lopez. If she says that she can help, she will."

"Thank you, Mr. Diamond. I'd like to compensate you for your time."

"Donate something to one of Lieutenant Lopez's pet youth projects, Mr. Harrison," I said, "and good luck."

While I was in my help-an-adolescent-in-trouble mode, I decided to call the woman worried about her daughter dating a drug pusher. The number she had given to Darlene was for her office at a large downtown financial institution.

I got the basic questions out of the way quickly, asking the name of her daughter's boyfriend, how the two had met, and what had led her to believe that the boy was involved in the drug trade.

"The boy's name is Pedro Sanchez," said Jane Miller. "Isn't it obvious, Mr. Diamond?"

Jane Miller was a single mother of three; Rachel was her eldest. Rachel and Pedro were students at the San Francisco Arts High School on Font Boulevard. They had been seeing each other since doing a show together in the Drama Department. I knew the school, knew of its reputation and requirements, and was almost certain that Jane Miller was doing her bit for racial profiling. I told her, as I had told Harrison, that I couldn't investigate juveniles. She said "Thanks for nothing" and hung up.

The call bothered me. A woman who was so vehemently against her daughter's socializing with a Hispanic boy that she would suggest criminality was dangerous to both the boy and her daughter.

I called Lopez and filled her in, asking if she would speak to the guidance counselor at the school to determine whether family intervention was needed. I also told Lopez that she might be getting a call from an attorney named Ted Harrison about another teen in a jam.

"What's with you, Diamond," Lopez asked when I was through, "you bucking for Concerned Citizen of the Year honors?"

"I'm just taking them as they come, Lieutenant," I said, "while I'm waiting for Judgment Day."

Two down and one to go, and I hadn't made a cent. I called the last number, hoping that the new manager suspected of skimming off sales was legal age. As it turned out, I knew the place and the owner. Gant's Loans, one of a row of pawnshops on Sixth Street between Stevenson and Market streets. I stopped into Gant's often, looking for used classical CDs, and Monty Gant usually gave me a call when something came in that he thought might interest me.

"Monty, Jake Diamond."

"Jake, thanks for calling. I got this new guy here and I think that he's robbing me blind, but I can't catch him at it. It's the nature of the business. Our salespeople are free to negotiate prices, and I'm almost sure that this guy is underreporting what he's taking in."

"You're calling me to play secret shopper, Monty?"

"Would you please, Jake?"

It almost made me grateful that an exciting case came along now and then, even it if held the threat that I could be killed if I couldn't find a few ghosts for Max Lansdale.

"Is the suspect working now?"

"He's here until six. I leave at five. There's a real nice Rolex, I'm asking three thousand dollars. I'll bring the cash over to you. See what kind of deal you can make with the guy."

"I'll meet you at the diner on Stevenson at five, Monty. Get any good music in?"

"Nab this fuck for me and you can take your pick, Jake."

"I'll see you at five," I said.

I opened the office window to determine what Angelo had prepared for his lunch special at Molinari's on the avenue below.

Despite the fact that the Catholic Church had lifted the ban on Friday meat consumption years ago for some esoteric reason, Angelo Verdi was a die-hard traditionalist. Since Angelo had featured fried calamari on Sunday, which I had of course missed when I was rudely whisked off to Chicago, Angelo went with baked clams that Friday afternoon.

Vongoli al forno. So much for putting the Lansdale dilemma out of my mind.

I picked up a salad for Darlene—romaine, cucumber, and Roma tomato, hold the dressing—and we dined together at her desk.

We talked about plans for the weekend. Hers, including a visit to Half Moon Bay, and mine, hopefully including some quality time with Sally French. Darlene donated her side order of garlic bread to Tug McGraw. It could only improve the mutt's breath.

Later in the afternoon I called Sally at her office, hoping for some luck that wasn't bad. Not yet. Sally had a function to attend, related to her work with the city arts council.

"You're certainly welcome to join me, Jake," she said, "but I don't think you would enjoy it very much."

I had great faith in Sally's disclaimers, so I politely passed.

"How about tomorrow?" I asked.

"I have a preordained brunch date with my mother."

I didn't have to be warned about the entertainment value of that program.

"And afterward?"

"I'll probably be free of Mom by two. Then I'm wide open through Sunday."

"How about I drop over at four, we can dream up a Saturday night on the town."

"Four it is," she said. "By the way, Jake, do I still need to be looking over my shoulder?"

"Just to be safe, at least until tomorrow afternoon. Then I'll do the looking for you."

"Okay, see you then," she said. "Stay on your toes."

Speaking of mothers, I had neglected mine for a while and decided that having dinner with Mom was as good a plan as any on a Friday night in the baseball off-season.

I gave Tom Romano a quick call, to thank him for his vigilance and to apologize again for missing the pinochle game with him and Ira Fennessy the night before. I had called him from Chicago when I was sure that I wouldn't make it back in time.

"Ira's brother sat in, but it wasn't the same, he bids like a maniac," Tom said. "How did it go in Chicago?"

"Not very far. I'm stuck in a holding pattern. I'm supposed to hear from the late Harry Chandler if and when he gets in from the far ends of the earth. Meanwhile I have to appear to be searching for him and Joe Clams, in case anyone is watching. Lansdale said he would take the heat off the women, but I have a problem with his sincerity. So, if time allows, keep an eye open."

"Sure. How did Eddie Hand treat you?"

"Like a brother, Tom. Thanks for that also."

"Eddie is a good man. And he'll do some follow-up for you if he said he would. How about a drink after work?"

"Can't tonight. I have to shop for a three-thousand-dollar watch at five, and then I'm hoping that my mother will feed me. I don't know about you, Tom, but if opening day at Pac Bell doesn't get here quickly I'm going to go stir-crazy."

I called my mother after finishing with Tom. She was delighted.

"It's Friday, Jacob, you'll have to settle for fish," she said.

"That's, Mom."

"I'll do linguini with clam sauce, and throw together some of the rice balls you love so much. I'll just use the peas and mozzarella and leave out the ham."

"Great, Mom, I'll bring the wine and dessert," I said. "Look for me at seven; I'll be the kid with the appetite."

Linguini con salsa vongoli. It figured.

The next morning, though I would have preferred to sleep in, I met Monty at the same diner where I'd picked up three thousand bucks in cash from him the evening before.

"Nice timepiece," I said, sliding the Rolex to him across the table.

"What did it set you back?" Monty asked.

"Here's the change," I said, placing two one-hundred-dollar bills beside the watch.

"Son of a bitch," Monty said. "Look at this."

He had stopped into his shop before meeting me and picked up the sales log. The last sale of the day was for a silver Rolex. The sale price was entered at $2,650.

"What will you do?" I asked.

"Look for a new employee," he said. "Too bad you already have a job."

"Sometimes I wonder."

Monty slipped the two hundred back my way.

"That's too much," I said.

"Did you make any money yesterday, Jake?"

"No."

"So don't complain. It was worth it. You can buy me breakfast."

Somehow I managed to squander the remainder of the morning and most of the afternoon doing absolutely nothing. At four, I was at Sally's house in the Presidio. We had a few drinks and planned an evening around dinner and a movie, with a working budget of two hundred dollars. When Sally invited me to stay the night, I nearly let out an audible sigh of relief.

If there was something strange about enjoying time spent with my ex-wife, I was ready to make *strange* my new favorite word.

We stayed together most of the day Sunday, talking, cooking, watching videos, generally having a grand old time. I made it back to my place in the Fillmore, brewed a pot of espresso, made up for the cigarettes I hadn't smoked at Sally's, read a couple of chapters of *Karamazov,* and hit the hay.

Monday and Tuesday were uneventful. I stopped over to Joey Russo's place on Monday evening to check on Vinnie Strings. Somehow he was managing to keep the basil plants alive. I was reminded of how much I missed having Joey around, being that whenever I found myself stuck between a rock and a hard place, Joey Russo had a natural talent for squeezing in beside me. Vinnie and I shared a pizza and a six-pack and we called it a night.

On Tuesday, I finally woke up to the realization that Darlene might need a little bit of attention. She claimed that her weekend down at Half Moon Bay had been a gas, but she wasn't entirely convincing. I can be pretty thick, but it was no excuse for neglecting the fact that Darlene had found her piece-of-crap football-player boyfriend in the sack with a girl sporting patent leather boots. There was a new health food restaurant recently opened in the Castro and I suggested that we try it out for dinner.

On me.

"What if you can't find anything on the menu to eat?" Darlene asked, as much as she appreciated the gesture.

"I called the place. They serve free-range chicken, whatever that is. I mean, if the bird was running around the range so free, how did the poor bastard wind up on the menu?"

"I'd love to have dinner with you, Jake," Darlene said.

Call me selfish, but it made me feel good to see her smile.

On Wednesday morning, I made it to the office at nine. Darlene was paying bills, so I did what I always did when Darlene was dealing with finances. I went to hide in my back room.

At half past ten Darlene buzzed me from her desk.

"Telephone call for you, Jake," she said. "A sweet-talker claiming to be Harrison Chandler."

Ten

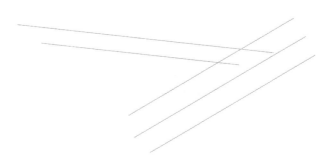

Harrison Chandler made it short, and he did most of the talking.

"Meet me at exactly five on Friday afternoon. There is a joint called the Pork Store Café on Haight, between Ashbury and Masonic. There's a green metal door off the alley behind the place, you can access the alley from Masonic. The door will be unlocked. Take the stairs to the second floor. Don't be late, don't be followed."

"Why not come here," I asked, "or meet in a public place if you're worried about safety?"

"Whether you realize it or not, your office and your apartment are being watched. And public places aren't well recommended for someone who is technically still wanted for murder," Chandler said. "It's the best I can do, and I'm going out on a limb. And it's a one-shot deal. I'll see you on Friday."

And the line went dead.

I had no clue as to what I could possibly do to keep myself occupied for two days waiting for the showdown with Harry Chandler.

A few minutes after Chandler ended his call, Tom Romano rang with a temporary solution.

Tom asked if I could meet him at his office.

"I got a call from Eddie Hand," Tom Romano said when I got

to his office. "He had no luck on the reporter, Phil Cochran. But he did get a line on Katherine Carson, the receptionist who iden-tified Chandler. Eddie found what may be a current address from a friend of his at the IRS."

"Oh?"

"Marina del Rey."

"You've got to be joking."

"Sorry, pal."

Tom let me use his telephone to call Willie Dogtail.

"Willie, Jake. I need a favor."

"Name it, paleface."

"I'm trying to find a woman."

"How tall?"

I gave Dogtail the Marina del Rey address.

"I need to know if a certain woman still lives there, Willie, and I wouldn't mind finding out where she works," I said. "The name is Katherine Carson, goes by Kit."

"Kit Carson? I'm Sioux, Jake. Are you trying to give me the shivers?"

"Scope it out, Willie, and try not to spook her. I need to talk with the woman, so keep your scalping knife locked up until I do."

"No problem, Wyatt. I'll get on it first thing in the morning, see if I can't ID the lady and maybe follow her to work. I'll give you a call as soon as I have something."

"Thanks, Willie."

"How about a card game tomorrow night, Jake?" Romano asked when I was through with Dogtail. "To make up for the one we missed last Thursday. I can give Fennessy a call, see if he's down for it."

"Sure, why not, if I can have a word or two with Kit Carson without having to haul my aching body back down there."

It was getting close to noon, so I offered to treat Tom to what-ever the greasy spoon down the street from his office was calling special that day. I made it back to my office just before two. I gave Vinnie Strings a call, to enlist the help I would need from him to make my Friday meeting with Harry Chandler.

Thoughts about leaving work early were interrupted when Max Lansdale called from Chicago at half past four.

"How are we coming along, Jake?" he asked.

I could feel the chicken-fried steak do a flip-flop in my stomach.

"I'm working a couple of leads, Max," I said. "Keep your shirt on."

"You know, Diamond, I've been very liberal with you. Please don't forget who you are talking to."

Fat chance.

"Look, Lansdale, I hate to burst your bubble, but you're really not doing me any favors. If you want to get talked nice to, call Regis. I'm doing the best I can. If you're unhappy with my work, call the Better Business Bureau."

Lansdale hung up.

I couldn't care less if the guy liked me or not. I was in the same spot, one way or the other.

A snake pit is a snake pit.

On the upside, Max Lansdale's call had held me long enough to catch a phone call from Sally. She had tickets to one of the semiprofessional theater productions over at Fort Mason.

Sally was an executive with the arts council. The theater company was looking for funding, and Sally wanted to check out the work. I realized that if the play was bad, it would be two hours of torture without escape. And if it was good, it would have me pining over the good old days Off-Off-Broadway. In any event, seeing Sally was worth the risk. And it would take care of another evening of waiting to see Chandler. I told Sally I would pick her up at seven.

I walked Darlene and the pooch back to her car at five, and grabbed an eggplant sandwich at Molinari's to take home. If someone was trying to watch my movements without being spotted, he was doing a damn fine job of it. I only hoped that Dogtail would do as well in the morning with Kit Carson.

He did. He called the following afternoon. I was out of the office picking up the beer and snacks for the pinochle game, so Darlene had him call me on my cellular.

Willie was able to confirm that Katherine Carson did in fact live at the Marina del Rey address, and he gave me both her residential and office phone numbers.

I thought it would be better to confront her at home and decided that I would call before I left for the card game.

"I don't understand it," I said, more to myself than to anyone else.

"What's not to understand?" Tom Romano said, arranging his cards, handling each one as if it would bite him. "It's Ira's night. It's always Ira's night. No matter how long I look at this hand, it still looks more like a foot to me. I pass."

I had reached Kit Carson, but try as she might, she was little help.

"So Ms. Carson tells me that when Randolph Lansdale learned that his sweetheart had fallen for Harry Chandler, he went on a two-day bender. Kit Carson nurses him through it and before you know it they're in the sack together. And Randolph Lansdale is suddenly head over heels for Katherine, she's always had a thing for him, and they're both hearing wedding bells."

"Nice rebound," Ira Fennessy said. "I'll bid three fifty."

"Jesus, Ira, have a heart," Tom said.

"Ira probably has a fist full of hearts," I said. "So, Carson asks me, and it's a very good question, why would Randolph Lansdale be dragging his ass to Los Angeles to stalk the slut who dumped him, let alone to blow the bitch to pieces? I'm paraphrasing, but I am trying to capture her tone," I said. "Four hundred."

"If you're looking to buy some meld, Jake, forget it," Ira said. "Four fifty."

"Don't let him intimidate you, Jake," said Tom.

"I haven't bought meld in about three months, so intimidation is futile. I only bid if I have it in my hand. Five hundred."

"I ought to stick you with it, Diamond," Ira said.

"So, I say to Carson, 'What about all of the photos he took of Chandler and Carla?' The pictures that brother Max said he found in Randolph's desk and warned Chandler about. And she says that Randolph Lansdale never took a photograph in his life and that he wouldn't know which end of a camera was up if he owned one, which he didn't," I said. "The bid is five hundred, do I hear five fifty?"

"I don't see how you come close to making five hundred, Jake," Ira said.

"Max Lansdale never told you personally about his brother's

jealous rage," said Romano. "Isn't that something you got from Ray Boyle?"

"Who probably got it from Chandler, so who knows? But Max did claim that he developed photos of Chandler from *his brother's camera*, so something gives. And the photograph that was used to identify Chandler to the police, the one that was taken in front of the newspaper building. Where did that really come from?" I said. "What's the bid?"

"Five hundred, and I don't think you can make it," said Ira.

"So pass," I said. "Harry Chandler was investigating Randolph Lansdale. He must have been onto something, and it scared Lansdale pretty bad. The question is, did Harry even know, or did he really believe that it had to do with love and romance?"

"You can ask Chandler tomorrow," Tom said.

"And why didn't Carson hear a gunshot when Chandler walked into the office and put one into Lansdale's head?" I said, thinking out loud. "The woman told me that she never heard a gunshot."

"A silencer?" said Tom.

"I don't know."

"You can ask Chandler tomorrow," Tom said again.

"If I can make it to tomorrow," I said.

"I pass," said Fennessy.

I turned over the cards in the kitty. Jack of spades. Nine of spades.

"What do you know," I said, flipping over the last card, "there's your second ace of hearts, Ira. Gives me one hundred aces, the run in spades with the double marriage in trump, and a pinochle."

"Jesus," said Ira.

"I don't know if I can add this high. Two hundred, two forty, three forty," I counted as I laid the cards down. "What do I need to make the hand?"

"One sixty," said Ira, "and you bid five hundred with what? Eighty points in your mitt?"

"Maybe your luck is changing, Jake," Tom Romano said.

I could only hope.

Eleven

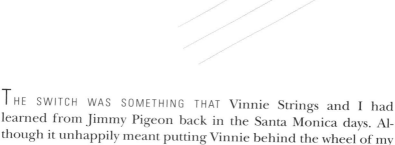

THE SWITCH WAS SOMETHING THAT Vinnie Strings and I had learned from Jimmy Pigeon back in the Santa Monica days. Although it unhappily meant putting Vinnie behind the wheel of my cherished 1963 Chevy Impala convertible, at least for the first part of the trip, I felt fairly confident that it would do the job of shaking any tails.

The logical choice was the Broadway tunnel. I left the office at twenty to five on Friday afternoon and drove the Toyota to the west entrance of the tunnel. I silently prayed that Vinnie would be on time, since stopping in the middle of the tunnel during rush hour was going to cause a great deal of commotion regardless of how quickly we could switch vehicles. For a change, the answer to my prayer was yes. At the center of the tunnel, I saw the Impala slow to a stop, halting the opposing traffic. I stopped the Toyota and hopped out. Vinnie and I brushed shoulders as we each crossed the traffic lane divider. I jumped into the Chevy, threw it into first, and took off. I saw Vinnie head off in the opposite direction in the Toyota. The whole deal had taken less than a minute. The riot of horn blasts in the tunnel could have raised the dead. I exited the tunnel at the place where I had entered.

I was already back out onto Powell Street before I realized that Vinnie had a tape going in the cassette player with the volume pumped. Joey Ramone screamed out of the speakers about wanting to be sedated. I quickly switched it off and pointed the car toward the Haight.

I parked the car on Masonic, near Frederick Street, and walked the few short blocks back down to Haight Street. I entered the alley off Masonic and found the green metal door. I glanced at my watch; it was exactly two minutes before five. I passed through the unlocked door and started up the stairs to the second floor.

At the top of the stairs I found another metal door, this one blue. I rapped lightly. I heard sounds of movement and then a voice.

"Diamond?"

"Yes."

"What was Jimmy Pigeon's middle name?"

How the fuck would I know?

"How the fuck should I know?" I said.

I heard footsteps approaching from the inside, and when the door swung open I found myself eyeball to eyeball with the legendary Harrison Chandler.

"Come in," he said.

I walked past him into the room.

Chandler closed the door behind us and led me into a large space crammed with what appeared to be multicolored cars from kiddie amusement park rides.

"How did you know it was me?" I asked.

"Your lack of hesitation answering the test question. Are you sure you weren't followed?" Chandler asked.

"Pretty sure," I answered. "What *was* Jimmy's middle name?"

"How would I know? Take a seat," he said, indicating one of two folding metal chairs sitting between two child-sized bright yellow cars in the shape of ducklings.

"What is this place?" I asked.

"A storage area for amusement park ride equipment," Chandler answered.

"I thought so," I said.

"What can I do for you, Diamond?"

Get me out of this pile of shit you put me in.

"Make Max Lansdale forget that I ever existed," I said.

"Let me tell you about Max Lansdale," Harry Chandler volunteered.

"Okay."

"Care for a drink while we talk?"

"Happen to have a bottle of Dickel handy?" I asked.

Chandler walked over to a tiny red car in the shape of a Volkswagen with a big goofy smile below its headlights.

"We'll have to make do without ice," Harry said, reaching into the car and pulling out a bottle of George Dickel Tennessee sour mash whiskey and two glasses.

Chandler filled both glasses, handed one to me, took a seat on the other folding chair, and unceremoniously began.

Harry Chandler's career as a private detective started immediately after Harry rearranged his captain's facial features at Parker Center. Chandler's credentials as an exceptional investigator helped him, but his reputation as a Boy Scout didn't. Harry had no lack of work, but it was not the challenging and lucrative sort of work that might have come from more questionable sources had he not been perceived as squeaky clean.

Chandler soon found himself working cases with Jimmy Pigeon before Jimmy moved his operation from Los Angeles to Santa Monica.

Chandler also spent a good deal of time working pro bono for himself, trying to nail the city councilman slash mayoral candidate who had contributed to Harry's fall from grace with the brass at the LAPD. Harry's efforts resulted in a fine portfolio of photographs of the councilman and a high school cheerleader, which ended the man's political career and sent him packing to sunny Arizona.

Soon after, Chandler received a call from an attorney in Chicago offering a large sum of money for what seemed a fairly uncomplicated surveillance job, and Harry could only consider the offer to be just in the nick of time.

So in the late spring of 1995, Harrison Chandler was retained by Max Lansdale.

Lansdale claimed that his older brother, Randolph, was regularly making unexplained trips from Chicago to LA. Max was worried that his brother might be involved with what he referred to as "unsavory characters of the Italian American persuasion." Max insisted that he had no desire to create any serious problems for his brother; his only wish was to protect Randolph from possible legal trouble or worse.

Harry watched the elder Lansdale's movements in Los Angeles long enough to determine that Randolph's business there, though perhaps stretching the limits of the law a bit, did not involve ethnic gangsters. Chandler reported his findings to Max Lansdale, who seemed satisfied and thanked and paid Harry accordingly. All might have been over between Harry and the Lansdale brothers except for the fact that on one of his visits to meet face-to-face with Max, Harry came cheek to cheek with Carla Rosario.

And later came nose to nose with Phil Cochran of the *Chicago Sun-Times.*

Cochran had been looking into the recent passing of Simon Lansdale. His interest was piqued by an anonymous phone call suggesting that even at the ripe age of eighty-five, the old man's death in his sleep might not have been entirely natural. Cochran's investigation included a short interview with Carla Rosario, who claimed to have nothing to offer. When Chandler heard, from Carla, about Cochran's inquiries, Harry's overpowering detective instincts kicked into gear. He made contact with the reporter and together they began snooping around. They agreed that there was a very good chance that the tip to Phil Cochran had come from Max Lansdale. Max may have felt that his brother Randolph was a little tired of waiting for the old man to check out and leave Randolph at the helm. Perhaps, though Chandler had found no evidence, Randolph Lansdale *was* in bed with the Italians and needed his father out of the way to consummate the marriage. Partly for the sheer love of the game, and partly to protect Carla Rosario from any danger working for a murderer could put her in, Harry Chandler began a quiet examination of the circumstances surrounding Simon Lansdale's uninterrupted sleep.

Chandler was able to dig up a few pieces of purely circumstantial evidence. It was established that Simon Lansdale was alone in the house on the night he expired in his sleep, his wife being out of state at a Giancana family get-together that Simon had elected to avoid. Harry also discovered that old man Lansdale had been given a clean bill of health by his physician just two days before his death. The Chicago Police Department, after a cursory investigation, dismissed both these points as immaterial. There was no evidence whatsoever that any other person had been inside the house between the time Simon's wife left him at home late that afternoon and the time his body was discovered the following morning by the housekeeper. The official line was that Simon had simply run out of steam.

Cochran and Chandler weren't convinced. Cochran put word out on the street through his many contacts that there would be a handsome reward to anyone who had information placing another person at the scene that night, and a few days later a call came in to his office at the newspaper. A neighbor, who had been walking his dog on the night Simon passed away, claimed to have seen a man leave Lansdale's home after two that morning. The neighbor felt fairly certain that it was one of the sons, but couldn't say which one. Cochran and Chandler set up a meeting with the caller, to take a signed statement and deliver the promised reward. The caller, who had never identified himself, failed to show up for the rendezvous and never contacted Cochran again.

A week later the investigation was stone cold.

Chandler took a breather from his narrative to refresh our drinks. He pulled a small black and white kiddie-ride car in the likeness of Snoopy over to his chair and used it as a footstool after retaking his seat. He quietly sipped his bourbon and seemed to slip away into thought.

I brought him back with the obvious question.

"So, then what happened?" I asked.

"Cochran lost his patience and jumped the gun with the story, alleging this and that," said Chandler. "A few days later he was out of a job and a few days after that he was gone."

"Gone?"

"Dematerialized."

"And?"

"And by then," Chandler said, "Carla was fired and I assumed she was safely out of danger, so I lost interest. And I thought I had left the Lansdale brothers to their own devices forever until Max called me in LA to warn me that his brother was badly overreacting to the loss of Carla's affections. And then the bomb went off, and when I came to all I could think about was killing Randolph Lansdale."

Chandler suddenly jumped up from his seat, knocking Snoopy for a loop. He pulled a large gun from the shoulder holster beneath his jacket and pointed it, I hoped, over my head. I nearly chipped a tooth on my bourbon glass. I instinctively went for my own gun but my reach wasn't long enough, since the .38 was where I had left it, four hundred miles away in the glove compartment of Willie Dogtail's pickup truck. Chandler stared past me to the door I had entered, knitting his eyebrows into a straight line. When he opened his mouth to speak, I expected to hear him say something like *Go ahead, make my day.*

"Did you hear something out there?" he asked.

I really hadn't.

"No," I said.

"Sit tight," he said, walking slowly to the door.

It would be no problem; I was tight as a drum.

Chandler reached the door and slowly opened it. He stuck his gun and his head out into the landing. Then he left the room.

I thought about trying to squeeze myself into the tiny red Volkswagen.

A few moments later, Chandler returned. He sat down in his chair, righted Snoopy, and made himself comfortable again, putting the handgun on top of the dog's black and white fiberglass head.

"You left the door open," I cleverly noted.

"It's harder to sneak up on an open doorway," he said. "Where was I?"

"Ready to waste Randolph Lansdale," I said.

"By the time we made it to Chicago and to Lansdale's office, Joe Clams had calmed me down considerably. Joe had lost a sister, and it had him twisted in knots, but Joe was always much more levelheaded. When I walked into Randolph Lansdale's office it was with the intention of wiping the floor with him until I could get a confession, and then turning him in to the LAPD. I found him behind his desk, slumped in his chair with a bullet hole in his temple. The gun on the floor at his feet belonged to me. I had thought the gun had been lost in the explosion, but apparently it had been taken from my apartment when the bomb was placed. I scooped up the gun and left the office, and we beat it back to Los Angeles. I talked it out with Ray Boyle and we agreed that no one was going to believe that Randolph Lansdale had killed himself with my weapon."

"So?"

"So, what may have been a suicide became a first-degree murder. With my name written all over it. Ray Boyle, Joe Clams, and Jimmy Pigeon helped me disappear."

"What happened to the weapon?"

"I left it with Ray."

"Did he check it for prints?"

"Yes."

"And he found only yours."

"Did he tell you that?" asked Chandler.

"I guessed," I said, "and I don't suppose Randolph was wearing gloves when he shot himself."

"No gloves. I may inadvertently have wiped it clean."

"It was great timing, Randolph putting one in his head just before you and Joe Clams arrived."

"Perfect timing," Chandler agreed.

"So maybe someone else killed Randolph, someone who knew that you were on your way there."

"Ray Boyle and I strongly considered the possibility," Chandler said, "but we had no way to prove it, and I had no choice but to vanish. And no matter how Randolph Lansdale bought it, at least the bastard paid for Carla's death."

"It wasn't Randolph Lansdale who had the bomb planted in your apartment."

"Do you know that as a fact?"

"Randolph had no motive; he was over his obsession with Carla. Randy was all set to tie the knot with his receptionist."

"Maybe he was afraid that I'd found something concrete to link him to his father's death?" Chandler suggested.

"If you're looking for facts, I can't help you. I'm not a rocket scientist. But I can tell you what I suspect. Randolph Lansdale had nothing to do with his father's death. He worshipped the old man. I believe that it had to be Max all the way. Max who was seen that night leaving his father's house. Max who killed Simon Lansdale. Max who was afraid that once you teamed up with Cochran, you might prove it. Max who had someone like Ralph Battle put a bomb under your bed and snatch your gun on his way out. Max who was reestablishing ties with organized crime, and needed his father and his brother out of the way. Max who was already planning to take Randolph out of the picture before he ever hired you. Max Lansdale began setting his brother up by hiring you in the first place. By casting suspicion on his brother's business dealings, allegedly dangerous dealings with organized criminals. By raising questions about the circumstances of his father's death with an anonymous call to Cochran, not expecting that you would get on the case. And ultimately by feeding you the bull story about Randolph's mental instability over losing Carla's affection. And when you survived the bombing, Max realized the perfect scenario. Max Lansdale knew that you would be hot for vengeance, so he waited and watched. And when he knew that you were on your way to Chicago, Max put one into his brother's head with your gun, or had Battle do it, just in time for your arrival. And when you went down in a shoot-out with the LAPD, Max was home free. Lansdale may have had some minor worries about Joe Clams popping up again, but he wasn't losing sleep over it, so he simply kept an eye out. But then Max learned that you were still alive and he felt the foundation tremble, and now he's looking to put you *and* Clams under the ground once and for all. Not to mention what he has in mind for me. How did Lansdale find out that you were still breathing?"

"Max Lansdale knew I was alive because I contacted him after Ray Boyle found the note from Jimmy Pigeon," Chandler said. "Jesus, now I understand why Max seemed so eager to pay me off."

"Oh?" I said, then took a healthy gulp from my glass.

Harry began to reach inside his suit jacket just as my cell phone rang. I grabbed for the phone with my free hand and hit the talk button as Chandler pulled an envelope from his inside pocket.

"Hold on," I said into the cell phone. "Harry, was there a silencer on your weapon when you grabbed it from the floor of Lansdale's office?"

The roar of a gunshot filled the room, and Chandler went down hard.

I dropped the cell phone, spun around, and hurled the glass blindly in the direction of the doorway. I heard the shattering of the glass as I ducked behind a pile of yellow duck cars, and I heard something other than shattered glass drop to the floor, bounce once, and roll toward me.

Three more shots were fired in my direction; both the cell phone and Harrison Chandler's weapon were out of my reach.

A concert of shouting and general commotion began in the restaurant below, and I could hear the intruder bound down the stairs toward the alley. The object the shooter had dropped rolled to a stop a foot from Chandler's body.

It was a metal ball, the size of a large marble.

Twelve

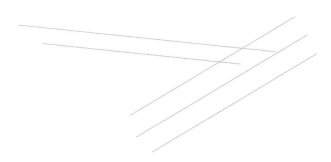

I COUNTED SILENTLY TO SIXTY before I considered coming out from behind my kiddie-car barricade.

While I counted, I listened for any sound indicating that the shooter was still on the landing or on the stairs. I heard none. I looked at Chandler's body for any sign of life. There was none. Harry Chandler lay on the floor, inanimate as the metal ball that had rolled to a stop at his feet. I pictured Ralph Battle running from the scene, clutching the matching metal ball in his sweaty palm. I stood up and went to Chandler's lifeless body.

I pulled the envelope from his hand and was slipping it into my inside jacket pocket when I heard the first of the police sirens coming nearer. Without additional thought, I scooped up the metal ball and dropped it into my pants pocket. I ignored the gun Harry had set on Snoopy's head and moved to retrieve my cell phone. As I reached down to pick it up, I could hear Darlene yelling my name from the other end of the line.

"Calm down, Darlene," I said into the phone.

"Jesus, Jake, are you okay? Were those gunshots?"

"Yes, I'm fine. Harry Chandler was killed. I must have been followed."

"Probably not," said Darlene. "That's why I called. Tom Romano phoned to check on me and heard something on the line that led him to believe the phone was bugged. Someone may have come in when we were down in Santa Monica. Whoever killed Chandler knew about the meeting time and place the moment Chandler set it up. I called Lieutenant Lopez when I heard the shots; she's on her way over there."

"I can hear the police cars coming," I said.

"Did you see the shooter?"

"No, but I have a good idea who it was."

"Who, Jake? And if he knew where to find Chandler, why did he wait so long to start shooting?"

I heard the door to the alley being opened, followed by movement and voices on the stairs.

"I have some ideas about that too, but I can't talk now. Get out of the office, go home. I'll call you later and fill you in."

"Jake."

"Go," I said, and ended the connection.

I put my arms straight up into the air just as Lopez entered, closely followed by my old friend Sergeant Johnson and two uniformed officers. All had their weapons drawn.

"You interrupted my dinner, Diamond," Lopez said after telling the others to stand down.

"Sorry, Lieutenant, I lost track of the time."

Lopez sent the two officers down to the alley entrance with orders to keep everyone out except the examiners.

"Sergeant Johnson, please check the body and call in the medical examiner and the crime scene unit," Lopez said. "Diamond, let's take a walk."

I brushed past Johnson as I crossed to trail Lopez to the stairs. Johnson gave me one of those looks that he had mastered so well, the one that made little daggers shoot out of his eyes. Down at the green metal door, Lopez said a few words to the uniforms and then she motioned for me to follow her down the alley.

"Who's the corpse, Diamond?" Lopez asked.

"Harrison Chandler."

"Who put him down?"

"I couldn't see the shooter, Lieutenant," I said. "I was busy ducking for cover."

"Uh-huh. Did you disturb any evidence, Diamond?"

My right hand was deep in my pants pocket, rolling the metal ball between my fingers. The envelope inside of my jacket felt as if it were burning a hole in my chest.

I tried to sound indignant.

"Of course not, Lieutenant," I said.

Lopez abruptly stopped walking, and I saw that we were at her car.

"Get in, Diamond. I prefer doing my grilling at the station."

Lopez opened the passenger door and I climbed in. She went around the car and slid in behind the wheel.

"My Chevy is up on Frederick," I said.

"There's a pencil and paper in the glove box," Lopez said. "Write it down so you don't forget where you left it."

"Mind if I call Darlene?" I asked, letting go of the metal ball and reaching for my cell phone.

"Make it fast," Lopez said.

I caught Darlene on her way out of the office.

"Jesus, Jake, where are you?"

"On my way to Vallejo with the lieutenant."

"Are you under arrest?"

"Am I under arrest, Lieutenant?" I asked Lopez.

"Not yet."

"Darlene, the Impala is at Masonic and Frederick. Can you get over there to pick it up?"

"Sure. I'll grab a taxi."

"Pick me up at the police station."

"I'll see you down there," she said.

I ended the connection just as we headed into the Broadway tunnel.

Fifteen minutes later, we were sitting face-to-face across a long oak table in an interrogation room at the Vallejo Street Station. The room had all the ambience of a post office break room. I wanted a cigarette badly, but not enough to bother Lopez about locating an ashtray.

"Don't you think we'd be more comfortable in your office, Lieutenant?" I asked.

"If I had comfort in mind I would have stayed at the small, can-dlelit French bistro sipping chardonnay and had Sergeant John-son torture you himself," said Lopez.

"Gosh, I hope I didn't break up a romantic moment."

"Can it, Diamond, before you make me forget my manners," said Lopez. "Who was this Chandler?"

"I really didn't know him," I said, changing my focus from pin-ing for a smoke to stonewalling the lieutenant.

"You just happen to meet him while you were shopping for spare merry-go-round parts?"

I was going to have to give her something.

"Do you remember me mentioning a visit from an ape named Ralph Battle last week?"

"Vaguely."

"Battle took me to a mandatory meeting with a Chicago lawyer named Max Lansdale. Lansdale made me an offer that was hard to refuse, to locate Chandler and another ghost known as Joe Clams. On Wednesday, I received a call from Chandler and he set up tonight's meet. Before we made it past the small talk, someone started blasting"

"Battle?"

"Like I said, I didn't see the shooter. But I don't see how Battle could have made it back into San Francisco, what with the exten-sive dragnet you had in place."

"You're making me angry, Diamond."

"I'm sorry, Lieutenant, please forgive me," I said. "I'm still a lit-tle shook up. A few of the bullets were aimed in my direction."

"Save it, Diamond. I know you're holding out, because it's all you ever do. I need to hear more about the victim and I have a lot of cute ways to keep you here until you start remembering some-thing."

"Call Ray Boyle at the LAPD, he should be able to tell you all about Harrison Chandler," I said.

Lopez looked as if she were debating whether to shoot me, lock me up, or tell me to get the fuck out.

"Get the fuck out of here, Diamond," she said.

Lieutenant Lopez didn't have to add that I would be hearing from her.

I walked out of the police station and immediately lit a cigarette. I spotted Darlene leaning on the Impala across Vallejo Street. I crossed to the car and invited her to take the passenger seat. As I drove her to her house near Buena Vista Park, I filled her in.

"And you're sure it was Battle?" she asked.

I reached into my pocket and handed her the metal ball.

"And why did he wait so long to plug Chandler?"

"I'm guessing that he was listening for something to help identify Joe Clams, and waiting to see if Harry was carrying this," I said, reaching into my jacket and handing her the letter-sized envelope I had taken from Chandler. It was addressed to Lieutenant Ray Boyle.

"What's this?" she asked.

"Haven't had a chance to look," I said, "but I know Jimmy Pigeon's handwriting when I see it. I'm guessing that there's something inside addressed to Chandler."

Darlene pulled out a second envelope. Chandler's name was written across it in Jimmy's distinctive script.

"Did Chandler identify Joe Clams?" Darlene asked.

"Never got around to it."

"And you told Lopez none of this?" asked Darlene.

"Not a word."

"Jesus, Jake. What about Battle? He's out there in the streets thinking about how disappointed Lansdale will be when he finds out that you have this letter. Not to mention wanting his ball back."

"I think that I gave Lieutenant Lopez just enough to inspire Ralph Battle to lie low, at least for the time being. I have a very strong desire to read the note from Pigeon before turning it over to Lopez," I said as we came up in front of Darlene's place. "We'll have to watch our backs. Let's go in and see what Jimmy Pigeon had to say to Harry. Do you have anything other than brown rice in there to eat? I'm starving."

"I picked up a veal parmigiana sandwich on my way to the police station," she said, reaching into the backseat.

"You're a saint," I said. "And to drink?"

"Coffee and Zambucca?"

"Perfect."

We climbed out of the car and entered the house.

Tug McGraw greeted us at the door and immediately began eyeballing the veal sandwich.

I ate, McGraw drooled, Darlene read Pigeon's letter aloud. It was dated just before Jimmy was killed more than a year earlier. Pigeon had never posted it. Somehow it had finally reached Boyle and then Chandler.

Jimmy had discovered evidence that Simon Lansdale had been suffocated on the night he died in bed. The medical examiner called to the scene had withheld the information after a phone call promised him a very large reward for the oversight. The ME, Richard Kearney, had retired to warmer climates shortly after. According to Pigeon, the doctor was willing to roll the rock over if the price was right. Kearney estimated the price to be "just enough to allow me to stay clear of the Chicago Police Department and anyone named Lansdale or Giancana, forever." Jimmy ended the note with the all of the information Chandler would need to get in touch with Kearney if he so desired.

"'Stay away from open windows. Best, Jimmy Pigeon,'" read Darlene, "that's it."

I lifted my plate off the table and looked to Darlene for a sign. She nodded reluctantly and I placed the plate on the floor at McGraw's feet. The dog restrained himself long enough to award me an adoring glance before devouring what remained of the sandwich.

"Mind if I use the telephone?" I asked.

"Are you going to call Ray Boyle?"

"No, I think I'll wait for Ray to call me," I said, walking over to the wall phone. "It won't take him long once he hears from Lopez. Read me the phone number that Jimmy gave to Chandler. Let's find out if Doc Kearney is still down in fun-filled Acapulco."

An answering machine at the Mexican end of the line informed me that Kearney was unavailable and that I could leave a message if I pleased. The recording then repeated what I supposed was the same suggestion in Spanish.

I declined both offers.

"So?" said Darlene, handing me a mug of coffee topped off

with a healthy serving of the clear, licorice-flavored Zambucca.

"So I guess I'll head home and try again later. I can check if there's a message from Ray Boyle. Stay away from the office until you hear from me," I said. "I'll try to get Tom Romano to look at the phones tomorrow."

"What if Ralph Battle is out there waiting for you, Jake?" asked Darlene.

"I'll tell you what. Call the police station. Ask for Johnson. Tell him that you're worried about me and ask if it wouldn't be too much trouble to have a patrol car cruise by my place a time or two," I said. "Sergeant Johnson might do it for *you*."

"What's the point, Jake?"

"The point?"

"You seem pretty sure that Max Lansdale is behind all of it. Why not hand it over to Ray Boyle or to Lopez or to the Chicago PD and let *them* iron it all out?"

"I have nothing to hand over. There's no proof and everyone seems to have lost interest. Chicago is happy with Harry Chandler as Randolph Lansdale's assassin, Los Angeles is happy with Randolph Lansdale as Carla Rosario's assassin, and all I have for Lopez and the San Francisco police on Harry Chandler's assassination is a metal ball just like a million other metal balls. There's only one person left who might really care to know how it all went down, and I have no idea how to find him."

"Joe Clams?"

"Joe Clams."

"So you're planning to stick it out for a while and try to dig Clams up."

"Cleverly put."

"It's not very smart, Jake."

"If I were smart I would have stayed married to Sally and made my living selling Taiwanese-manufactured sporting equipment."

"Thank goodness Joey and Sonny will be back from their island vacation on Sunday."

"The last thing I want to do is to get Joey involved in this mess, Darlene."

"Good luck trying to keep him out of it," she said.

Over the past year or so, Joey Russo had evolved from someone who leased me garage space to someone that I could hardly do without. Joey had pulled me out of a few very tight spots, at no small risk to himself. The Russos had adopted me into the family. Joey had taught me what I had never taken time to learn about friendship. Joey insisted that he loved the stimulation, the break from the backyard barbecue. But I felt that I had put Russo in harm's way too often and was very determined to keep Joey out of Max Lansdale's path.

"When you see Joey or Sonny," I said, "how about keeping Max Lansdale and Ralph Battle out of the conversation?"

"My lips are sealed," Darlene said, "but you'd better bring a roll of duct tape when you see Vinnie Strings."

"Great advice," I said. "Have a good weekend."

"Do I have to tell you to be very careful?" Darlene asked.

"You just did and I will. Thanks for the grub," I said. "Mind if I take the coffee to go?"

"Not at all. And you can trash the mug when you're done."

The mug displayed the logo of the San Francisco 49ers. Darlene was obviously ready to give up all that was left of her ex-boyfriend.

Darlene and McGraw walked me to the door and watched as I climbed into the Impala and drove off.

I parked a few short blocks from my building and approached with caution.

I spotted a police cruiser slowly driving past the apartment house, reaffirming my confidence in Darlene's unequaled charm.

In my apartment, I checked my answering machine for messages. No word from Boyle.

I needed more caffeine, so I put up a pot of espresso after dropping the empty mug into the kitchen wastebasket.

I decided to wait awhile before trying to telephone the doctor in Mexico again.

When the coffee was ready, I carried a demitasse of the espresso and a glass of bourbon to my reading chair.

I settled in and picked up the paperback lying on the side table. Old man Karamazov had been murdered by one of his sons. The question was which one.

I read and drank and drank and read.

Before I could solve Dostoyevsky's intricate puzzle, I was asleep.

Thirteen

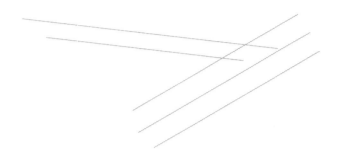

A LOUD RAPPING ON THE apartment door woke me.

The paperback dropped to my feet.

The pounding became louder and more insistent, nearly knocking me off the chair. I decided to keep my distance from the door and spoke from my seat.

"Who?"

"Ray Boyle."

I squinted at my Swatch. It was well before six in the morning. The door shook violently. I jumped up from the chair and rushed over.

"Ray? What did you do, hop the red-eye?" I called.

I opened the door. LAPD detective lieutenant Ray Boyle's eyes answered my question.

"What happened last night, Diamond?" he shouted.

"Jesus, Boyle, keep your shirt on," I said. "It's Saturday morning, you'll wake the whole building."

I made room for him to squeeze past me into the apartment.

I followed him in and shut the door.

"What happened last night?" Boyle repeated.

"Harry Chandler was shot to death," I said, heading for the kitchen. "I need coffee."

"I know he was shot, Diamond," Boyle yelled, following on my heels. "I just came from identifying his body."

I filled the percolator from the tap in the kitchen sink, went to the refrigerator and pulled out the can of Maxwell House and a container of half-and-half. I noted that one of my only two coffee mugs was sitting on a shelf in the Frigidaire holding water and cut celery stalks.

"Damn it, Diamond. Talk."

"Give me a minute, Ray, I'm not awake yet," I pleaded.

I spooned coffee into the basket and placed the pot over a high flame. I reached into the trash can, pulled out the discarded 49ers mug, and rinsed it in the sink.

Ray was tapping his right foot on the floor like Lawrence Welk.

"Take a seat, Ray, you're giving me a headache," I said, wickedly watching him squirm. "How about breakfast? I think I have all of the ingredients I'd need for a nice celery omelet."

"Are you through torturing me, Diamond?" Boyle said, sinking heavily into a kitchen chair.

"Okay," I said, placing the half-and-half and the two empty mugs on the table, "what was the question?"

"Who killed Harry Chandler, Jake?"

"Where can I find Joe Clams, Ray?"

"Christ, Diamond."

"Quid pro quo, Boyle."

"Where the hell did you pick that up, from *The Silence of the Lambs*?"

"Exactly, so don't ask me to spell it," I said.

"I can't tell you about Joe Clams, Jake," Boyle said. "What I can do is let him know you need to find him."

"We went that route with Chandler, Ray. I don't have to tell you how it worked out."

"Fuck."

"Okay, Ray, we'll get back to that," I said, pouring the coffee. "Can you at least tell me what you know about this?"

I pulled Pigeon's note to Chandler from the inside of the jacket I had draped over the kitchen chair and set the envelope down on the table in front of Boyle.

"Fuck."

"Give, Ray."

Boyle lightened his coffee and told me about Jimmy's note.

The envelope was discovered by the police in Jimmy Pigeon's apartment during the investigation into Jimmy's murder. It landed in an evidence room at Parker Center and was discovered by a clerk during an evidence-room cleanup six months later. The envelope was eventually released to Boyle. Boyle forwarded it to Harry Chandler.

According to Boyle, Chandler got in touch with the ex–Chicago medical examiner. Kearney had been having a good old time in Acapulco with the money he'd earned by covering up the fact that someone had pressed a pillow over Simon Lansdale's face on the night Lansdale died. By the time Harry finally reached the doctor, Kearney had run through his retirement savings wining and dining señoritas one-third his age. Kearney was willing to give Chandler the identity of his benefactor for fifty thousand greenbacks.

Chandler, assuming that Kearney would name Randolph Lansdale, got in touch with brother Max with the news that Harry Chandler was alive and well and looking to make a deal. Figuring that Max would want to protect the Lansdale name, at least what was left of it, Chandler promised that he could keep all pillow talk quiet for the bargain price of one hundred grand. Chandler was thinking that he'd pay Kearney off and keep the change. Lansdale told Harry that he needed time and asked Chandler to get back to him in a week. Chandler tried reaching Kearney with the news, but the doctor was not answering his telephone and not returning his messages. Finally understanding that Kearney was never going to resurface, and having nothing to sell, Chandler decided to go back to being dead and gone and to forget the Lansdales once and for all.

Boyle had taken the narrative far enough along for me to make it the rest of the way on my own.

"So Max Lansdale somehow tracked Kearney down and paid him off or knocked him off," I said when Ray took a breather, "and then Max started hunting for Harry to make sure he stayed dead this time. And Max succeeded. It was Max's boy, Battle, who was doing the shooting last night."

"Can you prove that?" Boyle asked hopefully.

"No. And I'll tell you what else I can't prove. That Max killed his old man, Carla Rosario, and his brother."

"How the hell do you get there, Diamond?"

"Harry Chandler's gun, the one that killed Randolph Lansdale, did it have a silencer?"

"No," Boyle said.

"So why didn't the receptionist hear the gunshot?"

"The gunshot?"

"Kit Carson claimed that Chandler went into the office and came out a few minutes later. She then tried to scare up Randolph on the intercom, got no answer, went in, and found Lansdale dead. Chandler had grabbed the gun off the floor. According to Katherine Carson, she and the victim had returned from lunch together an hour earlier. Randolph had never left the office nor had Carson left her desk. If Randolph Lansdale shot himself in the head, unless he took time to remove and hide a silencer before he died, Carson would have heard a gunshot."

"Jesus, Diamond, did you lay it out for Harry?"

"I didn't have the time, Ray, we were interrupted. No one entered Randolph's office through the reception area from the time they returned from lunch until Chandler and Clams arrived. The only access was from a door connecting Max's office to his brother's. Max Lansdale iced his own brother. And I don't know about you, Ray, but I think that the fuck deserves a little payback. And I think you're a very good cop, Boyle, but that's exactly why I don't think you can help. And exactly why you need to put me together with Joe Clams. I believe he deserves to know who really killed his sister."

"Fuck," said Boyle, for about the tenth time. "I'll see what I can do."

"You do that, Ray," I said. "How about the celery omelet?"

"Thanks, I'll pass," he said, draining the remainder of his coffee. "I need to be going, I have some thinking to do."

"Think hard," I said, escorting him to the door. "And get some sleep, Ray, you look worse than I do."

I closed the door behind Boyle and went back to the kitchen for a coffee refill. Six hours slumped in an armchair hadn't done much to heal my aching body. I flirted with the idea of crawling into bed; after all, it was still before seven on a Saturday morning. I fought off the urge and hit the shower instead.

Feeling close to human again, I ventured into the outside world. I crossed through Alamo Park and pointed my nose in the direction of the grease burning at the Hayes Street Diner near the Panhandle. I settled into a rear booth and ordered a breakfast combination that would make Darlene cringe.

As I ate, I thought about Harry Chandler.

Mostly, I was trying to assuage my guilt over having led Ralph Battle to the meeting with Chandler. I rationalized between bites of fried potatoes, eggs, and bacon.

Harry had written his own ticket.

It was greed that had moved Chandler to let Max Lansdale know he was still alive.

It was true that Max had used me to get to Harry, and it made me very angry, but I hadn't marked Harry Chandler.

I decided to deny culpability and concentrate instead on my own situation. I had no desire to be next on Ralph Battle's hit list.

I cleaned my plate and went back to my apartment building on Fillmore Street, feeling as if I'd swallowed a lead ingot.

I found myself looking over my shoulder. Often.

I ran into Mrs. Martucci on the first floor.

"Good morning, Jacob," she said, "could I talk to you for a moment?"

Mrs. Martucci lived in the apartment directly below my own. I was sure that she was going to remind me of Boyle's very early and very vocal visit.

"Good morning, Annie," I said, digging into my limited arsenal of charm. "I'm really sorry about all of the noise this morning. It really couldn't be avoided."

"It was no problem, Jacob, I understand how you young people are," she said. "And the excitement is good for me."

Mrs. Martucci wore a black dress, as she had every day since her husband passed away ten years earlier. The widow had to be ninety-five years old. She had shrunk at least six inches since I'd first met her.

"Thanks for your understanding, Annie," I said, moving for the stairs.

"Jacob."

"Yes?"

"I wondered if you could do me a favor."

Oh boy.

"What can I do for you, Annie?"

"I need to visit my older sister up in Santa Rosa; Millie's not feeling very well."

"I'm very sorry to hear that, Mrs. Martucci," I said, trying to picture someone older than Annie or shorter than four foot eight.

"I'll be gone until Monday afternoon," she went on. "I was hoping that you could see to Augie."

Augie was Annie's pet cat, a gift from her daughter as company for the old woman after Mr. Martucci died. Annie had named the animal after her dead husband and I'd often heard Annie talking to the cat in what I imagined was much the same tone as she had talked to the old man.

"Sure, Annie, I'd be happy to. It's always a treat to visit with Augie. I love that cat as if he were my own," I said, not meaning a word of it.

I'd "seen to" Augie more than a few times before and I knew the drill. I kept a spare key to Annie's apartment for emergencies, so I was all set.

"Thank you, Jacob."

"You're welcome, Annie," I said. "Have a safe trip and send my best to your sister. And don't worry about Augie, he's in good hands."

I bit my lip and took the stairs up to my apartment.

I glanced at my wristwatch; it was 8:26.

Saturday morning.

All dressed up and nowhere to go.

I undressed and crawled into bed.

I woke at noon, thinking that was more like it.

The ingot in my stomach had dissolved, sending molten saturated fats and cholesterol coursing through my circulatory system.

I hopped out of bed, feeling like a new man.

I found my cigarettes, fired one up, and went to the phone to call Sally.

I made a little wish that we were still on for dinner as I reached for the receiver.

The phone rang.

"Jake's den of iniquity."

"Jacob, how terrible."

"Sorry, Mom," I said, flicking the cigarette into the kitchen sink. "How are you?"

"Alone," she said. "Your aunt is down in Monterey with one of her numerous boyfriends."

Aunt Rosalie was Mom's younger sister. They shared a house in Pleasant Hill, east of Oakland and Berkeley. Mom couldn't live with Rosalie, and couldn't live without her.

"Good for Aunt Rosalie," I said, bracing myself for the outburst.

I heard my mother sigh deeply, and then to my surprise and relief she let it pass.

Mom had other fish to fry.

"How are you, sweetheart?" she asked, warming up for the pitch.

"Fine, Mom," I said.

"How long has it been, Jacob?" she asked.

"It depends on what you're referring to, Mom," I said.

I knew exactly what my mother was referring to, but I also knew that she loved the game as much as I did.

"I have a lovely roast in the refrigerator," she said, "packed with garlic and ready for the oven."

"Baked potatoes?"

"Of course."

"Would you mind if I brought Sally along?" I asked, which was like asking my mother if she would mind winning the lottery.

"Not at all, dear," she said, which was her way of saying she would be thrilled.

"Seven thirty okay?"

"Fine, Jacob. We can sit down to dinner at eight," she said, "but you can come as early as you like."

"We'll bring wine, Mom," I said, "and we'll be there early if we can. Thanks for the invitation."

"Don't be silly, Jacob."

"You love it when I'm silly, Mom," I said. "See you later."

I ended the connection and rang Sally's number.

"Are we still on for dinner?" I asked, after Sally sang hello into her end.

"Who is this?" she asked.

"America's most eligible bachelor."

"Clooney? I told you never to call me here, George."

"Mary would like to feed us meat and potatoes at eight," I said.

"Let's go over early; I can be ready at six."

"I'll pick you up at six."

"How will I know you?"

"I'll be driving a 1963 Impala convertible and look a lot like your ex-husband."

"It's going to be tricky getting the hair right."

"No problem, I've got it figured out. I slept on it."

"You're funny, Jake," Sally said.

"I know, but looks aren't everything," I said, beating her to the punch line.

"Six sharp," Sally said.

"Bring a large appetite," I said, "over and out."

Sally French was okay. We'd been getting along real well lately.

Sally's career change, from a sporting goods magnate to executive director of the San Francisco Arts Council, had done a great deal to brighten her disposition.

Recent events had done a good job of darkening my own mood, so I was looking forward to spending time with Sally. I was hoping that some of her sunny attitude would rub off on me.

Meanwhile, I needed to see a man about a bug.

I phoned Tom Romano and asked if he had time to help me check the office for listening devices. Romano said he could meet me there at three.

I ran water over my face from the bathroom sink and thought about the first time I set eyes on Sally French.

Sally French walked into my office in North Beach, a referral from Jimmy Pigeon, to initiate a search for her birth mother. Sally had the kind of looks that belonged in a forties film, the kind of looks that would have had GIs tearing up their footlocker photographs of Betty Grable.

Not long after, Sally had a new mother and I had a mother-in-law.

The marriage lasted two years, at least half of it bad. Circumstances surrounding Jimmy Pigeon's death had brought me and Sally together again, much to her displeasure at the time.

But one thing had led to another.

Now we were taking it slow.

As I towel-dried my face, I caught myself wondering if Sally and I would ever remarry. Something that I was sure my mother wondered about often. I anticipated an evening of dinner and dodging. I glanced into the bathroom mirror and decided that a haircut would not be a bad idea.

I wondered if I could find a barber who could make me look more like George Clooney.

Fourteen

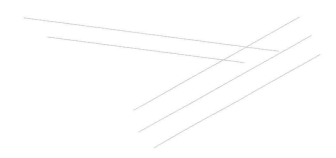

At two, I was sitting in Vito's Barber Shop near my office leafing through a two-month-old *Newsweek* magazine. I was waiting for Vito to give me an ear lowering. I'd decided to go the safe route and get a haircut that would make me look more like Jake Diamond. Vito was busy with another customer. The guy in the chair must have showed Vito a photograph of Rod Stewart.

Vito's assistant, unsympathetically known as Sammy the Butcher, was free. I made the mistake of looking up from the Science page. Sammy stood in front of his chair glaring at me.

"Are you certain I can't help you, Mr. Diamond?" Sammy asked.

"Pretty sure, thank you, Sammy," I said. "I'll wait for Vito."

The Butcher turned away sullenly and I went back to my magazine.

A team of researchers in Seville, Spain, had dug up what they *believed* to be the remains of Cristóbal Colón, aka Christopher Columbus, aka the well-known alleged Italian for whom the avenue I sat on was fondly named.

"I'm ready for you, Jake."

I looked up from the *Newsweek.*

Vito stood with a clean sheet in his hand, the Rod Stewart lookalike was crossing to the door, and Sammy the Butcher was spinning in his chair.

"Just a trim, Vito," I said, taking a seat.

"Did you find anything interesting in the magazine?" Vito asked as he safety-pinned the sheet around my neck.

"Not really," I said. "They're trying to find out where Christopher Columbus is buried."

"Guess they've given up on Jimmy Hoffa," Vito said, closing in with scissors clicking.

The fruit of a thorough search of all the rooms that constitute the humble headquarters of Diamond Investigation rested in my open palm. I sat on a corner of my desk and looked down at the thing. It was approximately the size of a wristwatch battery.

"How does it work?" I asked.

"It's fairly rudimentary," said Tom Romano, who had orchestrated the bug hunt. "Basically a wireless, voice-activated microphone transmitting to a tape recorder. The signal could be monitored live with an earplug, or recorded for future listening pleasure."

Romano had discovered the device concealed within the handset of my desk telephone. Tom suggested that the tiny microphone was capable of picking up anything spoken in my "private" office, as well as the voice of any person on the other end of the phone line.

"What's the range of something like this?" I asked.

"Not much farther than just outside of the building," Tom said. "Battle could have planted the recorder inside of the building and later come back for it, or he could have listened from the street, maybe from a car parked on the avenue."

"Could he be listening right now?" I asked.

Tom walked over to me, took the device from my hand, placed it on the floor, and stomped on it with the heel of his shoe.

"If he was, that would have rocked his world," said Tom. "But I doubt Battle is anywhere near, what with the vigilant gang at Vallejo Street Station just a few short blocks away. But that's not to say he's out of your hair, Jake. I think you're exactly right. Battle waited until you arrived because his orders included listening for any mention of Joe Clams, finding out what if anything Harry Chandler had on Max Lansdale that was concrete, and then killing both you and Chandler. Max Lansdale doesn't like loose ends, and he counts on Battle to tie them up. And it appears Ralph Battle's one ambition in life is to be a man who Max Lansdale can count on."

"The thing is, I have nothing at all on Lansdale," I said. "I have a letter from one dead man to another about a doctor in Mexico who is probably in no better shape."

"True, Jake, but don't forget that it's also all that Chandler had, and Max Lansdale wasn't real happy with Harry still in the world. At the risk of sounding crude, the man is one paranoid motherfucker. Max Lansdale is very, very afraid of something. And that is the chink in his armor. You need to find out what it is that frightens Lansdale, what it is that scares the shit out of him, what it is that gives him nightmares, his personal pit of snakes. And then you have to throw him right into the pit."

"It would be easier to just kill the fuck," I said.

"There is that," said Tom. "What about Ralph Battle?"

"If you're correct about Battle's raison d'être, with Max gone, Ralph will be too busy looking for an alternative meaning of life to find time to be thinking about me."

"Good point, Jake, but there's a major flaw in that scenario. You're not a killer; it's simply not in you."

"Ain't that a bitch," I said.

"Hey, don't beat yourself up, pal," Tom Romano said. "Nobody's perfect."

I sat in the living room of the house shared by my mother and Aunt Rosalie, filled to the eyes with roast beef and baked potato. I was randomly entering numbers into the TV remote control.

Sally and my mother were in the kitchen, cleaning the dinnerware while the coffee percolated. Mom was bending Sally's ear mercilessly. I was tempted to charge into the kitchen to rescue Sally, but I'd left my shining armor at home. I stopped playing with the remote. I found that I had landed in the middle of the court scene at the tail end of Oliver Stone's *JFK*. Kevin Costner was making a strong argument against the lone-assassin theory.

The argument failed because it was not impossible.

"Jacob," said my mother, carrying a plate of Italian pastries into the dining area, "coffee is ready."

I turned from the television. Sally followed behind my mother with the coffeepot.

"Jacob."

"I heard you, Mom," I said, struggling out of the chair.

"Sally won't give me a straight answer," my mother complained.

Since Sally was famous for giving straight answers, I had a good idea what the question was.

"Oh?" I said, moving to the dining table.

"All I wanted to know, dear," said my mother, "was if it's possible that you and Sally may someday marry again."

I looked past my mother. Sally gave me a wicked smile that told me what her unstraight answer had been.

Ask Jake.

"Anything's possible, Mom," I said, with all of the conviction of a Warren Commission member. "Great-looking cannolis by the way."

"Sorry my mother tortured you, Sal," I said.

We were in the Impala, crossing the Bay Bridge back into San Francisco.

"It wasn't that bad," she said, "although I thought I would lose it when she used the words *biological clock.*"

"Jesus, she's unbelievable. It's not like she doesn't have grandchildren," I said, "and if you saw photos of my brother's kids you'd wonder why she would want to risk it again."

"Jake, that's terrible."

"I'm joking."

"To sidestep a touchy subject?" Sally asked.

"Marriage?"

"Children."

"I can't see myself being much of a father," I said. "Kids make me very nervous. I don't know how to talk to them. When I do manage to choke out a few words I usually find myself saying, 'Do you think you could maybe keep it down to a roar?' Have you been thinking about children?"

"I do occasionally. But then I read all about morning sickness, weight gain, labor pains, postpartum depression, diapers, child maladies, kidnappings, and adolescence, and I get over it," Sally said.

"There you go," I said.

"Are you going to spend the night?" she asked.

"I'd love to," I answered.

We were on California Street heading for Sally's house in the Presidio when I remembered Augie.

"Damn," I said, "I need to swing by my place for a minute to feed Mrs. Martucci's cat."

I hung a left onto Divisidero and headed over to Fillmore.

The only empty spot close to my building was at the fire hydrant, so I parked there. I thought about asking Sally to wait down in the Chevy for a minute, but then I thought about Ralph Battle.

"Why don't you come in with me," I said.

"Will it be okay leaving the car here?"

"Sure," I said.

Though with my luck, if Sergeant Johnson still had a patrol car occasionally cruising past my apartment, the uniforms would probably stop just long enough to give me a parking citation.

I casually glanced up and down the street as we walked to the building.

I stopped in front of Mrs. Martucci's door.

"Why don't you wait down here, Sal," I said. "I'll run up and get the keys to her apartment."

"I'll come up with you, Jake," Sally said. "I need to use the ladies' room."

The spare set of keys to Mrs. Martucci's apartment was in the drawer of my bedside table. As I pulled them out, I felt Sally wrap her arms around my waist.

"We could spend the night here, Jake," she said. "Save some time."

"The bed isn't big enough for what I have in mind," I said. "Let's go feed the beast and get out of here."

"I'll be right behind you," Sally said, heading toward the bathroom.

I was halfway down the flight of stairs when the phone in my apartment rang. I hesitated and took another step down. When the telephone rang a second time, I turned and started quickly back up. Then I was running up, shouting Sally's name above the sound of the third ring. An intense flash of light blinded me, followed by the deafening sound of a massive explosion.

Followed by darkness and silence.

Part Three

ONE TO TEN

Fifteen

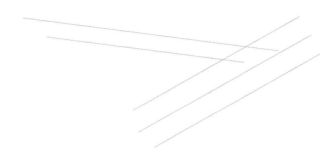

CONSCIOUSNESS RETURNED WITHOUT CEREMONY.

I could feel my head. I could feel the pressure at each temple, pushing inward.

Then the first sounds. The muted roar of the ocean, the incessant clanging of a distant buoy bell thrown in. As if heard from a large seashell. Heard from two large seashells, one pressed to each ear and trying to meet at the middle of my eyes.

I thought my eyes were open but couldn't be sure.

I was in darkness.

I thought that I was lying down flat but I couldn't swear to it. I tried to move my legs, no dice. I tried my arms, the right arm responded. I moved my hand up to my face and felt the bandages wrapped tightly across my eyes and over my ears—no seashells there. I tried working on the bandages. A woman's voice called my name. *Jake.* The sound of the voice was like an explosion. The clanging of the buoy became the ringing of a telephone. I tore at the bandages as the ringing continued. I cried out.

"Sally."

A hand covered mine, pulling my fingers away from my face.

"Sally," I cried out again.

"It's Darlene, Jake. Please don't touch the bandages."

"Sally?" I said.

"I'm sorry, Jake," said Darlene.

The telephone in my head stopped ringing. I passed out.

Sound returned. A quite constant buzzing.

"Darlene?"

"I'm here, Jake."

"Sally?" I said.

"I'm sorry, Jake. Sally didn't make it. The medical examiner is certain she died instantly."

I could feel tears in my eyes. Burning.

I couldn't speak.

I raised my good arm, telling Darlene not to speak.

I fell asleep.

I heard more than one voice now. A man's voice added to Darlene's. A muffled conversation.

"Darlene?"

"I'm here, Jake. The doctor is here. He wants to answer your questions. About your condition."

"I don't care," I said.

"Please, Jake," said Darlene.

"I can come back," said the doctor.

"Please, Jake," Darlene said again.

"I'll come back," said the doctor.

"I don't care," I said.

I heard someone leave the room. Darlene took my hand into hers. She didn't speak. Time passed, indeterminable. I tried to put Sally's face out of my mind. There was only one way to do that.

"Am I blind?" I asked.

"No, Jake. It was the flash of the explosion, like looking into the sun too long. They'll heal. Your vision will be fine."

"I can't feel my legs."

"Both are set in plaster casts, Jake," Darlene said. "A dislocated right knee, a grade-three left ankle sprain. And the left wrist is broken. Miraculously, they found no other bone fractures and no broken ribs. A very ugly gash above your left eye, there'll be a scar."

"What day is it?"

"Sunday. You were in the emergency room most of the night.

It's early afternoon. I haven't called your mother yet. Tom Romano and Vinnie Strings are out in the visitors' waiting room."

"I don't want any visitors, Darlene," I said.

"Fine," said Darlene.

"I don't know what to do about my mother."

"I'll take care of it, Jake."

Sally's face broke through again. Smiling.

"I loved her, Darlene."

"I know."

"It's my fault."

"Even you know that's not true, Jake."

"I'm scared, Darlene."

"It's going to be okay, Jake. I promise."

"I'm tired."

"Sleep, Jake. I'll be here."

Darlene held my hand in hers. Tightly. As if she were afraid to let go.

I closed my damp burning eyes beneath the bandages. I tried to put Sally's face out of my mind.

There was only one way to do that.

I thought about Max Lansdale and Ralph Battle and how they would pay.

I felt Darlene squeezing my hand.

"Jake."

"Yes."

"The doctor is back. His name is Whitman. He needs to ask some questions."

"Okay."

"I'm going out to Pleasant Hill to see your mother. I'll ask Vinnie to drive me out there; it will get him out of the hospital. Tom Romano left; he said that you should call him if you needed anything at all."

"Tell my mother that she doesn't have to come here," I said.

"Don't be foolish," said Darlene. "I'll be back with your mother."

"Thank you, Darlene."

"You're welcome, Jake," Darlene said, letting go of my hand.

I heard her move away, and a moment later the doctor spoke.

"We're going to need some health background information, Mr. Diamond," he said. "If you feel up to it I'd like to send a nurse in to do a short interview."

"Sure," I said.

"How do your eyes feel?"

"On fire," I said.

"It's the medication. I'll see you later this afternoon with an eye specialist to remove the bandages and take a look," Whitman said. "We'll move you into an examination room where we can control the lighting; we'll want to bring it in gradually. We have an extremely positive prognosis from the ophthalmologist. We are very optimistic."

Whitman paused and waited. When he realized that I had nothing to say he went on.

"The right knee has been reset in place. The X-rays showed stretching of ligaments, but none were torn. There will be considerable swelling, and the cast will have to remain intact to ensure proper healing. I estimate three to six weeks, followed by rehabilitation. There were no breaks or fractures evident, no damage to the artery or to any nerves. The left ankle was badly sprained but should heal fairly quickly. The knee will keep you off your feet long enough for the ankle to heal. We will be doing follow-up X-rays and will do an MRI if the orthopedist feels it is necessary. The wrist should mend successfully. The scar above your eye will be noticeable but not horrible. All in all, Mr. Diamond, I would say that you were very lucky."

"I don't feel very lucky," I said.

"Do you have any questions?" Whitman asked.

"Do you have a spare cigarette?"

"I'd like to send the nurse in now to ask you about your medical history, if you feel up to it."

"Sure," I said.

"We'll be back later to check your eyes," Whitman said. "I'll see you then."

"I hope I'll be able to see you also," I said.

Now it was my mother holding my hand. Mary knew me well enough not to say much. Darlene told me she would be waiting outside, trying to keep Vinnie under control. He was jumping out of his skin trying to get into the room to see me. Darlene casually mentioned that Joey Russo would be getting back later that night. It was the best news I'd heard in a long time.

Darlene came in again; I could hear her whispering to my mother.

"They're ready to take you to the examination room, Jake," Darlene said, "to remove the bandages."

"I'll be waiting, Jacob," my mother said.

"Let me talk with Darlene for a minute," I said. "Can you do something with Vinnie, Mom? Maybe get him something to eat."

"Of course, son," she said.

I heard my mother cross the room to leave and waited to hear the door close behind her.

"Darlene?"

"Yes, Jake."

"Will you come with me?"

"Absolutely, Jake," Darlene said. "I'll go tell them you're ready."

They rolled me on a gurney down a long hallway and into another room. Darlene held my hand. Whitman introduced the ophthalmologist as he unwrapped the bandages.

"We would like you to keep your eyes shut until we dim the lights, Mr. Diamond," Whitman said. "Then we will bring them back up slowly."

I closed my eyes. When the bandages were removed, I felt a warm cloth gently wiping my eyelids.

Darlene held my hand.

"All right, Mr. Diamond," Whitman said, "you can open your eyes, slowly."

I opened my eyes.

The room was pitch-black.

I panicked for a moment before the darkness began to recede. The room remained dim, but I could see a face come up close to mine.

"I'm Dr. Michelle Donaldson, Mr. Diamond," the face said. "Please hold still."

She came closer and stared into my eyes.

"Please bring the lights up to seven," she called behind her.

The room brightened.

Donaldson brought a small scope up to my left eye and took a long look. She repeated with the right. She pulled back and her face came into focus.

"You can bring them up all the way," she called.

"Did anyone ever tell you that you look like Julia Roberts?" I asked.

Darlene gave my hand a hard squeeze.

"Mr. Diamond, the good news is I'm confident that your eyesight will be fine," Donaldson said.

"And the not-so-good news?" I asked.

"It might be a while before your vision is completely back to normal."

"How long?"

"Just until you realize that I look nothing like Julia Roberts," she said.

I passed the remainder of the afternoon and early evening drifting in and out of sleep, either flat on my back or tenuously propped up in the bed, with Darlene and my mother drifting in and out of the room separately and together.

The worst part of being able to see again was seeing the condition I was in. I looked like Boris Karloff. As Frankenstein or the Mummy, take a pick.

My right leg was wrapped in a plaster cast to the hip, the left leg to midcalf, the left arm to the elbow.

I looked like a kindergarten art project.

The surgical stitching above my left eye ran from just above the bridge of my nose up to my lower forehead. The scar would split my eyebrow in two.

Vinnie Strings had finally worked his way into the room. I was thankful he had waited for the bandages to be removed; it was better to see Vinnie than to imagine him lurking there in the darkness. The poor kid was genuinely upset. All of my efforts at trying to assure Vinnie that I would be all right almost helped me to convince myself.

Sometime after I had rejected what the hospital called dinner,

Darlene slipped out and returned with a contraband chicken burrito. I shared it with Vinnie.

When a nurse came in and insisted it was time for all visitors to give the patient a chance to rest, I wanted to kiss the woman.

Darlene said she would drive my mother home and would visit again in the morning. I asked her to stay away from the office for the time being, to check calls from home.

Darlene and my mother gave me awkward hugs and headed out of the hospital room. Vinnie didn't budge.

"Can I talk to you for a minute, Jake?" Vinnie asked once the women were gone.

"Sure, Vin, what's on your mind?"

"I wanted to tell you how sad I am about Sally."

The kid was close to tears. I was initially resentful that Vinnie had reminded me about Sally. Then thankful.

"And whatever you decide you need to do, Jake, *whatever*," Vinnie went on, "I'm there."

"Thank you, Vinnie," I said. "Really."

"Okay, Jake, I need to go," Vinnie said. "The Russos are coming home tonight and I want to make sure the house looks all right. Somehow I managed to keep the basil plants alive."

"Can you do me a favor, Vin?"

"Sure, Jake, anything."

"Ask Joey Russo to come see me," I said, "as soon as he can."

"You got it, pal. I'll drop back by to visit you tomorrow."

"You do that, friend," I said.

Vinnie left and I was alone.

Terribly alone.

Sixteen

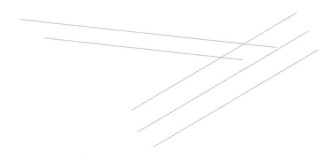

I STOOD IN THE VESTIBULE of the Payless shoe store. Even though I was in my father's heavy wool overcoat, the wind coming off Lake Michigan sliced through me. A woman studying the window display was crowding me with a baby stroller. My hand was deep in my coat pocket gripping the handgun.

Ralph Battle had walked out of the adjacent building minutes before and crossed South Wacker. Where I stood, I could see Battle in the bagel shop across the street. A young woman behind the counter was placing bagels into a paper bag. Battle took the bag and a moment later he was back out at the curb, waiting for an opening in the busy morning traffic. Battle crossed the avenue, the baby in the stroller said something unintelligible, my grip on the gun tightened. Battle reentered the building and I moved to follow. I watched from outside the entrance as Battle waited for the elevator. The elevator car arrived and I moved quickly into the lobby as Battle stepped into it.

I raced to the elevator and used my foot to stop the doors from closing completely, pulling out the .38 as the doors reopened. Battle looked up at me in recognition and shock as the doors shut. I pointed the weapon at his chest and as the car began to rise I pulled the trigger twice.

The body crashed heavily to the floor of the elevator. I reached to push the button for the twelfth floor.

The late Ralph Battle had beaten me to it.

Battle stared up at me, dark circles of blood on his shirt growing larger. I knelt down and used my fingers to close his eyes. I picked up the paper bag. The elevator doors opened on the twelfth floor. I stepped out, the bag in one hand and the gun in the other.

I walked to the door of Lansdale's office suite.

I managed to get the door opened using the top of the paper bag. I went into the receptionist area; no one was at the front desk. I quietly moved on to the door of Lansdale's private office. The door was ajar; I pushed it open with my foot. Max Lansdale looked up from his seat. I tossed the bag, landing it in the middle of the desk in front of him.

"Bagels from Ralph," I said, "and this is from Sally French."

I pulled the trigger of the gun until it emptied.

I closed my eyes and kept squeezing the trigger, the hammer clicking.

Someone grabbed my arm, seemed to take the gun from my hand. Then someone was holding my empty hand, slapping it gently and calling my name.

"Jake. Jesus Christ, Jake."

I opened my eyes and tried to focus.

"Jake, snap out of it. You're scaring the shit out of me, buddy."

"Joey? What are you doing here?"

"Calm down, Jake. I came as soon as I heard."

"How did you find me? Where am I?"

"You're lying in a hospital bed, Jake," said Joey Russo, "soaking wet. What the hell happened? You look like you were just pulled out of McCovey Cove."

"It was a dream," I said.

"Must have been one hell of a dream, pal," Joey said. "I can't wait to hear about it. But first I need to wring you dry. And then I want you to tell me who put you here. Jesus, if I'd known I'd find you this way, I'd have brought a couple of Angela's Martha Stewart towels along. Don't go anywhere; I'll see what they have in the bathroom."

Joey moved off toward the bathroom. I was shaking like a leaf, and dripping wet. He came back quickly and mopped my face dry.

Joey threw the towel into a corner of the room, poured a glass of water from the pitcher on the bedside stand, and handed it to me.

"Take a drink, slowly," he said, "and settle down. And when you're ready, I want every single detail."

I took a long, slow drink.

"I could use some bourbon with this," I said.

"That can be arranged, but first things first."

"God, I'm glad to see you, Joey."

"From what I've heard, I'm sure that you're glad you can see anything. But I'm going to forget everything I've heard, Jake. I need to hear it all from you," Joey said, "from the beginning."

And so I told Joey everything. From the beginning. From the moment two weeks earlier when Ralph Battle came into the office of Diamond Investigation waving a cannon, up to the moment I sent Max Lansdale to hell in my dream.

"I don't need to tell you how sorry I am about Sally. Do I, Jake?" Joey asked when I had told the tale.

"No, Joey, you don't."

"And do you believe me when I say that I have a very good idea how *you* feel about it?"

"Of course I believe you, Joey."

"The dream, Jake. It's no good and I'll tell you why," Joey said. "Because it's not going to happen that way, it's a fantasy. It's a wish that can't come true, not that way. Do you understand?"

"I think so," I said.

"In Ralph Battle's dream it's *you* with the bullets in *your* chest, lying on the stairs up to your office. In Max Lansdale's dream it's *you* who picks up the telephone."

"I understand," I said.

Joey Russo reached into his jacket pocket and pulled out a pint bottle of George Dickel bourbon. He filled two plastic cups and handed one to me.

"Do you trust me, Jake?" Joey asked after we had both taken a healthy drink.

"Absolutely."

"You need to put Battle and Lansdale out of your mind until

you're back on your feet," Joey said. "You need to heal, and not only physically. You need to come to terms with what happened to Sally. I'll help you get Lansdale, Jake. And we *will* get him. And Battle. I promise you. But not before you're strong again."

I took another drink. My hand was shaking.

"Trust me, Jake. I will work on it while you recover. Six, maybe eight weeks tops," Joey said. "Just don't ask me about it. Play cards, read books. Take a trip, somewhere warm, stare at the ocean. You're welcome to use our place in St. Martin, it's all set up. Take Darlene along to see that you eat. Close the office; refer any clients to Tom Romano. You can't work and you can't stay alone."

"I don't know, Joey."

"You know what they say about patience, Jake."

"That it's difficult."

"That too. Try counting."

"Counting?"

"When you feel you're about to blow, count to ten."

"Six to eight weeks is a long time, Joey," I said. "What if I get to ten and the fuse is still burning?"

"Then you keep counting."

"Counting to infinity?"

"As high as you need to go," Joey said. "What's important is that you think about something else for a while."

"For instance?"

"For instance, like where you're going to live. Even if you could make it up the stairs to your apartment, it's going to be some time before the place is habitable again. If ever."

"Jesus, I didn't think of that."

"Think about it. You're more than welcome to stay with us here in the city, but a month in a wheelchair with Angela's cooking and you'll look like Marlon Brando. It would be the same if you moved in with your mother. Get away, Jake. Go to the island. They have doctors there, take Darlene. At least Darlene will save you from cardiac arrest and she'll be glad to have something to do for you if she can't be at the office. Or we could get a nurse to come in. The windows look out on the ocean. There's more than enough room and plenty there to distract you."

"I'll think about it," I said.

"Good," Joey said. "I need to get going."

"What time is it?"

"One in the morning."

"Pretty late for visiting hours," I said.

"Visiting hours don't apply to me, Jake. I'll be here or anywhere you want whenever you need me, just don't ask me about Chicago until you're able to walk. Understood?"

"Understood."

"Good," Joey said, rising to leave. "I'm out of here."

I tried to find a way to thank him before he left. It wasn't the first offer of help I had received that day, but it was the one with the most teeth.

The sharpest teeth.

"Joey," I said as he crossed to the door.

"I know, Jake. Just get well," Joey Russo said.

And then he was gone.

But I didn't feel terribly alone anymore.

Seventeen

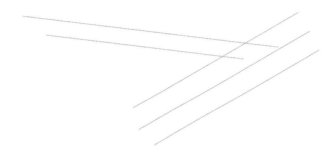

My OPTIONS WERE DICTATED by my circumstances.

For the first five days, I wasn't going anywhere.

There would be follow-up X-rays, physical therapies, eye exams, counseling sessions, and patient education. I learned a lot about my handicaps. Humbling and dreadful.

I would not be able to get up on my feet at all, at least until the ankle cast was removed and the joint was strong enough to carry weight. Two to three weeks, minimum. At that point, maybe I'd be able to get around with a walker or with crutches, and in time very tenuously with a cane while the right leg was still in plaster.

While both legs were incapacitated, I would require assistance getting into and out of the wheelchair until the wrist was healed and strong enough to lift my body.

The thought of having to take Vinnie Strings along on every trip to the bathroom was horrifying. It was almost as disheartening as trying to figure out where I would have to *put* Vinnie to keep him handy.

Particularly since I wasn't very clear about where I was going to put myself.

I wasn't feeling quite ready for a Caribbean vacation.

I wouldn't be in any shape to attend Sally's funeral, physically or emotionally. I tried finding courage to call her mother and her adoptive parents, but I didn't know what *I* could possibly say to help them deal with their loss.

On Monday morning, my mother called the hospital with news that, under the circumstances, could only be considered a lucky break.

My cousin, Bobby Senderowitz, known in the biz as Rob Sanders, was coming up to the Bay Area to act in a motion picture. Bobby would be staying at his mother's house, the house in Pleasant Hill where my mother lived. It meant that I would be rooming with Mom and Aunt Rosalie, at least for a while, but Bobby would be there to help when he wasn't working. I told my mother that it didn't sound like such a bad idea. I insisted she promise she would not try to move my weight class from light heavyweight up to sumo.

Darlene came bouncing into my hospital room just after I had sealed the deal with my mother.

"Look, Jake," she said, "you can stay with McGraw and me at my place when they cut you loose. I'll have time on my hands to care for you and you don't have to worry about help getting to the bathroom, since I've helped you before."

"Oh?"

"Joey Russo's New Year's Eve party."

"I don't remember."

"I'm not surprised."

"I'm all set, Darlene, thanks," I said. "My mother and Aunt Rosalie will take me in, and Cousin Bobby will be around. What exactly happened at Joey's party?"

"Nothing," Darlene said. "I was bluffing."

"What do you have there?"

"I brought you something to read."

Darlene walked over and handed me a worn paperback copy of *The Brothers Karamazov.*

"Where did you get this?" I asked. "It looks a lot like mine."

"You don't want to know."

"Tell me anyway."

"Everything in your apartment that was salvageable has been moved into storage while the landlord works at trying to clean the place up. I took a quick look last night. I spotted the book and thought you could use it," Darlene said. "There's not very much left, Jake. Fortunately, you won't be called upon to wear long pants for a while."

I tried not to picture it.

"Where did they take my things?"

"A small room at one of those storage places over on Army Street. It's not very organized, just thrown into boxes. I was looking for the letter from Jimmy to Harry Chandler and Battle's metal ball when I came across the book," said Darlene. "No luck on the other items."

As was very often the case, Darlene had answered my question before it was asked.

"I see," I said.

"Look at it this way, Jake," said Darlene. "If Battle grabbed the letter and metal ball, maybe Lansdale will give up thinking of you as a threat."

"I doubt it, Darlene. I'm more of a threat to him now than I ever was, and I'm sure he knows it."

"What are you thinking, Jake?"

"I'm trying not to," I said. "Joey Russo asked me to put it out of my mind, to put it on hold for a while. I have to trust him on that. I need his help."

"Okay, then, let's change the subject. Any word on when you're getting out?" asked Darlene.

"Probably Friday, Thursday at the earliest."

"Just let me know, and I'll take you out to Pleasant Hill. And my offer of room and board is always good, in case you change your mind or it doesn't work out at your mother's."

"Thank you."

"Okay, next topic. Lopez needs to talk with you."

"Now there's something to look forward to."

"The lieutenant said she would give you a little time to recuperate, but she sounded as if she's on a very short fuse," said Darlene. "Lopez seems to think that there is a lot you know that you're not telling her."

"You would think she'd be used to it by now," I said. "The joke is that I don't know a damned thing."

"You should be used to *that* by now," Darlene said, taking a wild stab at lightening the mood.

"Nice try," I said. "Darlene, I want you to stay away from the office until this business is settled. Check calls from home, or have calls forwarded. If there is something worth following up, shoot it over to Tom Romano or to the Fennessy brothers. I don't want any arguments, Darlene. Diamond Investigation is on sabbatical. There is enough money in the account, make sure that you cut yourself a check every week until we're back to work. Are we clear?"

"Yes."

"Say it."

"We're clear, Jake," Darlene said, "crystal clear."

"Good. Now go do something fun. Please ask a nurse to come in; I need to visit the water closet."

"Jake."

"No thanks. I'll go with trained medical personnel."

"Would you like me to bring you something for lunch?"

"No, thanks, Darlene. Come back tonight if you like, we'll see what's on TV."

"Okay, have a good day."

I resisted the urge to tell Darlene that I had other plans.

The next four days went very slowly. Most of my time was spent sleeping, reading Dostoyevsky, or being poked by nurses and doctors.

My eyes seemed to be fine. X-rays of the ankle showed that the sprain was not as serious as first diagnosed, and that once the swelling went down I should be able to lose the cast and begin strength exercises. In as soon as seven to ten days, I might be able to walk with crutches. The stitches were removed from the gash above my eye. As I had predicted, I was going to have three eyebrows henceforth.

Darlene visited often; Joey Russo stayed away.

Tom Romano and Ira Fennessy came in Tuesday night with a pizza and a deck of pinochle cards. Romano had tried to smuggle in a six-pack of beer but was busted at the nurses' station.

Lieutenant Lopez finally nabbed me Wednesday morning.

Fortunately I was warned by Vinnie, who spotted Lopez coming into the hospital. When the lieutenant came into my room, I tried my very best to look even more pathetic.

"I didn't come here for a song and dance, Diamond," she began.

"I won't be dancing for quite some time, Lieutenant."

"Do you have any proof that it was Ralph Battle who set the bomb in your apartment?"

"Not really," I said.

"I reached out to the Chicago Police Department," said Lopez. "They did some asking around. There are three men in Detroit who will swear that Battle was in the Motor City with them from Friday morning until Sunday evening playing poker. All weekend, no breaks."

I knew better. I suppose it was possible that someone else had placed the explosives on behalf of Max Lansdale, but I had no doubt that Battle was nowhere near Motown on that Friday evening when Harry Chandler was gunned down.

"How did he do in the card game?" I asked.

"Don't be cute, Diamond."

"I can't help it, Lopez, it's a curse."

"Look, Jake, I don't want to badger you," Lopez said, "you look too damned pathetic. But if that's all you can give me, there's not much I can do for you."

To the lieutenant's credit, she didn't try to throw guilt my way for putting Sally in the line of fire.

Lopez was smart enough to see I needed no help in that department.

"I appreciate the good intention, Lieutenant," I said, meaning it.

"You need to learn how to be better at accepting help, Diamond," Lopez said.

"I'm working on it," I said.

"Good luck," she said, and then she was gone.

Vinnie was back on Wednesday evening, his third visit of the day. He walked into the hospital room struggling with a large cardboard box.

"I hate to ask," I said.

"I have two sandwiches from Molinari's," Strings said, reaching into the box. "Eggplant parmigiana or sausage and peppers?"

"I'll take the eggplant," I said.

Vinnie tossed the sandwich. I made a stabbing catch with my good hand to save it from smashing into the wall above my head. Vinnie placed the other sandwich to the side and reached into the box with both arms. He pulled out a thirteen-inch television.

"There's a TV up on the wall, Vin," I said.

"This one has a VCR built in, Jake," Vinnie said, setting the TV up on a chair facing the bed. "I brought two videos, my favorite and your favorite. Which do you want to watch first?"

I was well aware of Vinnie's favorite flick, a 1960 French New Wave film directed by Jean-Luc Godard. Vinnie had a large poster of Belmondo on a wall in his apartment. I had no idea what Vinnie considered my favorite movie; I was only certain it wasn't one that I had a bit part in. I hoped that trying to figure it out might keep me alert enough to read subtitles.

"Let's start with *Breathless*," I said, trying to get the foil wrapping off the sandwich single-handedly.

"Need help with that, Jake?"

"I think I've got it, Vinnie."

"Are you sure you wouldn't like to watch *Mean Streets* first?" asked Strings, ruining the suspense.

"Let's save it, Vinnie," I said.

I held the large sandwich in my one good hand. I decided that it was going to be a challenging evening.

I was released into my mother's custody on Friday morning. Joey Russo had arranged transportation.

Russo had leased a large van with a hydraulic lift. The lift carried me in the wheelchair up into the rear of the van. As I rose off the ground, I felt like Raymond Burr in *Ironside*, which brought to mind the importance of watching my diet while at my mother's. The van took me to Pleasant Hill, Darlene and Mom following in the Toyota.

I lasted two weeks with Mom and Aunt Rosalie. The cast came off the ankle and I was able to hobble around on my own. Bobby finished his work on the movie and needed to get back to Los Angeles. The sisters bickered constantly. I called in an SOS to Darlene and she came running to rescue me.

Two weeks later, the cast came off my wrist. By that time, sharing a one-bedroom house with Darlene and the mutt was getting very claustrophobic. I told Darlene that I was thinking about taking Joey Russo up on his offer. She said that she would love it and began brushing up on her French. Joey agreed to look after Tug McGraw, and Darlene and I took the trip to St. Martin.

Two and a half weeks later, the cast came off my right leg. The next afternoon, I gazed out the window of Joey Russo's condominium. Out to the Caribbean. Down at the poolside, Darlene was batting off hopeless Casanovas like flies.

I limped down with a cane and a tennis racket to give Darlene a hand.

I sat at the edge of the pool and hung my legs into the water. The knee pad on my right leg soaked up the chlorine like a sponge. Darlene came over and sat down beside me.

"This is too much fun, Jake," Darlene said. "I don't know how much more of it I can take."

"I called Joey this morning," I said. "I told him we would be flying back the day after tomorrow."

"Thank God," she said. "What's the tennis racket for?"

"I couldn't find a flyswatter."

Darlene and I came off the plane at San Francisco International.

It was a Saturday evening, exactly eight weeks after the explosion. Joey Russo and Sonny the Chin met us at the baggage-claim area and helped us collect our bags.

Sonny and Darlene walked ahead, toward the parking garage. Sonny carried Darlene's suitcase and was talking to her in whispers. Joey Russo carried my suitcase and I limped alongside with my cane.

"Is it my imagination," I asked Joey as we followed, "or do I sense something conspiratorial?"

"Sonny will take Darlene home," Joey said; "you'll be riding with me."

"Should I ask where to?"

"Not yet," Joey said.

We parted at the vehicles. Darlene gave me a hug and hopped into Sonny's car. She seemed to know what was going on. I climbed into Joey's car and we headed out of the airport.

"You look a lot better, Jake," Joey said as we drove.

"It was the only way to go, Joey," I said.

"How do you feel, Jake?"

"Not too bad, Joey."

"Good," he said.

And then Joey remained silent until we pulled up in front of the house in the Presidio twenty minutes later.

"What is this, Joey?" I asked.

Joey killed the engine and turned in his seat to face me.

"Hear me out before you say anything, Jake," he said.

"Okay."

"Sally's will was read two weeks ago. She left the house to you."

I looked up at the house. The house Sally and I had shared when we were married.

I looked back at Joey and started to open my mouth to speak. He held up his hand and stopped me.

"Hear me out, Jake," Joey said. "There are three good reasons for you to walk into that house and make yourself at home as quickly as possible. First, you have no place to live. Your apartment is uninhabitable, it will be for quite a while, and, no offense, it was never what could be called a showplace to begin with."

"No offense taken," I said.

"This house was as much your home as it was Sally's before you split up. I really think you might have been living back here before too long even if this tragedy had never occurred," said Joey. "I believe you belong here."

"And reason number three?"

"It is what Sally wanted. Look, Jake. I'm not going to drag you in there; I can find you a place to stay. I'm only asking that you feel it out. Sonny and I brought your things over from storage, what little there was. We picked up a few new shirts and two suits to help get you started. No ties, I know how picky you are about neckwear. There is food inside. There is a bottle of George Dickel. There is a working telephone. If you have a problem being here, you just pick up the phone and I'm on my way back."

"Want to come in for a drink?" I asked.

"No, thank you, but I'll walk you to the door," Joey said, handing me the house keys.

We both got out of the car, I grabbed my cane, and Joey grabbed my suitcase from the backseat. As we moved to the entrance, I spotted my Toyota in the driveway.

"The Impala is in my garage," Joey said. "We can move it over here when you're ready."

I unlocked the front door and pushed it open. Joey placed the suitcase just inside and reached for my hand.

"Welcome home, Jake," he said.

"Thanks, I guess," I said.

"You have tonight and all day tomorrow to get settled, Jake," Joey said as he turned back to his car. "First thing Monday morning we get to work."

I stood and watched Joey drive away. I stepped into the house and closed the door behind me. I went looking for the bottle of bourbon.

I drank to Sally French.

Again and again.

Eighteen

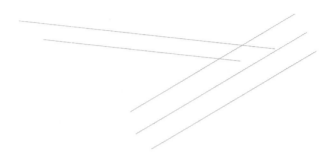

By NOON THE NEXT DAY, Sunday, thanks to a forty-five-minute scalding hot shower, a fistful of extra-strength Excedrin, and a pot of black coffee, I was able to focus for the first time on the details of my surroundings.

Most of Sally's personal belongings were gone. There were basic furnishings, including the sofa I had passed out on the night before, but the walls were bare. Missing was the assortment of multisized framed photographs that Sally had scattered throughout the house. Opposite a large glass-topped coffee table, which ran the length of the sofa in the front living room, sat the weary reading chair from my own apartment. On the floor beside the recliner were a number of cardboard boxes, which held all that remained of my humble possessions. And a small metal safe box.

The coat tree from my apartment stood just inside the front door, looking very much as it had the last time I saw it. My three-quarter-length leather coat, my City College of New York bomber jacket, and my father's Harris Tweed topcoat had survived the blast. As had most of my shoes, which I customarily removed and left sitting at the front door of my apartment at the foot of the coat tree.

There were also two baseball caps, Giants and Mets.

All of Sally's clothing, shoes, and accessories were gone. The closets were bare, except for the two new suits that Joey and Sonny had afforded me. All but the bedroom dresser's bottom drawer were empty. That drawer held some of my own things, kept handy for those times when I spent the night with Sally—a few pairs of casual slacks, polo shirts, socks and underwear. There was enough on hand to throw together a marginally presentable postshower outfit.

The bathroom was also cleared of everything belonging to Sally. It was instead supplied with an unopened toothbrush, toothpaste, soap, shampoo, a package of disposable razors, and shave cream.

The kitchen was equipped with a toaster, a coffeemaker, and the espresso pot from my place. The cookware, plates, glasses, and eating utensils Sally had accumulated remained. Much of it had been with us when we were married and shared the house and the domestic duties. The kitchen dry-goods cabinets were bare, with the exception of a few essentials such as salt, pepper, coffee, and the bottle of George Dickel that I had located and put a good dent into the night before.

There was a carton of Camel nonfilter cigarettes, a bottle of Excedrin, and an Entenmann's raspberry Danish ring on the counter beside the kitchen sink.

The refrigerator had been cleaned out and restocked with a few basic items. A dozen eggs, a quart of half-and-half, a half gallon of orange juice, a loaf of sliced whole wheat bread, and two sticks of unsalted butter. I put up a second pot of coffee, prepared a few slices of toast, and took my breakfast into the living room.

I sat in my chair and began going through the boxes that Joey and Sonny had delivered from storage.

The contents were primarily books, both paperbacks and hardbacks, mostly classics. There was a photograph album; I put it aside. There were videotapes and compact discs. Joey and Sonny had not delivered any electronic components, so I had no idea about the fate of my TV and stereo. But the house was already well equipped for sound and video.

I threw a disc into the CD player, Wang Chung, *To Live and Die in LA,* and went back to the boxes.

The rest was odds and ends, dust collectors.

The small safe box was badly battered; it had been in my bedroom. On a shelf under the table near my bed, below the telephone. The box was unlocked, but the contents were intact. Personal documents, ranging from little to moderate importance, including the titles to both the Impala and the Toyota, my birth certificate, marriage and divorce papers.

And a baseball autographed by Sandy Koufax.

I needed to do some shopping and I needed company.

I went to the kitchen wall phone to call Darlene. Joey Russo had taped a note across the keypad, letting me know that phone calls to my number on Fillmore Street were being forwarded here to Sally's and calls to Sally's phone number were being forwarded to her mother.

Darlene answered on the first ring.

"What are you doing?" I asked.

"Sitting by the phone waiting for you to call."

"Want to go food shopping?"

"Sure. I can pick you up," she said.

"Do me a favor, swing by the office and grab whatever I have for neckties from my desk drawer."

"Jake, I thought you were going to have those ties dry-cleaned and burned."

"I need more time."

"I'll be there in an hour," Darlene said.

Darlene insisted we do some clothes shopping before we hit the grocery. She helped me choose a few pairs of pants, a couple of shirts, new socks and underwear, a wool sweater, and a cotton blazer. She twisted my arm until I agreed to choose at least one new tie to have handy for "when the time was right."

We returned to the house and filled the cupboards and the refrigerator with enough food to suggest that someone lived in the place. Darlene had brought a bottle of wine along and enlisted me to uncork and pour while she prepared dinner.

All afternoon I had been trying to coax information from Darlene. Joey Russo had announced that we would be "getting to work" first thing Monday morning, and I wanted a clue as to what he had in mind. Darlene kept begging me to be patient.

As much as I hated torturing her, I couldn't stop myself from giving it one more try over dinner.

"Please, Jake," Darlene pleaded, "I can't talk about it. Joey has a plan, but I don't know all of the details. None of us do."

"None of *us*?"

"Joey is putting a team together; I have no idea who exactly is included. Joey said that he was bringing us all together tomorrow morning and that he would lay it all out. He asked that we keep our shirts on until then," Darlene said. "Don't you trust Joey?"

"Of course I do," I said.

"Good, then stop bugging me and eat."

"I'm impossible, right?"

"Unbearable is more like it," Darlene said.

"Give me something, Darlene, anything."

"And you'll leave me alone?"

"I swear," I said.

"Joey mentioned that the biggest challenge to his plan would be getting Ralph Battle out of the picture."

"Jesus, Darlene, without knowing a thing about what Joey has planned, I could have told you that."

"Jake, I'm warning you, one more word about it and I'm out of here."

"Have some more wine, Darlene," I said.

I didn't say another word about it.

After dinner we watched a repeat of *The Sopranos*.

"Darlene?"

"Yes, Jake."

"Do you find Tony Soprano attractive?"

"Are you kidding? The guy is as appealing as a garden slug."

"So why do women fall all over him?"

"Because they are all morons, Jake, including his idiot wife."

"Oh," I said.

"I need to get going; we have a big day tomorrow."

I walked Darlene to the door. I stood on the porch and watched her drive off before going back into the house.

A few minutes later the doorbell rang.

"Forget something?" I said as I swung the door open.

Ralph Battle stood in the doorway with his right arm extended, the large gun in his hand pointed at my chest.

"Before I kill you, Diamond, I want you to know that I never intended the woman any harm."

"That's very sensitive of you, Ralph," I said.

"What I'm telling you, Diamond, is that I don't work that way. I'm very careful not to hurt innocent bystanders. I don't hurt women or children, no matter who's giving the orders. I had nothing to do with the bomb in your place; I was in Detroit all that weekend playing cards."

"Jesus, Battle, just fucking shoot me and get it over with," I said. "You are some piece of work. I can't decide what's worse, someone who would continue to lie right up to his last dying breath or a piece of crap like you who would lie to someone he's about to kill."

"Fuck you, Diamond. I said I was in Detroit, Friday afternoon through Sunday night. You can decide to believe me or you can decide not to. I really don't care all that much, now that I think about it," Battle said, "but you'll need to decide quickly—your time is about up."

I really couldn't make up my mind; I prepared myself to take a bullet.

I caught sight of a shadow moving very quickly behind Battle and suddenly he was violently knocked to the floor. Battle tried to rise. I clobbered him with the metal safe box and he went still. I looked up at the figure standing over me.

"Vinnie Strings told me where I could find you, Jake. I came by to return this; you left it in the glove box of my truck. I suppose that it could have waited until Joey Russo's big powwow tomorrow morning, but it seems that my timing wasn't too bad."

Willie Dogtail stood there with my .38 in his hand.

I picked up Battle's weapon from the floor and handed it to Dogtail.

"Cover him, Willie," I said. "Shoot him in the leg if he moves."

I went to the kitchen to telephone Joey Russo.

Joey's wife, Angela, answered and called Joey to the phone.

"Jake, is everything all right?" Joey asked.

"Joey, I heard you were looking for a way to get Ralph Battle out of the picture."

"Can't this wait until tomorrow, Jake?"

"I don't think so, Joey," I said, taking a quick peek to check the situation in the front room.

"What about Battle?"

"Battle is lying here unconscious on the living-room floor."

"Keep him there, I can't wait to meet him, I'm on my way," Joey said, quickly ending the conversation.

I walked back into the living room to join Willie and our honored guest.

Willie found clothesline in his vehicle and was using it to immobilize Battle while I started a pot of coffee.

"Do you have any duct tape, Kemosabe?" Willie called. "I know there's a roll somewhere in the back of my truck, but it would take me a week to find it."

"I'm not sure, Willie, what do you need to do?"

"I thought we should gag this guy, unless you want to have to listen to his bullshit when he wakes up."

"Absolutely not. There are some socks in the Kmart bag on the sofa. Use a pair of those."

When I walked back into the front room, Ralph Battle was roped like a rodeo calf. Two athletic socks, knotted together, were tied around his head, with the knot in his mouth. Battle was beginning to stir, but he wasn't going anywhere. I invited Willie Dogtail into the kitchen for coffee and Danish.

Twenty minutes later the doorbell rang.

"You might want to take one of these along, Wyatt," said Willie, indicating the two handguns on the kitchen table as I rose from my seat.

"I'll look out the window before I open up this time," I said. "Wait here."

I glanced at Battle on my way through. He seemed very uncomfortable. He stared back at me without affection.

I checked the porch through the window and opened the door to Joey Russo. Sonny and LAPD lieutenant Ray Boyle stood behind him. I moved aside to let them in. Joey walked directly over to Ralph Battle to take a look.

"I wasn't expecting you, Ray," I said. "How did you get up here so fast?"

"I came up earlier this evening, for the meeting in the morning."

"The last time we spoke you said you would put me in touch with a certain character nicknamed for a shellfish, Ray. That was two months ago."

"Lay off him, Jake," Joey said. "Ray is here to help. He's been helping us out all along. Try to be friendly. Offer Ray a cup of coffee while we wait for the others."

"The others?"

"I decided we may as well take care of the meeting tonight," Joey said. "We need to decide what to do about Battle and how his visit affects our game plan. Who is that in the kitchen, Jake?"

"Willie Dogtail," I said.

"He showed up early," said Sonny.

"Actually, not a moment too soon," I said. "How would you like your coffee, Ray, buddy?"

"Sonny, help me get this gorilla out to the garage," Joey said. "I don't want to have to look at him when the others arrive, and I don't want him taking notes."

Joey and Sonny got to work moving Battle; I invited Boyle to join me and Willie for coffee.

A few minutes later, Sonny came into the kitchen to make it a quartet.

"Where's Joey?" I asked.

"In the garage, having a little man-to-man talk with your friend Ralph."

"Are you sure Joey's all right out there, alone with Battle?"

"No problem," Sonny said. "We didn't untie the guy, we just removed his socks. Any of that coffee left?"

"Plenty," I said, as the doorbell rang.

"I'll get that," said Sonny, "and save me a piece of the Danish ring."

I poured coffee all around and put up another pot.

Sonny returned with Tom Romano and Vinnie Strings.

I looked around the room, which was getting very crowded. Boyle, Willie, Sonny, Tom, Vinnie, me. And Joey out in the garage.

"Joey put together quite an impressive crew," I said.

"No shit," said Vinnie, doing the math. "We're like the Magnificent Seven."

"More like Snow White and the Seven Dwarfs," Darlene said, suddenly appearing at the kitchen doorway.

"Maybe we'd better hi-ho it out to the front room before we all suffocate in here," I said.

"I'll go check on Joey," Sonny said.

The rest of the crew began the exodus out to the front room.

We waited for Joey and Sonny.

And waited.

Darlene and Tom Romano played five hundred rummy at the glass-topped coffee table.

Ray Boyle paced the room.

Willie Dogtail browsed through my photo album.

Vinnie Strings scouted my videotapes. I watched as he put one aside, as if we might have the time to get in a screening.

I shuttled back and forth from the kitchen, keeping the coffee coming.

Finally, Joey Russo came in from the garage. I had since been dealt into the rummy game.

"So, what did you decide to do about Battle?" I asked, laying down a four-card straight in hearts.

"We decided that we would allow him to help us out," Joey said. "Come in and join the party, Ralph."

Battle walked into the room, unbound and unhappy, Sonny close behind him.

Joey asked that we all find a comfortable seat.

Nineteen

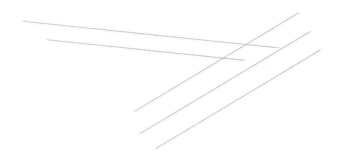

R ALPH CLAIMS HE DIDN'T KILL Harry Chandler and had nothing to do with placing the bomb in Jake's apartment," said Joey Russo when we were all settled.

"And you believe him?" I asked.

"If I didn't believe him, he wouldn't be sitting here with us, cracking his knuckles," said Joey. "Relax, Ralph."

Battle sat in my reading chair, apart from the others. Sonny stood silently behind him. Ralph was the center of attention. Darlene glared at him unlovingly.

"I checked it out, Jake," Sonny said. "Battle's alibi is airtight. He was in Detroit all that weekend, no doubt about it."

"It doesn't change the fact that he came here to kill me," I said.

"I never killed anyone," Battle said. "I was sent to put a good scare into you, maybe to find out what you know or think you know. Lansdale uses me to scare people. It's my looks, I'm intimidating. I might rough somebody up once in a while, but I don't kill anyone. Lansdale has someone else for that, who probably looks more like a choirboy."

"Who?" I said.

"I don't know, I only know he calls himself Tucker."

"How does it work?" asked Joey. "How is it arranged?"

"Lansdale calls a phone number, leaves a message. An hour later, Lansdale takes a call at the phone booth in the bagel shop across from his office. Max names the mark and waits. When the contract is complete, Lansdale receives a flower delivery. A card is included, with information on how to make payment."

"And you're sure you have no idea who Lansdale calls?" asked Ray Boyle.

"None," said Battle. "Lansdale doesn't even know who the guy is."

"I suppose you know nothing about what happened to the medical examiner down in Mexico or to the Chicago newspaper reporter, Cochran," said Tom Romano.

"I'm told only what I need to know, but it's a pretty good bet that they're both as dead as Stan Riddle," Battle said, "and Max Lansdale put out the contracts, obviously. I have no clue exactly who iced any of them or where the bodies are buried."

"So what *do* you know that can help us hurt Lansdale?" asked Ray Boyle.

"Not very much, really."

"So how are you supposed to do us any good?" I asked.

"Russo has an idea or two," Battle said.

"And why would you help us?" asked Darlene.

"Because I shared these with our new friend," said Joey. "I apologize for borrowing these without letting you know, Jake."

Joey Russo reached into his jacket pocket, pulled out the letter and the metal ball that I had taken from the Chandler murder scene, and placed them on the glass table.

Ralph Battle rose from the chair and slowly moved to the table, Sonny watching him like a hawk. Battle picked up the metal ball with one hand while he reached into his pocket. He came out with two more, exactly alike, and began rolling them between his fingers.

"Someone wanted to make it look as if I was Chandler's killer, wanted Diamond to find this," said Battle. "Russo helped me put two and two together. I'm stating it mildly when I say that it makes me very angry. If Lansdale wanted you killed that day, you'd be dead, Diamond. Lansdale left you alive to finger me, and because he couldn't be sure if you really had anything on him."

"So why would Lansdale have a bomb set in my apartment the next day?"

"Lansdale realized that you had kept the evidence from the

cops. He decided to gamble that you were sitting on it and that anything you knew would be buried with you."

"And when Lansdale misses finishing me off with the bomb, why doesn't he come right back after me? I was an easy target—for the past two months I could hardly get out of my own way," I said. "Why would he wait until I'm back on my feet? And why would he send a measly thumb breaker to call on me tonight—no offense, Ralph—and not a bona fide choirboy-looking assassin?"

"The stakes have been raised somewhat for Lansdale since the explosion," said Joey. "I've been tossing bait into the slimy pond that Lansdale hides in. And sending Battle to visit you tonight is clearly a nibble. Which brings us around to why I've brought you all together."

"It's about time," said Ray Boyle, who was up and pacing again. Joey Russo let it pass.

"Our goal is to destroy Max Lansdale," said Joey, "to strip Lansdale of everything, his power, his privilege, and his protection. And I believe we can do that. But there are two things we will not do. We will not kill Lansdale. If I wanted him dead, it would have been over and done two months ago. I have something much more dismal in mind for Max Lansdale. I need to be sure that everyone here understands and agrees."

Russo waited. No one disagreed and he continued.

"The second condition," Joey said, "is that Lansdale will not be handed over to the police. Not the Chicago PD, not the San Francisco PD, not the LAPD. I have very good reasons to insist on this provision, personal reasons, and it is nonnegotiable. If any of you find this problematic, speak now and we can all go home."

All eyes turned to Ray Boyle.

"No problem," Ray said.

"In order to proceed we need to take what we know as fact, decide what these facts imply, and then accept the implications as fact. We need to begin with convictions, a set of *givens*. From what we learned from Kit Carson and from Harry Chandler, we know that Randolph Lansdale did not commit suicide. There were no fingerprints on the weapon, no silencer, and Carson did not hear a gunshot. No one had entered Randolph's office from the reception area and no one was present in the office suite other than Carson and Max Lansdale. Max Lansdale murdered his brother. Fact."

Joey waited. There was no argument.

"I visited John Carlucci at San Quentin six weeks ago and asked for a favor," Joey continued. "I asked Johnny Boy to find out if Max Lansdale had any business with organized crime and, if so, when it had begun. Tony Carlucci called me last week with information from his brother. Eight years ago, Max Lansdale was approached by a group of 'businessmen' from New York City. Lansdale was offered a contract to launder cash, a great deal of cash, at twenty-five percent commission. Max was told that he could expect his end to be at least a million every year. Lansdale brought the proposition to his brother. Max needed Randolph's support to get it past the old man, Simon Lansdale, who would never have let the brothers get anywhere near it. Randolph said no way. Max said okay, forget that I asked. Less than two weeks later, Simon Lansdale died in his sleep. Max began to launder gambling money. Carlucci couldn't say exactly how Lansdale pulls it off. Anonymous cash donations passed through a maze of phony nonprofit corporations, tax-exempt grants for community outreach programs, smoke and mirrors, whatever, it doesn't much matter. In any event, according to Ralph, Max Lansdale is in New York as we speak picking up two hundred fifty thousand dollars in undeclared cash from a Connecticut casino. Max killed his father. We're going to consider this a fact."

"What a guy," said Darlene, turning to Ralph Battle. "How could you even bear to look at a man like Lansdale, let alone work for the sick bastard?"

"Simon Lansdale took me in from the streets when I was a kid," Battle answered, hardly above a whisper. "The man was like a father to me. I never suspected that his death was anything but natural. I want Max Lansdale as badly as anyone here."

"Why did Lansdale send Battle here tonight?" I asked.

"I took the liberty of contacting Max Lansdale on your behalf, Jake," said Joey. "I told Lansdale that you needed to see him about a former Chicago medical examiner who died mysteriously in Mexico and left a copy of an autopsy report in a safe-deposit box for his son. A report indicating that Simon Lansdale died of suffocation, along with a statement explaining how this report was replaced by a false report and why. I told Lansdale that you were representing Dr. Kearney's son in negotiating a purchase price. I was sure that Lansdale wouldn't do anything to hurt you until he had more information, though I'll have to admit I didn't expect Ralph to show up so quickly."

"Lansdale was pretty shook up about it," said Battle. "He was just about to leave for New York; he had me take the first flight out here. And he'll be expecting me to call him sometime tonight."

"When does he get back from New York?" asked Joey.

"Tuesday night."

"Call Lansdale now," said Joey. "Tell him that Diamond verified he has access to the documents and that Jake wants a meeting with him on Friday. Jake, go with Ralph in case Lansdale wants to hear it from you. I'll get another pot of coffee going, and then we'll work out the details."

Lansdale did want to speak to me. I told him what he needed to make his problem go away. One hundred thousand dollars in cash by Friday. I told him I would be coming up to Chicago and that I would call him to arrange a meeting when I arrived in town.

When Battle and I came back to the front room, Joey was pouring coffee all around and Vinnie had broken into the package of anisette toast Darlene and I had picked up earlier at the grocery.

"Max Lansdale murdered his father and brother," said Joey Russo. "This is our working hypothesis. Now, all we need to do is to convince a certain person that these are truly the facts. A certain person who will not believe a single word of it unless it comes straight from Max's own lips. What we need to do is to get Max Lansdale to confess to patricide and fratricide, make sure the choirboy hit man doesn't get in the way, and be extremely careful not to step on the toes of anyone with Connecticut casino interests, and we all need to be in place by the time Max Lansdale gets back to Chicago Tuesday night."

"That's all?" Darlene said.

"I think that's it," said Joey. "Am I forgetting anything, Sonny?"

"I don't think so, Joey," said Sonny. "I thought that you handled the plot synopsis pretty well."

"Good," said Joey Russo. "Now all we have to do is get all of our roles straight."

It was nearly two in the morning. Joey Russo and I stood on the front porch, watching the two cars pull away.

Darlene was heading home to pack a travel bag and drop the dog off with her sister. Tom Romano would be packing as well, after dropping Vinnie off at home. Darlene and Tom would be on the first flight to Chicago Monday morning. Vinnie would be flying to Chicago on Tuesday night.

Sonny had left earlier to drive Ray Boyle back to his hotel. Ray would be returning to Los Angeles. Sonny would be flying to New York City on Monday afternoon.

Willie Dogtail was asleep on the sofa inside. Willie would be driving home to Santa Monica to keep an eye on Kit Carson, in case she needed to be brought into the mix. We hoped to avoid involving her.

Ralph Battle had gone back to his hotel.

"Do you think Battle will play along?" I asked Joey while we waited for Sonny to return.

"Yes. I think we convinced Battle that he doesn't have much of a future with Max Lansdale. And when Ralph understood that Max had killed the old man, he jumped on board with both feet. Ralph will do just fine."

"Joey."

"Yes, Jake."

"Why are you taking this on?"

"I want to help you get the fuck who murdered Sally."

"I'm sure you do, Joey, and I appreciate the help," I said, "but there's something personal in this for you—you said so yourself."

"If things go well, you will know everything in less than a week, Jake," Joey said. "Can you give me that much time?"

"Sure."

"Good," said Joey. "Here's Sonny. I'll call you tomorrow."

Joey went down to the car and climbed in beside Sonny.

I lit a cigarette as I watched them drive off.

Part Four

TEN TO
INFINITY

Twenty

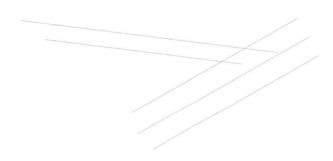

MONDAY MORNING. Chicago.

"That's her," said Eddie Hand.

Tom Romano and Darlene peered out the window of the bagel shop. A young woman was stepping out of a taxi in front of the office building across South Wacker Drive.

"Her name is Jill Ballard. With Lansdale and Battle both gone, she should be alone in the office," said Eddie.

Eddie Hand had collected Tom and Darlene at O'Hare an hour earlier. They had come directly downtown and taken a table at the window of the bagel shop to await the woman's arrival. They watched as Ballard walked into the building. Tom Romano wore a dark blue suit; Darlene wore a dark blue dress that nearly matched. Darlene's hair was pulled back severely and pinned up high on her head. Tom and Darlene wore matching dark glasses.

"You guys look scary," said Eddie.

"Let's hope so," said Darlene. "We'll give Jill a little time to settle in before we spook her."

"Do you have everything that you need, Tom?" asked Eddie.

"Right here," said Romano, tapping the briefcase on the floor at the foot of his seat.

"I'm dead tired, and this coffee isn't cutting it," said Darlene, removing her glasses. "How do my eyes look?"

"Perfect," said Tom Romano.

"Have you decided on names?" asked Eddie.

"I'm going with Tom Romano, it will be pretty easy to remember," said Tom. "How about you, Darlene?"

"How about Clarice Starling?" said Darlene. "I'm just kidding. I always liked the name Amanda Bonner."

"Katharine Hepburn in *Adam's Rib*," said Eddie.

"That's very good," said Darlene. "Do you think Max Lansdale will know it?"

"How would anyone know it?" asked Tom Romano.

Thirty minutes later, Tom Romano and Darlene walked into the reception area of Lansdale's office suite. They carried overcoats on their arms; Romano held a briefcase. Jill Ballard looked up from her desk as they came in.

"Can I help you?" Ballard asked.

"Is Mr. Lansdale available?" asked Darlene.

"No. Mr. Lansdale will be out of town until tomorrow evening," said the receptionist. "Would you like me to set up an appointment?"

"I'm Agent Bonner; this is Agent Romano," Darlene said, "Federal Bureau of Investigation."

Darlene flashed a badge, something that Ray Boyle had scared up for the occasion. Jill Ballard's eyes went wide.

"FBI?" Ballard said.

"That's right," said Darlene. "We have a warrant to search these offices."

Tom Romano removed a convincing facsimile of a search warrant from his suit jacket pocket. Something else that Lieutenant Boyle had pulled out of his hat.

"I should phone Mr. Lansdale," said Ballard.

Well, here goes, thought Darlene.

"Miss Ballard, calling Mr. Lansdale is not a very good idea," said Darlene. "You may be in danger or in serious trouble or both. I need to question you while Agent Romano looks through the offices. Please trust me; we are only trying to protect you."

"Danger? What kind of danger?"

"Avoidable danger, Miss Ballard," said Darlene, "if you'll try working with us."

"What kind of trouble?" asked Ballard. "I haven't done anything."

"Why don't we leave that up to me to decide," said Darlene. "Agent Romano, why don't you get started while Miss Ballard and I have a little talk. I'm sure that she is very willing to cooperate."

"I am," said Ballard, "totally willing."

"Good," said Darlene, "that's very good."

Darlene took a seat opposite Ballard's desk and pulled a notepad and pencil from her shoulder bag as Romano headed off for Max Lansdale's private office.

"Miss Ballard," Darlene began. "Would it be all right if I call you Jill?"

"Jill would be fine. Do you have a first name?"

"Agent will be fine," Darlene said. "Jill, I need to know about everyone who works out of these offices."

"It's only Mr. Lansdale and me, basically," Ballard said.

"Mr. Lansdale works all of his cases alone?" Darlene asked.

"For the most part. If Mr. Lansdale has a case that requires assistance, I mean beyond what I can provide, he contracts outside help. Someone may use the other private office occasionally, for a place to sit, to use the phone or the computer, but it's rare. Of course, Mr. Battle is usually close."

"Mr. Battle?"

"Ralph Battle," said Ballard. "Ralph works for Mr. Lansdale, runs errands and drives, that sort of thing."

"Is Battle with Lansdale now?"

"No, Ralph isn't with Mr. Lansdale. I don't really know where Ralph is right now."

"Can you tell me where Mr. Lansdale is? You said that he was out of town."

"New York City," Ballard said.

"Could you be more specific, Jill?"

"I have everything in my desk drawer. The hotel, the phone number," said Ballard. "Mr. Lansdale will be there until tomorrow morning, and then he will be driving up to Connecticut and will be flying back here from Hartford. I have that information also."

"Good, we'll be needing that," said Darlene.

"Would you like it now?" Ballard asked, reaching for the drawer.

"No, it can wait. Please leave your hands visible on top of the desk," said Darlene, thinking it a nice touch.

Ballard placed both hands palm down on her desktop.

"Do you have any knowledge, Jill, as to the nature of Mr. Lansdale's business in New York and Connecticut?"

"None at all. Mr. Lansdale makes the trip often, but he has never specified his business there."

"You said Mr. Lansdale would be returning to Chicago tomorrow evening," said Darlene. "Will someone be picking Mr. Lansdale up at the airport?"

"I suppose Ralph will pick him up; he usually does," said Ballard.

The woman's hands were shaking.

"Relax. You are doing very well, Jill," Darlene said, "and we appreciate your help. Would you please show me the information from your desk, Lansdale's itinerary. Slowly."

Jill Ballard carefully opened the drawer and removed a sheet of paper. She handed it across to Darlene.

"Can we trust you, Jill?"

"Yes."

"Okay, I'm going in to check on Agent Romano. Please stay at your desk, and do not use the telephone."

"What if the phone rings?"

"Is there an answering service?"

"Yes."

"Let them pick up the call," Darlene said. "I'll be back in a few minutes. Will you be okay?"

"I need to go to the bathroom."

"Sure, go ahead," said Darlene.

Both women rose from their seats.

"It's there," said Ballard, indicating a door that displayed a small painted sign: Washroom.

"I see," said Darlene, moving toward Max Lansdale's private office.

"I could make some fresh coffee," said Jill Ballard. "It's hazelnut."

"Not for me, thanks," said Darlene.

When Darlene walked into Lansdale's office, Tom Romano was working on the telephone.

"How are you doing?"

"I'm almost done," said Romano. "We will be able to monitor all calls, incoming and outgoing. How is Ballard doing?"

"A little shaky, but I think she will work with us," said Darlene. "Here's Lansdale's itinerary. Give Sonny a call. You should catch him before he leaves for the airport. If he's not at home, call his cell phone number. Give Sonny all the details on where Lansdale will be and when. I'll go back and tell Jill what she needs to do."

Jill Ballard was sitting back at her desk, both hands in full view. Darlene sat.

"Jill, we're almost done here. We need your help."

"Can you tell me what this is all about?"

"The less you know, the better off you will be," said Darlene. "Where are you from, Jill?"

"Billings," Ballard said. "It's in Montana."

"Do you have family there?"

"Mom and Dad, four sisters, and two brothers."

A bit more information than Darlene really needed. Ballard was trying very, very hard to be helpful.

"Does Mr. Lansdale know where your family lives?"

"I don't think so; he never took much interest in my personal life," said Ballard.

"Is Lansdale married?" Darlene asked.

"Widower. His wife passed away about a year ago. Cancer. No children."

"And you and he?"

"Oh, no," Ballard said. "Nothing like that, honestly. I do my work and I go home."

"Jill, we need you to call Mr. Lansdale in New York. We need you to tell him that your mother is ill and that you need to get home to see her and that you need to leave tomorrow afternoon. Don't say where to. If he asks where, say anything except Billings. Tell Lansdale that you will arrange with a temp agency to have someone come in to cover for you until you return and that you will use the rest of today and tomorrow morning to school the temp in the basic office duties. Tell Lansdale that you expect to return to the office next Monday morning. Are you with me?"

"Yes," said Ballard.

"After you speak with Lansdale, I need you to show me where everything is, anything that Lansdale might ask for in the course of the next few days, and tell me enough to be able to at least handle any telephone calls."

"I can do that," Ballard said.

"You are being very cooperative, Jill," Darlene said.

"I'm trying very hard, Agent Bonner."

"Good. After you give me the lay of the land, you are going to Billings to stay with your family until you hear from us. You should be able to return by next week," said Darlene. "I'm sorry."

"Sorry?"

"I'm afraid that you are going to be looking for a new job."

"Maybe I could work for the FBI," Ballard said.

"You never know," said Darlene. "Let's get started."

Monday. New York City.

Vito Ventura stood gazing out of his forty-sixth-floor window down onto Central Park.

The office intercom buzzed on Ventura's desk.

"Yes?"

"There's a collect call for you, Mr. Ventura," said his receptionist, "John Carlucci from California."

"Accept the charges and put him through to me," said Ventura.

"Vito."

"John. It's been a long time."

"Don't remind me."

"How are they treating you?"

"Hotel San Quentin has undesirable checkout policies," said Carlucci. "Listen, Vito, I don't have very much time to talk."

"What can I do for you, John?"

"It's what I can do for you, Vito."

"Oh?"

"A little heads-up on your friend Max Lansdale," said Carlucci.

"What about Lansdale?"

"Word has it that Ralph Battle, Max Lansdale's muscle, is being looked at for homicides in Santa Monica and San Francisco. I don't know what kind of a case they have, but I thought that you might want to know. In the event Battle gets tagged and has to do some dealing. If Battle sold out his boss, it could have an effect on your interests."

"I suppose it could," said Ventura.

"That's all I can tell you," said Carlucci.

"How do you hear these things from the inside?"

"I hear everything, Vito."

"I'll keep that in mind. Thanks, John, I owe you one."

"I won't forget you said that, Vito," said Carlucci. "Watch your back."

Ventura placed the receiver down, thinking he would have a little extra business to talk about with Lansdale over dinner that evening.

Monday. San Francisco.

Joey Russo picked up the phone on his desk after the second ring.

"Yes."

"Joey, this is Tony Carlucci. I just got a call from my brother John. John said that he talked to Ventura in New York and relayed the message."

"Great, thanks, Tony," said Russo. "Tell your brother that I owe him one."

"I will, Joey," said Carlucci, "and Johnny Boy won't forget that you said so."

Joey Russo called Sonny's cell phone number.

"Yes?"

"Where are you?"

"I'm on my way out to the airport," Sonny said. "Tom Romano called. Lansdale is at the Regency Hotel on Sixty-first and Park Avenue. I booked a room there and I'll follow him to Connecticut in the morning. One of the casinos up there, where Lansdale will likely pick up the cash. I bought a seat on the same flight that Lansdale will be taking from Hartford to Chicago tomorrow evening."

"Good."

"Is Battle all set?"

"Yes," said Russo. "Ralph will be at the airport to pick up Lansdale when the plane gets in from Hartford."

"Okay."

"Call me when you get into New York, Sonny."

"Will do, Joey," said Sonny, and they ended the call.

Monday afternoon. Chicago.

In deference to Darlene, they chose a vegetarian restaurant for a late lunch.

"So, no snags?" said Eddie, after testing the chili.

"Not yet," said Tom Romano, who had ordered the same. "The office phone is taken care of, and I can monitor the phone booth in the bagel shop when the time comes."

"And Lansdale's receptionist?" asked Eddie.

"Off to Big Sky Country," said Darlene. "We gave her three thousand in cash, for a plane ticket to Billings and a little cushion while she's hunting for a new job."

"Where's the cash coming from?" asked Eddie.

"Joey Russo put together a budget to bankroll the whole setup," said Darlene. "Joey is confident that one way or another Lansdale will pay back."

"How did Lansdale take the news from Ballard about her ailing mother?" asked Eddie.

"I listened in," said Darlene. "Max wasn't thrilled, but he sounded as if he had more important things on his mind. So he'll be expecting a fill-in receptionist when he comes in to the office on Wednesday. Ballard showed me what was what and then we sent her packing. The place is stocked to the teeth. I wouldn't mind pillaging the supply cabinets before we go back home to San Francisco. Diamond Investigation would be flush in Post-its and invisible tape for the next ten years. How's the chili?"

"Could use some beef," said Tom. "How is the sun-dried tomato tempeh? What is sun-dried tomato tempeh?"

"It would be tough to explain. What do we do while we're waiting for Lansdale to get back?" asked Darlene.

"We need to run out to the airport to pick up Battle this evening," said Tom. "Tomorrow evening we go back to O'Hare to pick up Vinnie."

"That's something to look forward to," said Darlene.

"Sonny ran it by me when I called," said Tom. "Vinnie will be getting in just before Sonny and Lansdale arrive. At the airport, I'll hook up with Sonny. Sonny and I will follow Battle and Lansdale. And you get custody of Vinnie, Darlene."

"Terrific," said Darlene.

"It sounds like you guys are free tomorrow afternoon," said Eddie. "How about box seats for the Cubs opener?"

"Now we're talking," said Darlene.

Monday afternoon. San Francisco.

Jake Diamond had been leafing through the pages of his old photo album when the phone rang. He put the book down and went to the kitchen. Reaching for the telephone, he glanced at the refrigerator and was reminded that he hadn't eaten all day.

"Yes."

"Have you had anything to eat today, Jake?"

"Nope."

"How about a late lunch?" asked Joey Russo.

"Sure. Is everything moving right along?"

"Seems to be," said Joey. "Sonny left for New York. Battle is heading back to Chicago late this afternoon."

"Have you heard from Darlene?"

"Sonny heard from Tom Romano," said Joey. "They've secured Fort Lansdale."

"I'm missing all of the fun," said Jake. "It's nerve-racking. I'm feeling very impatient."

"Your time will come, Jake. I'll pick you up in about thirty minutes."

"Where are we going for lunch?"

"Pac Bell Park," said Russo. "I have tickets for the Giants' season opener."

"I'm feeling less impatient already," Jake said.

Twenty-one

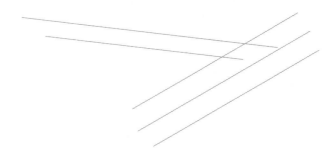

MONDAY AFTERNOON. San Francisco.

Jake Diamond and Joey Russo sat directly behind the Giants' dugout at Pacific Bell Park. Barry Bonds stood swinging a bat in the on-deck circle thirty feet away.

"If I eat one more of these garlic fries I'm going to explode," said Jake, placing the box of potatoes on the ground at his feet.

"Try not to do it while Bonds is at bat," said Joey.

"So, what's Max Lansdale up to?" asked Jake.

"He's in New York. According to his receptionist, he has a dinner engagement with Vito Ventura this evening and he's off to Connecticut in the morning."

"And Sonny?"

"Sonny will call us from the hotel in New York when he gets in. He'll follow Lansdale to Connecticut and fly back to Chicago on the same flight."

"Will Lansdale get suspicious if he spots Sonny before Chicago?" asked Jake.

"If everything goes as planned, Lansdale will have made Sonny's acquaintance before they board the plane in Hartford," said Joey.

"How will that work?"

"It will depend on whether or not Ventura is making the trip to Connecticut. Sonny should be able to find out one way or the other and go from there," said Joey. "I'll run it all by you in a minute, but right now Bonds is up."

Monday. Late afternoon. New York.

Sonny Badalamenti checked in at the Regency Hotel and went up to his room. He phoned the office of Vito Ventura.

"Ventura and Associates," the receptionist answered. "This is Maggie. How can we help you?"

"Maggie, this is Sonny Badalamenti. I'm an associate of Anthony Carlucci's. Would it be possible see Mr. Ventura sometime tomorrow?" Sonny asked.

"I'm sorry, Mr. Badalamenti; Mr. Ventura will be away in Baltimore all day tomorrow. I can possibly get you in to see him sometime on Wednesday."

"Anytime on Wednesday will be fine," said Sonny, "the earlier the better. I'll call back first thing Wednesday morning to find out what you were able to arrange."

"Can I tell Mr. Ventura what you wanted to see him about?"

"Sure," said Sonny. "Wait. I'm sorry, I have another call that I really need to take. Let me get back to you Wednesday morning. Thank you for your help."

Sonny disconnected and went down to the check-in desk.

"Can I help you, sir?" asked the desk clerk.

"I'd like to make arrangements for transportation to the casino in Connecticut tomorrow morning."

"Which casino?" asked the clerk.

Sonny told him which casino.

"Would you like a van ride or a limousine?"

"I would prefer a limo."

"Okay, let's see what we can do," said the desk clerk, punching the keyboard of his computer. "I have a limousine leaving at ten in the morning, if you wouldn't mind sharing a ride with another passenger."

"Just one other passenger?" asked Sonny.

"Yes, only one," said the clerk. "One of our guests. Mr. Lansdale.

Mr. Lansdale specified he would be willing to share the limousine with one other passenger only."

"That would be fine," said Sonny. "Sign me on."

Sonny went back up to his hotel room to call Joey Russo.

After filling Joey in, Sonny phoned Louis Russo. Louie was Joey Russo's eldest son, Sonny's brother-in-law, and a resident physician at New York University Medical Center.

Sonny and Louie made plans for dinner.

A few blocks away, in his office on Fifty-ninth Street, Vito Ventura buzzed his assistant.

"Yes, Mr. Ventura?"

"Maggie, set up a dinner reservation for two," Ventura said. "Make it for seven thirty. Someplace fairly close to the office, nice but not too formal. Then please give Max Lansdale a call at the Regency Hotel and let him know where he can meet me."

"I'll take care of it right away, Mr. Ventura."

"Thank you, Maggie."

"By the way," said Maggie, "Sonny Badalamenti called earlier. He said he was an associate of Anthony Carlucci's and that he would like to see you on Wednesday."

"Did he state his business?" asked Ventura.

"No, he said he would call back Wednesday morning."

"Next time he calls, put him through to me," Ventura said.

"Great game, Joey, thanks," said Jake as they exited the ballpark.

"They're always good when the Giants win," said Joey. "Listen, Angela is over at our daughter Connie's house. I expect that there is some serious cooking going on there. You're more than welcome to join us."

"Thanks, Joey, I think I'll pass. It's still painful when I'm on the leg too long."

"Will you be all right alone for a few days?"

"Sure, I'll take some time to settle into the new place," said Jake.

"And you'll call me if you need anything?" said Joey.

"I'll do that," said Jake.

"Otherwise, I'll keep you up to date by telephone and I'll see you when you get into Chicago Thursday night."

"Good."

"Do you remember the first time we met, Jake?"

"Sure, Jimmy Pigeon sent you to me," said Jake. "You were my second client."

"I met Jimmy through Harry Chandler."

"I didn't realize that you knew Chandler," Jake said. "Did you know him well?"

"Not all that well, and not for very long," said Joey. "Harry Chandler made some poor choices along the line, but he was a decent man, Jake. Harry didn't deserve the hell that Max Lansdale put him through."

"Okay," Jake said as they pulled up in front of the house.

"Thursday night," said Joey.

"Thursday night," Jake said as he left the car.

Jake watched Russo pull away. He smoked a cigarette on the front porch before going into the house.

Max Lansdale walked from the Regency Hotel over to the restaurant on Sixth Avenue between Fifty-eighth Street and Central Park. A hostess showed him to Vito Ventura's table in back. Vito rose to greet Lansdale. The two men shook hands.

"Good to see you, Max," said Ventura.

"Same here, Vito," said Lansdale.

"Sit, you look like you could use a drink," said Vito, waving for a waiter.

Lansdale and Ventura exchanged small talk and nursed twelve-year-old scotch. After the waiter went off with their food order, Vito Ventura opened the meeting to new business.

"How are things on the home front?" asked Ventura.

"I'm not sure what you mean," said Lansdale.

"Word has it Ralph Battle is attracting the attention of police up and down the California coast," Ventura said. "They're trying to connect him to a couple of homicides."

"Battle hasn't killed anyone, Vito," said Lansdale.

"It's not so much what Battle has actually done or not done, Max," said Ventura. "It's more a question of what he knows and how much he may want to deflect the heat."

"What are you suggesting, Vito?"

"It might be a good idea if you had Battle lay low for a while," said Ventura.

"As a matter of fact, Vito, I've been thinking the same thing lately. It might be time for Ralph Battle to lay *very* low. Don't worry about it; I've got it under control."

"Glad to hear that," said Ventura. "Great. Here comes the food. You're going to love the steak here, Max."

Monday evening. Chicago.

Darlene, Tom Romano, and Eddie Hand sat in the kitchen of Eddie's house near Wrigley Field.

"Battle gets into O'Hare at eight thirty," said Tom. "We're going to check out the route he'll be using with Lansdale tomorrow. I want to be sure I'm familiar enough with the spot to find it if we lose Battle's car when Sonny and I follow them from the airport. We'll need to leave here in about thirty minutes, Darlene."

"Would you mind terribly if I passed on the airport tonight, Tom?" asked Darlene.

"No problem," said Tom. "Are you feeling all right?"

"I'm feeling fine," said Darlene, "and I'd like to stay that way. I realize that Joey feels we need help from Battle, and maybe Battle's reasons for helping us are benevolent. But it doesn't change what kind of man Battle is. I'm just not a big Ralph Battle fan. I'd rather not deal with him."

"As I said, Darlene, no problem," said Tom. "I can handle it alone. Maybe Eddie will be kind enough to give you a little taste of Chicago nightlife."

"My pleasure," said Eddie Hand.

An hour later, Tom Romano met Ralph Battle as Battle came off the concourse. They walked out to the car that Romano had rented earlier in the day. They didn't have much to say to one another.

Romano drove, Battle navigated. They crossed over the river. Battle had Tom exit the expressway and turn off the service road into the Chevalier Forest Preserve. It was a heavily wooded area. They turned again at a sign for Camp Fort Dearborn. The access road was dark and deserted.

"Slow down here," said Battle. "This is where you and Sonny can stop. I'll continue around the bend. It's about thirty yards, and you can't see this spot from there."

Tom rolled by slowly, looking the place over. He then continued around the sharp turn in the road.

"Right here," said Battle.

Tom stopped the car and both men got out.

Tom looked back, confirming that he and Sonny would be out of view from this location the following night.

"This is good," said Romano. "This should work well. Lansdale is going to ask why you exited the highway."

"He hardly pays attention when I drive," said Battle. "If Max says something, I'll tell him I think there's a problem with the car and need to check it out. Just be sure that you guys are very careful coming in. Kill your headlights as soon as you can and get over to our car as quickly and quietly as possible."

"You'll need to disappear for a while, Ralph," Tom said. "Any problem with that?"

"No. I'll go up to Detroit until it's done," Battle said. "I already have the plane ticket. You can take me right back to the airport from here tomorrow night."

"Where to now?" asked Tom.

"You can take me to my house in Cicero. I'll have to throw together what I need for a week or so. We can put my things in this car for my trip to Detroit tomorrow," Battle said. "The company car is over at my place. Lansdale can use it to get himself home from here when it's over."

"Okay," said Tom as he turned the car around to exit the park. "I hope we're not forgetting anything."

"I hope Badalamenti knows what he's doing," Battle said.

"Don't worry about Sonny, Ralph," said Tom. "He knows exactly what he's doing. How do I get to Cicero?"

Monday evening. New York.

Vito Ventura walked Max Lansdale back to the Regency.

"Sorry that I can't make it up to Connecticut with you tomorrow, Max," Vito said. "I need to be in Baltimore all day. Paul Sacco will take very good care of you. Anything you want, food, drink, just sign for it, it's on the house. And I held two tickets for the show tomorrow night if you'd like to catch it. Frankie Valli and the Four Seasons, and Frankie can still knock out the tunes."

"And Paul Sacco has the cash ready?" asked Lansdale.

"It will be all set to go when you're ready to leave for the Hartford airport."

"Thanks, Vito," Lansdale said as they came up to the hotel entrance.

"Don't mention it," said Ventura. "Have a safe trip. Take good care of my money."

Lansdale didn't know quite how to respond, so he said nothing. He went into the hotel lobby and from there directly into the lounge. He sat at the bar and ordered scotch.

Lansdale was still sitting at the bar an hour later when Sonny came into the hotel, returning from dinner with his wife's brother. Sonny spotted Lansdale in the lounge. He debated whether he should go into the lounge or wait until the limousine ride in the morning.

"What the hell," Sonny said to himself. He went to the bar and took a seat close to Lansdale.

"What can I get for you, sir?" asked the bartender.

"Scotch," said Sonny, "the oldest you have. Do you have anything that's reached adolescence?"

"How does sixteen years old sound?"

"Sounds great," said Sonny. "Better make it a double; I probably won't be able to afford it after my visit to the casino tomorrow."

"Atlantic City?" asked the bartender, pouring the scotch.

"Connecticut. The limo leaves at ten."

"I guess we'll be riding together," said Lansdale from a few seats down.

"Are you Mr. Lansdale?" asked Sonny.

"Yes."

"Sonny Badalamenti," Sonny said. "What are you drinking, Mr. Lansdale?"

"Same as you, Mr. Badalamenti."

"Call me Sonny, and allow me buy you another while I still can."

"Let me get yours instead," said Lansdale.

"Sure," said Sonny. "I'll get the next round."

"I *will* have another," Lansdale said to the bartender. "Why don't you slide over, Sonny. If we're sharing a ride together in the morning, then we may as well start getting acquainted."

"May as well, Mr. Lansdale," said Sonny, moving over to the adjacent stool.

"Call me Max," said Lansdale.

"Here's to filling the inside straight, Max," Sonny said, lifting his glass.

After dropping Ralph Battle off in Cicero, Tom Romano had come back to Eddie's place. He had nodded off watching TV. Romano was awakened when Darlene and Eddie came in.

"Have fun?" Tom asked.

"Loads of it," said Darlene. "I'd ask if you had fun, but I think I can guess."

"It's business, Darlene," said Tom. "It went well. I believe it will fly."

"Coffee?" asked Eddie Hand.

"I could drink some," said Tom.

"Do you have any herbal tea, Eddie," Darlene asked as the telephone rang.

"Cinnamon apple spice?" Eddie said.

"Perfect," said Darlene.

Eddie went to the kitchen and answered the phone. A few minutes later he called to Darlene. "Darlene, phone call for you. You can take it in my study if you like."

Darlene walked into the study and picked up. "Hello?"

"Hey, partner."

"Jake, what a surprise. How are you?"

"Okay. How are you doing?"

"What's up? You sound blue."

"I don't know. I think it's all the waiting," said Diamond, "or being in this big house, alone."

"I knew that I should have left Tug McGraw with you," said Darlene.

"I don't know that the dog would help much in this case, Darlene."

"Aw, shucks, Jake. Do you miss me?"

"Sure I miss you," said Jake. "I miss a lot of other things, also. Nothing seems the same since the explosion, Darlene."

"It will never be the same. Maybe you'll never be the same. That's the deal," said Darlene, "those are the cards. You're a pinochle player, Jake; you play what you have in your hand. And maybe, if you're lucky, you get some help from the kitty. You'll be here Thursday evening; I'll take you to dinner. And on Friday you're going to be right in the thick of it. Meanwhile, try to get some rest. Spend a little time at the office; it might make you feel better. Who knows, there might even be some work waiting."

"All right, Darlene. Thanks for talking."

"Anytime, pal," said Darlene. "Anytime."

Monday night. New York.

Sonny excused himself after two hours at the bar with Lansdale. He displayed appropriate surprise when he learned that he and Lansdale would not only be sharing a limousine to Connecticut, but would also be traveling on the same flight to Chicago. "Small world," Max Lansdale had said.

Sonny had simply agreed.

It was nearly midnight when the telephone in Sonny's room rang.

"Hello?"

"Hey, tough guy. How are you doing?"

"Well, you know, Connie. New York is a lonely town when you're the only surfer boy around. How are you?"

"Same."

"And the baby?"

"Which one? The one I had to read Dr. Seuss to for an hour before she gave up the fight against sleep or the one trying to kick his or her way out a month early?" asked his wife. "They are both fine. Are you drunk?"

"I had a few too many with Max Lansdale."

"Are you kidding?"

"Nope," said Sonny. "We hit it off famously. He even offered me a ticket to see Frankie Valli and the boys."

"Is Lansdale hitting on you?"

"No, I don't think so. I think that the poor bastard is in dire need of friends."

"Either way, it's going to tickle my father," Connie said. "How did my brother treat you?"

"Louie treated me very well," said Sonny. "He took me out to Mario's Restaurant."

"Mario from the Food Network?"

"The very one. He came to our table, Bermuda shorts, ponytail, the works. The food was very good, although it looks like Mario might enjoy it a little too much himself."

"When are you coming home?"

"I have to come back here to New York for a meeting on Wednesday, hopefully an early meeting. I should be back by late afternoon."

"What you're doing for my father, Sonny?"

"Yes?"

"Is it dangerous?"

"No, Connie, not at all. Joey would never put me in danger. You should know that about your father."

"Be careful anyway," Connie said. "We need you."

"I'll be extremely careful, Connie. I love you."

"Glad to hear it. How long have we been on the phone?"

"I don't know," said Sonny, "five minutes maybe. Why, are you worried about the phone bill?"

"No," said Connie. "I'm just timing how long it took you to say those three little words."

Twenty-two

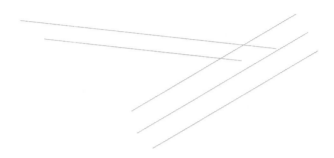

EARLY TUESDAY EVENING. Chicago.

After the Cubs game and dinner at a restaurant on the North Side, close to the ballpark and Eddie's house, they prepared for the trip to the airport.

Darlene would be riding with Eddie in his Bonneville; Tom would be driving the rental.

Ninety minutes later, the three stood watching at the concourse security checkpoint.

"Here he is," said Tom.

Vinnie Strings strolled up the concourse toward them.

"He looks like he's in his own little world," Eddie Hand said.

"Wait until you hear him speak," said Darlene.

Vinnie spotted them and picked up his pace, a wide smile across his face.

"When did you start wearing glasses, Vinnie?" Darlene asked.

"They're clear glass," Vinnie said. "I thought that it would help me get into character."

Darlene held her tongue.

"Vinnie, this is Eddie," said Tom.

"I've heard a lot about you," said Vinnie.

"Ditto," said Eddie.

"I'm looking forward to getting to know you, Eddie," said Vinnie.

"You guys can bond in the car," said Darlene. "Let's get Vinnie checked into the hotel. Sonny and Lansdale will be arriving soon, and Battle is close. I can feel it."

"Okay," said Tom Romano. "Wish us luck."

"Let's hope that luck won't have to figure into it," said Darlene.

Ralph Battle stood watching as Max Lansdale and Sonny approached. Battle took Lansdale's suitcase when the two men reached him. Lansdale held on to the briefcase that held the cash.

Lansdale quickly introduced Ralph to Sonny.

"Are you sure you don't need a ride?" asked Lansdale.

"I'm set, Max," said Sonny. "I have a ride waiting."

"Give me a call if you find the time while you're in town," Lansdale said, handing Sonny a business card. "We can have lunch."

"I'll see how it goes," said Sonny.

Tom Romano stood some distance away, waiting. Romano had run across Battle earlier, and each had ignored the other. He moved to Sonny as Battle and Lansdale walked off.

"I'm parked in the same section as Battle," Tom said. "We should be able to drive out right behind them."

"Let's do it," Sonny said.

They hurried out to the parking lot.

"What does Diamond actually have, Ralph?" Lansdale asked as they exited the airport.

"The retired medical examiner, who mysteriously passed away in Mexico, left his son an inheritance with your name all over it," said Battle. "It would be embarrassing if the documents came to light, to say the least. They suggest you had something to do with your father's death."

"You know that's absurd."

"Sure, I know," Battle said as he exited the freeway at the Chevalier Forest Preserve.

"Where are you going?" Lansdale asked when he suddenly found they were off the highway and in the park.

"There's something wrong with the car, Mr. Lansdale," Ralph said. "I'm going to stop up here out of traffic and take a look."

Romano was able to keep Lansdale's car in view on the expressway. He followed the car off the exit and into the large wooded area.

"Great choice," said Sonny as they turned at the Scout camp entrance.

"Battle will be stopping the car up around the bend. You'll need to get over there quickly," Tom said, turning off the headlights. "I'll duck down in the seat when I see Lansdale coming back this way. The gun is in the glove compartment."

Romano began slowing down as they watched Lansdale's car move out of sight.

Battle stopped the car and pulled out his weapon.

"Get out, Max," he said.

"What is this?"

"Get the fuck out. Don't touch the briefcase."

Lansdale climbed out of the car; Battle jumped out and moved quickly around to Lansdale.

"Get down on your knees, Max."

"You're insane, Battle. You're committing suicide."

"You killed your own father, you fucking maniac," said Battle. "Diamond convinced me. If anyone gives a fuck about what happens to you, they can come after me. I think I can get lost pretty well with a quarter million bucks."

"Ralph, please don't do this," Lansdale pleaded from his knees. "I can explain. I'll take care of you."

"Go to hell, Lansdale, it's over," said Battle.

Lansdale heard the terrible sound of Battle chambering a bullet. He closed his eyes.

There was a muted shot and Battle fell on top of him. He clawed his way out from under the body and looked up to find Sonny Badalamenti standing over him.

"You?" Lansdale cried. "Battle was going to kill me."

"It would appear so," said Sonny. "Lucky for you that Mr. Ventura asked me to keep an eye on his money."

Sonny moved to the body and put a finger to Battle's neck.

"Is he dead?" asked Lansdale, standing and brushing himself off.

"Oh, yeah," said Sonny.

"And all along, you're working for Vito?"

"Mr. Ventura had some concerns about Battle," said Sonny. "Well founded, I would say. I'll take care of the body, Max. Take the car and go home. And I'll take the cash. Mr. Ventura would insist. When you're ready to do whatever you do with it, call me at the Allegro Hotel on Randolph Street, downtown. I'll meet you with the money."

Sonny opened the car door and reached in for the briefcase. "Go, Max," Sonny said.

Lansdale looked once at Ralph Battle's body and then at Sonny holding the briefcase. He couldn't say a word. Lansdale climbed behind the wheel, started the car, and turned it around to exit the park. Tom Romano sat up in the seat of the rental after Lansdale passed.

"Okay, Ralph," Sonny said. "Get up and dust yourself off. You have a plane to catch to Detroit, and I need to get back to New York."

Tom dropped Ralph Battle and Sonny off at the airport and headed into town.

Romano called Eddie's cell phone number.

"How did it go?" asked Eddie.

"So far, so good," said Romano. "Where are you and Darlene?"

"Downtown at the Burnham Hotel on State," said Eddie, "getting Vinnie settled in. Darlene is helping him work on his *character* and making sure that the kid has everything straight. Why don't you head to the house? We should be back there soon."

"How is Darlene holding up?" asked Tom.

"She looks pretty tired, but she's doing great," said Eddie. "Jake Diamond is a very lucky guy."

"I hope he realizes how lucky," said Tom.

"Darlene is all pumped up for tomorrow morning," said Eddie. "She said that she can't wait to meet Lansdale, that she's always been fascinated by reptiles."

"From what I've seen of the guy," said Tom, "she won't be disappointed. I'll catch you guys back at the house."

Early Wednesday morning. New York.

It was well past midnight when Sonny checked into the hotel. He chose the Regency again, so he could walk over to Ventura's office in the morning. He phoned Joey Russo as soon as he reached his room.

"Hello?" Angela Russo answered sleepily.

"Hello, Angela," Sonny said.

"Sonny, what time is it. Is anything wrong?"

"No, everything is fine. It's late, I'm sorry," Sonny said. "Joey asked that I call when I got back to New York, no matter what time."

"Hold on, Sonny, I'll get him," Angela said. "Take care of yourself."

"I will, Mom," Sonny said.

"Sonny, how did it go?"

"Smooth as silk, Joey. You should have seen Lansdale after Ralph Battle fell on him. I'm surprised Max didn't have a heart attack. He was white as a ghost."

"Battle?"

"Tom and I put him on a plane to Detroit," said Sonny, "and Vinnie made it in okay. I'm back at the Regency."

"The money?"

"Right here. I'll bring it over to Ventura in the morning. I don't know what kind of briefcase this is, but Lansdale carried it right on the plane at Hartford. It went through the X-ray machine and never raised an eyebrow. I decided not to press my luck, and put it into my suitcase; I checked it in at the ticket counter," said Sonny. "Figured if they lost it, Ventura could sue the airline."

"I spoke with Tony Carlucci. Tony said it was okay to drop his name when you see Ventura."

"I think I already dropped it."

"I thought for a minute about having you drop *my* name, but I'm not quite ready to come out of the closet," Joey said. "Pray it won't be long."

"Every night before I go to sleep, Joey."

"Good work, Sonny."

"I'm hoping to be back by late afternoon. When are you heading to Chicago?"

"We'll see how things go up there tomorrow," said Joey. "I'll probably fly up on Thursday morning."

"Okay, then I guess I'll see you tomorrow."

"Need a lift from the airport?"

"No, thanks, Joey," Sonny said. "Connie wants to pick me up."

"Good. I'll see you tomorrow."

Early Wednesday morning. San Francisco.

Jake Diamond was jolted awake by a stabbing pain in his right knee, a consequence of tossing and turning in his sleep. Jake had been tossing and turning a lot during the past two nights, and much of the unrest had to do with Joey Russo.

Something about Joey's plan was nagging Diamond. He had confidence in Joey Russo's plan. He had confidence in Joey Russo. It was Joey's conditions that puzzled Jake.

Jake could understand Joey's insistence that Lansdale not be killed. After all, who among them was a murderer? Jake could not imagine Joey or Sonny any more capable of cold-blooded killing than he or Darlene would be.

It was Joey's admonition against involving the police that bothered Jake. Lansdale *was* a murderer, a multiple murderer. Short of assassinating Max Lansdale, what better punishment than to see him rot in a jail cell for the rest of his miserable life? What could Joey Russo possibly have in mind? And why was Ray Boyle willing to comply?

Jake recalled something Tom Romano had said about how to bring Max Lansdale down. *You need to find out what it is that frightens Lansdale, what it is that scares the shit out of him, what it is that gives him nightmares, his personal pit of snakes. And then you have to throw him right into the pit.*

Maybe Joey Russo had located the snake pit.

Joey had promised to tell all by the weekend.

Jake would have to wait.

Diamond looked at the illuminated digits on the clock radio near the bed. Five in the morning. Jake wondered if Darlene would be awake yet in Chicago, if Sonny would be up and ready to go in New York. Diamond was losing track of all of the time zones. Jake reached for the painkillers on the bedside table and swallowed two. He closed his eyes and tried to sleep.

Twenty-three

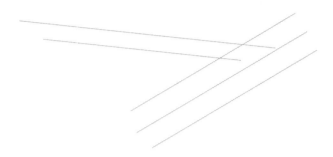

WEDNESDAY MORNING. Chicago.

They were all up and moving at Eddie Hand's house at daybreak.

At seven thirty, Darlene was walking into the lobby of Lansdale's office building. She rode the elevator to the twelfth floor and used the key she had taken from Jill Ballard to enter the suite. She started a pot of coffee and made herself comfortable behind the receptionist's desk.

In the parking lot below the building, Tom and Eddie sat in the rental car. Romano had two sets of headphones for the listening device so that both he and Eddie could monitor calls to and from Lansdale's phone. They parked close to Lansdale's designated garage space, where they would spot him when he arrived and let Darlene know that Lansdale was on his way up. From what they had learned from Ballard, Lansdale usually arrived at the office by nine. But after the drama of the previous evening, it was difficult to predict how well Lansdale could stick to routine.

Eddie ran across Wacker Drive for bagels and coffee, and they waited.

Across town, Max Lansdale woke in a sweat.

Lansdale couldn't push the images from his mind.

Down on his knees in the dirt, trembling, a gun aimed at the back of his head, being pinned down under Battle's body, crawling like a terrified child, and every pathetic move being watched by Vito Ventura's man. Granted, it took care of the problem of Ralph Battle, but it would do little to inspire Ventura's confidence in Max's ability to handle Vito's money. And the money. Having the cash taken out of his hands as if he were a helpless fool was the hardest pill to swallow.

All this, and having to deal with the fucking private investigator from San Francisco. Somehow, giving Diamond credit for all of his problems made Lansdale feel calmer.

Jake Diamond would pay.

Lansdale checked his table clock. Almost eight. He had a lot of cleaning up to do. He climbed out of bed to get ready for dirty work.

Wednesday morning. New York.

Sonny had time to kill.

He had called Ventura's office at nine sharp. He was told by Maggie the receptionist that Ventura was running late and would not be in until eleven. She asked that he call back after lunch to set up an appointment.

Sonny told the woman that he would call after one. He had every intention of being at Ventura's office in person at eleven.

Sonny went to a restaurant on Lexington for breakfast. He ordered an omelet that cost him more than a steak dinner would cost in South San Francisco, where he'd grown up.

After breakfast, Sonny checked out of his hotel room. He left his suitcase with the bell captain at the service desk, to be picked up before his ride to the airport. He carried the briefcase filled with money and walked north on Fifth Avenue.

Sonny walked the aisles of FAO Schwarz, searching for something to bring home to his daughter. He had looked in the display windows of Tiffany Jewelers as he passed on his way up. He spotted one or two items that Connie would not mind owning, and he certainly had enough cash handy. He resisted the temptation and moved on to the toy store.

With a gift for his daughter Carmella in one hand and the briefcase in the other, Sonny came into the office at precisely eleven. He identified himself and asked to see Mr. Ventura. Maggie asked

Sonny to please take a seat as she buzzed Vito Ventura's desk. Sonny remained standing.

"Yes, Maggie?" Ventura answered.

"It's Mr. Badalamenti, sir," she said.

"Put the call through, Maggie."

"He's out here in the reception area, Mr. Ventura."

"Well then," Ventura said, "you had better send him in."

Ventura stood behind his desk when Sonny walked in.

"I understand you are an associate of Tony Carlucci's," Ventura said.

"I believe this belongs to you," said Sonny, lifting his arm to indicate the briefcase. "Can I put it on your desk?"

"Go ahead," said Ventura, "and then please have a seat."

Sonny placed the briefcase on the desk and sat down. Ventura sat behind the desk. Ventura looked at the briefcase.

"You can open it, Mr. Ventura, it's safe," said Sonny.

Ventura looked up at Sonny and back down at the case. He turned it to face him, opened the latches, and lifted the top. He looked into the briefcase and then back to his guest.

"What does this mean?" Ventura asked.

"It means that you're going to have to find a new washing machine," said Sonny.

"Is Max Lansdale dead?"

"No, but he's about to go down, and he's going to fall hard," said Sonny. "You'd be smart to stay out of the way."

"I appreciate the advice, Mr. Badalamenti," Ventura said, "but Lansdale could cause me a world of grief if he can still use his tongue after he falls."

"Max Lansdale will cause you no trouble, Mr. Ventura," said Sonny. "All you need to do is to forget that you ever knew the man."

"I can do that."

"Good. Now if you'll excuse me, I'm anxious to get home," Sonny said, rising from his seat.

"Who can I thank for this?" asked Ventura, tapping the briefcase. "I have a feeling that it has nothing to do with Carlucci."

"There may be a way you can show your gratitude, Mr. Ventura.

I'll let you know. Unless you hear from me again, just forgetting Lansdale is thanks enough," Sonny said.

And he walked out of Ventura's office.

Wednesday morning. Chicago.

Eddie and Tom watched Max Lansdale leave his car and waited until he moved toward the elevators.

Romano took out his cell phone and called Darlene.

"Lansdale and Sons, can I help you?" Darlene answered.

"He's on his way up, Darlene," Tom said. "Will you be all right?"

"I'll be fine, Tom," Darlene said, looking up at the wall clock. "Listen. Call Vinnie at the hotel and make sure he wakes up. The kid will sleep all day if you let him. Tell Vinnie to call here in about an hour, no later than ten thirty."

"I will," said Tom. "We'll be right here, Darlene. All you need to do is speak into the phone and we'll be able to hear you."

"Okay, Tom, I'll talk to you later."

A few minutes later, Lansdale walked into the office suite. He looked at Darlene at the reception desk. For a moment he was confused; then he remembered Jill Ballard's phone call.

"Good morning, sir," Darlene said. "Can I help you?"

"That's what I'm paying you for, isn't it?" said Lansdale.

"Mr. Lansdale, I'm sorry," said Darlene. "I didn't realize. I'm Amanda Bonner from the temp agency. It's good to finally meet you."

Creep.

"Bring me a cup of coffee," said Lansdale. And he quickly disappeared into his private office.

Darlene poured a cup from the coffeemaker. She remembered that Jill Ballard had said black, no sugar. She carried the cup to Lansdale's door. She tapped on the door and Lansdale called her in.

Max Lansdale sat at his desk, nervously drumming his fingers on the desktop. Darlene placed the coffee cup on the desk.

"I want you to call the Allegro Hotel. Find out if Sonny Badalamenti has checked in yet," said Lansdale. "If he has, try to get his room number."

"Yes, sir," Darlene said, and she left the office.

A few minutes later she tapped on his door again.

"What the hell is it?" he called.

She opened the door and remained in the doorway.

"Mr. Badalamenti is not at the Allegro Hotel, sir," Darlene said. "They don't seem to have any record of a reservation, and the hotel is booked full."

Lansdale stared up at her; she stood waiting for him to speak.

"Mr. Lansdale?" she finally said.

"That will be all," Lansdale said. "And from now on use the office intercom. You don't need to come beating on the door every time we get a phone call."

"Yes, sir," Darlene said, closing the door behind her.

She stood there for a moment. The finger drumming on Lansdale's desktop got louder. She couldn't resist smiling as she walked back to the receptionist's chair.

Fifteen minutes later Darlene took a call and buzzed Lansdale.

"What is it?"

"A Mr. Hamilton on the telephone, sir," she said.

"Put him through," said Lansdale. "Carl."

"Max, how was Connecticut?"

"Great, Carl. Always is."

"Just wanted to let you know that we're ready for you on this end. Whenever you want to come by to make the exchange, just give me a call."

"There was a slight delay over on the other end, Carl, nothing very serious," Lansdale said with forced nonchalance. "It may be a day or two."

"Whenever, Max, call me. I just wanted you to know we were ready on this end."

"Thanks, Carl," said Lansdale.

Lansdale disconnected and immediately buzzed Darlene.

"Call the Allegro again," he said when she picked up, "and keep calling until you hear that Badalamenti has arrived."

"Yes, sir," Darlene said.

Down in the garage, Eddie Hand turned to Tom Romano. "Our boy sounds a little edgy."

"Wait until he hears from Vinnie Strings," Tom said. "I'd better call the kid and make sure he's good to go."

Darlene took the call from Vinnie a few minutes before ten thirty. She buzzed Lansdale.

"What?"

"Phone call for you, sir."

"Is it Sonny Badalamenti?"

"No, sir. No word on Mr. Badalamenti yet," Darlene said. "It's a Mr. Vincent Kearney."

"I don't know who that is. Take a message."

"He said it was very important, Mr. Lansdale. He said you knew his father, Dr. Richard Kearney."

Darlene held the phone, waiting for Lansdale to break the silence.

"Put him through," Lansdale finally said.

Lansdale took a deep breath.

"Mr. Kearney, how can I help you?"

"I think you know why I'm calling, Mr. Lansdale."

"I'm not certain that I do."

"I have documents that I believe you're interested in. I believe you heard about them from Jake Diamond."

"Yes, I do seem to recall hearing something about some documents," said Lansdale.

"Let's not waste time, Mr. Lansdale. I want to make a deal and decided there was no reason why I needed a middleman. We can leave Diamond out of this. I have the papers with me."

"What did you have in mind?"

"I'll be in town through tonight. I want one hundred thousand dollars. Bring the cash to my hotel and I'll hand over the documents. Otherwise, I pass them on to Diamond, and you can deal with him."

"That's a large amount of cash to come up with this afternoon, Mr. Kearney."

"It is entirely up to you, Mr. Lansdale. I am at the Burnham Hotel on State Street. Suite 712. I'll be back at the rooms at eight this evening. If you are not there by ten, Jake Diamond will see you on Friday."

"I'll be there," said Lansdale.

"Great. Have a good afternoon."

The line went dead.

"Thank fucking God," Lansdale said aloud, holding on to the phone receiver as if it were unburied treasure. "It's about fucking time something went my way."

He hung up the phone.

In the car down in the garage, Tom Romano smiled.

"Did Kearney actually have a son?" asked Eddie.

"Who knows, Joey Russo dreamed it up."

"Vinnie did a terrific job," said Eddie.

"Oh, yeah," Tom said. "Even Darlene will be proud of the kid."

"Do you think Lansdale will make the call?"

"Oh, yes. Lansdale will make the call," said Romano. "Joey Russo read this guy like a road map."

Lansdale made the call a few minutes later.

As he punched the office phone keypad, the digits were displayed on the LCD device sitting on the car seat between Eddie and Tom. Romano jotted down the phone number.

After three rings, a recorded voice asked the caller to leave a message. Lansdale simply stated his last name and disconnected.

"According to Battle," said Tom, "Lansdale should get a call-back at the bagel shop in an hour. I'll go over in a while to place the microphone and listen in. You'll wait here and keep an ear on the office."

"Got it covered," said Eddie Hand.

Max Lansdale came out of his private office at eleven fifteen. He stopped at the reception desk long enough to tell Darlene that he was going out for a quick errand.

He took the elevator to the lobby, crossed the street, and went into the bagel shop. Going to the phone booth, he sat down on the seat and waited.

Romano was sitting at a table near the window. The listening device in his left ear was no larger than a hearing aid.

The telephone rang. Lansdale grabbed the receiver.

"Lansdale," he said.

"Who, where, when?"

"Vincent Kearney, Burnham Hotel on State, suite 712, after eight and before ten tonight," Lansdale said.

"Twenty thousand, tomorrow, I'll send flowers."

"I need something else," said Lansdale.

"What?"

"Kearney has papers that I need to have. You need to get him to give them up before you kill him."

"No problem. Thirty thousand."

"Thirty?"

"If I have to talk to the mark it's going to cost you an extra ten, nonnegotiable."

"Okay, thirty thousand," said Lansdale. "Kearney will be expecting me to bring a payoff, so carry a briefcase or something. Just make sure that you don't leave without the documents."

"Just make sure that you have the cash tomorrow. I'll send flowers."

The line went dead.

Lansdale rose from the seat, left the booth, and went out to the street. Tom Romano watched him go back into the office building before he left the table and headed back to the garage.

"Any word on Badalamenti?" Lansdale asked when he walked back into the suite.

"No, sir," said Darlene. "I'll try again in a few minutes."

Lansdale went back to his office without another word. He phoned Vito Ventura in New York as soon he reached the desk.

In the garage, Tom was climbing into the rental.

"Lansdale is making a call," said Eddie, handing Tom the second set of headphones.

"Ventura and Associates, this is Maggie. How can we help you?"

"This is Max Lansdale for Mr. Ventura."

"Please hold, Mr. Lansdale."

"Yes, Maggie?" Vito Ventura answered when she buzzed him on the interoffice.

"Mr. Lansdale is on the telephone, sir."

"Tell him that I'm out, you don't know when I'll be back."

"Yes, sir."

Maggie gave Lansdale the message.

"Please tell Mr. Ventura that I called, the minute he comes in," said Lansdale. "Please ask Vito to phone me."

"I certainly will, Mr. Lansdale," she said.

"Fuck," said Lansdale as he slammed down the receiver.

"Ouch," said Eddie in the garage below. "How did it go at the bagel shop?"

"Like clockwork," Tom said. "The delivery is set for tonight between eight and ten. Ray Boyle will be flying into O'Hare from LA at six. Boyle wants to take this guy alive."

"Your friend Joey Russo is a genius. I can't wait to meet him," said Eddie Hand.

"It shouldn't be long," said Tom Romano.

At four, Lansdale came out of his private office. After hearing from Darlene that there was no word about Sonny Badalamenti and no word from Vito Ventura, he growled at Darlene that he was leaving for the day and stormed out of the suite.

Darlene waited thirty minutes before picking up the phone to talk to Tom.

"I'll be down in a few minutes," she said.

Darlene climbed into the car, and Tom and Eddie filled her in.

"Let's get something to eat," Darlene said, "before we go out to the airport to fetch Lieutenant Boyle."

"How do you like Lansdale?" Tom asked as he started the engine.

"A real sweetheart," Darlene said. "It sounds like our Vinnie did very well."

"The kid was beautiful," said Eddie. "Cool as ice."

"I imagine Vinnie is getting a little warmer every minute, worrying about tonight. Let's take him to dinner and pump him back up. We don't want him to melt," Darlene said, pulling out her cell phone. "I'll let Vinnie know that we're coming to get him."

Twenty-four

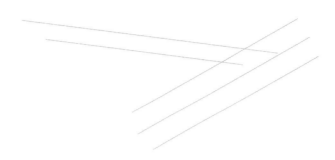

WEDNESDAY EVENING. Chicago.

After dropping Vinnie Strings and Darlene back at the Burnham Hotel after dinner, Eddie and Tom had driven out to the airport to pick up Ray Boyle.

Darlene worked on Vinnie while they waited for Ray.

"Don't try pulling a Belmondo, Vinnie," she said. "We all know how cool you are without further proof. This guy is a killer; it's what he does for a living. Follow Ray's instructions to the word."

"Don't worry, Darlene," Vinnie said. "I'm not feeling very heroic at the moment."

"And lose the eyeglasses, Vinnie," she said. "They look ridiculous."

Vinnie removed the glasses as Darlene's cell phone rang.

"Yes?"

"We're a block away, Darlene," said Tom Romano. "We can wait for you at the hotel entrance. Come down when Boyle gets up there and we'll go to Eddie's house."

"I'm not leaving until this is over and I know Vinnie is okay, Tom," Darlene said. "There's a bar here in the hotel. You can join me down there if you like."

"We'll be there," said Tom as they pulled in front of the hotel. "Boyle is on his way up."

A few minutes later, Ray Boyle rapped on the door of suite 712. He carried a small shoulder bag.

"Be cool, Vinnie," Darlene said, "but not too cool."

Darlene opened the door for Boyle.

"Don't let anything happen to him, Ray," she said as she came out into the hall.

Boyle went into the room and Darlene headed down to meet Tom and Eddie at the bar.

There were two rooms in suite 712. The sleeping area was separated from the entry room by a dividing wall with a wide door.

"This is perfect," said Boyle. "He won't do anything threatening at first, Vinnie. He'll want to get his hands on the documents with as little coaxing as possible, and the simplest way is to let you hand them over. Don't ask to see the money; he's not coming here to pay off. When he asks for the papers, tell him they're in the bedroom. Walk in and get out of the way. I'll take it from there."

Boyle pulled the gun from his shoulder harness. He took a silencer from his jacket pocket and screwed it onto the end of the barrel.

Vinnie stared at the weapon.

"Jesus, Ray," Vinnie said, "I didn't realize that the LAPD used those things."

"We're not in Los Angeles," said Boyle. "Come on. We'd better wait in the far room."

The knocking on the door came just past eight. Vinnie went and opened the door; the man standing there held a small rope-handled shopping bag.

"Mr. Kearney?" he said.

"Yes, are you Lansdale?"

"I'm here on behalf of Mr. Lansdale," the man said. "Can I get in out of the hallway."

"Sure," said Vinnie, "come in."

"Thank you, Mr. Kearney," the man said, coming into the front room.

Vinnie closed the door and followed.

"What do I call you?" asked Vinnie.

"You can call me Tucker," the man said, "and I'm in a bit of a hurry, Mr. Kearney. Do you have the papers that Mr. Lansdale asked me to pick up?"

"Sure," said Vinnie. "I have them in the other room. Give me a minute."

Vinnie Strings walked into the far room. Tucker pulled a silenced gun from the shopping bag. Ray Boyle stepped into the connecting doorway. Ray held his arms fully extended, his gun held in both hands. He locked on Tucker's face. Boyle was about to speak when he caught a glimpse of Tucker's hand, and Tucker's gun, coming up.

There were two muted gunshots. Boyle was knocked into the bedroom, landing on his back. His weapon hit the floor and slid toward Vinnie. Vinnie grabbed the gun, sat on the floor beside Ray's body, and pointed the weapon at the open doorway. His hands were trembling. When he felt another hand cover his, Vinnie nearly pulled the trigger.

"Easy, Vinnie," Ray Boyle whispered, sitting up. "Let me have the gun."

Boyle took the gun from Vinnie's hand and slowly rose to his feet, motioning to Vinnie to stay down. Boyle stood at the side of the open doorway and cautiously looked into the other room. Tucker was facedown on the carpet, his weapon on the floor less than a foot away. Boyle slowly moved to the body, kicked the weapon away, and turned the body over. There was a clean bullet hole in the center of Tucker's forehead.

"So much for taking him alive," Ray said as Vinnie came up behind him.

"Great shot, Lieutenant," said Vinnie.

"Pure luck," Boyle said, taking off his jacket and undoing his shirt buttons to reveal the Kevlar vest; when he took that off, Vinnie saw a large red welt at the center of his chest. Ray replaced his shirt and jacket, pulled a plastic bag from his jacket pocket and a handkerchief from his pants, and moved to Tucker's gun.

"Packs a punch," Boyle said, bagging the gun. "Vinnie, go down to the hotel bar and join the others. Take that shopping bag. I'll clean up this mess."

"Can I help, Lieutenant?"

"No, thanks, Vinnie, you did fine," said Ray. "When you get down to the bar, I want you all to leave the hotel. Go back to Eddie's place. Tell Darlene that I'll call you there when I'm done."

Vinnie picked up the shopping bag and left the room.

Ray Boyle got to work.

Wednesday evening. San Francisco.

Carmella sat in her playpen, having a chat with her new stuffed animal from FAO Schwarz. Connie and Angela washed the supper dishes while waiting for the coffee to brew. Joey Russo and Sonny sat talking in front of the television, the Giants game in the background.

"Have you heard from Ray Boyle?" Sonny asked.

"Not yet. It should go down by ten their time."

"And if it goes well?"

"I'll leave for Chicago in the morning," Joey said.

Connie set a plate of pastries on the dining-room table. Angela followed her in from the kitchen with the pot of espresso.

"Would you like your coffee in there?" Angela called.

"No," answered Joey, "we'll come to the table."

"Sonny, bring the baby in with you," said Connie.

Sonny reached into the playpen and lifted Carmella into his arms.

"Graff," she said, clinging to the stuffed animal.

"That's right, sweetheart," said Sonny, "giraffe."

Sonny looked at Joey with concern as they moved to the dining room.

"I'll be all right," Joey said.

Wednesday night. Chicago.

Ray Boyle had little choice.

He walked out onto the small terrace of the hotel suite; it looked down on an empty courtyard. Boyle went back to the body, dragged it onto the terrace, and lifted it over the rail. He let go and watched just long enough to see the body hit the ground. He went back inside and checked the rooms.

He folded the bulletproof vest and put it into his shoulder bag along with Tucker's gun. Boyle was confident that ballistics testing would tie the weapon to the Stan Riddle and Harry Chandler shootings. He would have to call in a few markers, favors owed to him within the department, to have the testing done discreetly. Explaining how he came by the murder weapon would be difficult.

Boyle took a final look around the suite and went down to the hotel lobby to call Darlene.

"Jesus, Ray, are you okay?"

"Yes, Darlene, and I'd rather skip the details," Ray said. "I have enough time to catch the last flight back to LA; I'll grab a taxi to O'Hare from here. Do me a favor?"

"Sure."

"Give Joey Russo a call. Tell him what happened."

"I will, Ray. Thanks for your help."

"Yeah, well, I did what I had to do," said Ray. "Good luck with the rest of it. Take care."

Darlene called Joey Russo and told him how it had gone.

"Thankfully, none of the good guys got hurt," Russo said. "I'll be up there tomorrow. I'll phone when I'm ready to hook up with you."

"All right," Darlene said. "Tom Romano and Vinnie will be flying back to San Francisco late tomorrow morning. Eddie will continue to monitor the office phone from the garage."

"Okay, Darlene, make sure the flowers are delivered to Lansdale's office first thing in the morning," Russo said. "You know how the card should read."

"I do and I will," said Darlene.

"Good."

"How is Jake doing?" asked Darlene.

"I haven't spoken to Jake, I thought I'd let him alone for a few days."

"Well, maybe I'll give him a quick phone call," said Darlene.

"Sure," said Joey. "Why don't you do that."

"I'll see you tomorrow, Joey."

"Good," Joey said.

Wednesday night. San Francisco.

Jake Diamond closed the paperback, drank what remained of the Dickel in his glass, and crushed out his cigarette.

He had spent a few hours at the office earlier in the day, taken a couple of calls, set up several meetings with prospective clients for the following week.

Going through the motions.

Acting exactly as if all of this business with Max Lansdale would be over and done by week's end.

Diamond couldn't decide on espresso or bed.

Jake wished he had someone to talk with. Casual talk. A distraction more animated than the worn pages of a paperback Russian novel, more interactive than the thirty-one-inch Sony TV. Less incoherent than the voices in his head.

When the telephone rang, he jumped at it.

"Hello."

"Hey, partner."

"Hey, Darlene," Jake said, "I'm real glad that you called."

Twenty-five

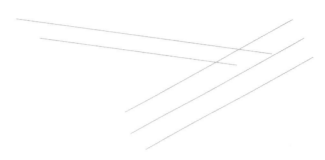

THURSDAY MORNING. New York.

The intercom button on Vito Ventura's phone blinked.

"Yes, Maggie?"

"Mr. Badalamenti is on the phone, Mr. Ventura."

"Put him through," Ventura said. He waited for the call to be transferred and greeted Badalamenti.

"Mr. Ventura," Sonny said. "I would like to take you up on your offer of gratitude."

"I'll do what I can, Mr. Badalamenti," Ventura said, hoping to settle the debt. "What did you have in mind?"

"Have you heard from Lansdale?"

"He's called a few times. I'm avoiding him. Isn't that what you wanted?"

"I did," Sonny said, "but the next time he calls, I would like you to speak to him. Lansdale won't admit to you that he's lost track of your money, but he'll want to ask about me. Tell Lansdale that you've never heard of me and ask him when you can expect to receive your end of the transaction. Show impatience; give Lansdale a deadline, a subtle ultimatum."

"Are you certain that this won't backfire?" Ventura asked.

"Absolutely," said Sonny. "Max Lansdale is going to be very busy for the next few days trying to save his skin. I assure you, as

I did earlier, Lansdale will cause you no trouble. And if you can do this for me, you'll never need to deal with him again."

"And will I ever need to deal with you again, Mr. Badalamenti?" asked Ventura.

"You can forget that we ever met, Mr. Ventura," Sonny said. "I'll do the same."

"I'll do my best to rattle his cage," said Ventura.

"Thank you," said Sonny.

Thursday morning. Chicago.

Max Lansdale came into his office suite at nine. Darlene looked up from the reception desk.

"Good morning, Mr. Lansdale, sir," Darlene said. "You received flowers this morning. I put them in water. Would you like me to move them into your office?"

"Was there a card?"

"Yes, there was," said Darlene. "The card is sitting next to the flowers in the kitchenette. Would you like me to get it for you?"

"I can get it myself," said Lansdale.

"And the flowers?" asked Darlene.

"The hell with the flowers," Lansdale said. "Have you been calling the hotel for Badalamenti?"

"Twice already this morning, Mr. Lansdale. Nothing."

"Keep trying. And let me know if Mr. Ventura calls," Lansdale said, moving to the small kitchen.

He grabbed the card and disappeared into his private office.

Lansdale tore open the small envelope and read the card:

"Ghost Bar. Randolph Street. Three this afternoon. Bring 20,000."

Lansdale examined the note again. He wasn't mistaken. It read "20,000." Unless he was being afforded an unexpected discount, which he seriously doubted, something had gone wrong.

He tore up the card and flung it into the wastebasket. He sat at the desk debating whether or not to try calling Vito Ventura again.

Thursday morning. Chicago.

The receptionist rang the desk of Jack LoBianco.

"Yes?"

"A phone call for you, Mr. LoBianco."

"Who?"

"The gentleman wouldn't identify himself, sir," said the receptionist. "He would only say it was important and that it has to do with your aunt, Mrs. Lansdale."

"Put the call through," LoBianco said.

"Mr. LoBianco?"

"Who is this?"

"I need to speak with Anna Lansdale. I plan to visit her at eleven this morning. I wanted to let you know."

"Who is this? And what is this about?"

"My name wouldn't mean anything to you, Mr. LoBianco; hopefully it will mean something to Mrs. Lansdale. And my business is personal; I need to speak to your aunt face-to-face."

"My aunt is eighty-four years old. I'm sure that she has no interest in your personal business," said LoBianco. "And you will not bother her, whoever the fuck you are. Is that understood?"

"I only called as a courtesy. I will be visiting Mrs. Lansdale's home at eleven. If you feel that you need to be there, I will see you then."

The line went dead.

"What the fuck," LoBianco said aloud, then buzzed the receptionist.

"Yes, sir?"

"Cancel my appointments. Please ring the garage and ask them to get my car ready," LoBianco said, glancing at his wristwatch. "Tell them I'll be down in ten minutes."

Thursday. Late morning. New York and Chicago.

"Yes, Maggie?"

"It's Mr. Lansdale on the telephone, Mr. Ventura. He sounds very eager to talk with you. Are you in?"

"Yes, Maggie, please put him through."

"Yes, sir."

"Max," said Ventura, picking up the call, "how was Connecticut? Did Paul Sacco treat you right?"

"Terrific, Vito," said Lansdale. "Paul treated me like royalty."

"Good. Sorry I haven't returned your calls, I've been swamped. What can I do for you?"

"I wondered if you could tell me how to get hold of Sonny Badalamenti."

"I don't know a Sonny Badalamenti, Max."

Lansdale nearly lost his ability to speak.

"I met him at the casino, Vito; he mentioned that he knew you," Lansdale was finally able to choke out.

"A lot of people know me up there, Max," said Ventura. "It's hard to keep track of everyone I meet."

"I suppose that it would be," was all Lansdale could manage.

"If I met Mr. Badalamenti at one time or another, I don't recall. Is there some kind of problem, Max?"

"No, not at all, Vito."

"Because I checked the accounts this morning, and I didn't find a deposit."

"There was a little delay on this end, nothing to worry about."

"It's when someone tells me there's nothing to worry about that I begin to worry, Max," said Ventura. "Can I expect to see the transfer showing up by tomorrow?"

"Sure, Vito, no problem," said Lansdale. "It should be taken care of by tomorrow afternoon."

"I'd rather hear you say that it *will* be, Max."

"It will be, Vito."

"Good. You know how much my people dislike being disappointed."

"I do," said Lansdale.

"Good. Take it easy, Max. Speak to you soon."

The line went dead.

Lansdale slammed down the receiver.

In the garage below, Eddie Hand's ears rang.

Lansdale stormed out of his office. "I'm going out. I don't know when I'll be back," he grunted as he passed Darlene at her desk.

"Should I keep trying the hotel for Mr. Badalamenti?" she asked.

Lansdale left the suite without answering. He rode the elevator down and went directly to the bank.

He could come up with the twenty thousand in cash for his meeting at three, but the two hundred grand for Ventura and the hundred grand to purchase the documents from Jake Diamond were another story. And that story was only twenty-four hours away.

Lansdale put his head down against the wind and tried to think about something else, but he could not think of a single other thing.

He walked up the drive to the front door of the house. It was a small mansion in the Astor Street district north of downtown Chicago, with a view of Lake Michigan.

As he pressed the doorbell, he adjusted the collar of his coat.

Jack LoBianco answered the door, entirely prepared to remove the intruder physically if necessary. He was momentarily halted by the visitor's commanding appearance. The man at the front door was tall and strikingly handsome. He wore his graying hair short; his suit was expensive and perfectly tailored; his full-length coat was cashmere.

"Mr. LoBianco, I spoke with you on the phone earlier," said the man. "I'm here to see Mrs. Lansdale."

"And I told you earlier that it wouldn't be possible," said Lo-Bianco. "Now, either you leave on your own or I can have you escorted."

The man slowly raised his hand, unthreateningly. He held an envelope.

"Mr. LoBianco, I understand your wanting to protect your aunt," said the man. "I find it commendable. I only ask that you show this note to her and let her decide if she will see me or not. I would not forget your consideration."

"And you won't tell me who you are or what this is about?" asked LoBianco.

"With all respect, I would prefer that Mrs. Lansdale decide whom to share this with," the man said, holding the envelope out to LoBianco.

LoBianco looked at the envelope and then up into the visitor's eyes. After a moment of hesitation, he took the envelope.

"Wait here," LoBianco said.

He moved back into the house, closing the front door behind him.

The man waited on the porch for a full ten minutes, gazing out over the lake. The front door opened and Jack LoBianco ushered him in.

"Follow me," LoBianco said.

He led his visitor into a large room walled with bookcases. Anna Lansdale sat in one of three overstuffed chairs placed around a high oak table.

"Please sit, Mr. Vongoli," she said. "Can I offer you coffee?"

"No, thank you, Mrs. Lansdale."

"Please explain this to me," Anna Lansdale said, holding up the note.

Vongoli looked from the woman to LoBianco and back again.

"Jack is my late sister's eldest," the woman said. "He is like a son to me, and he handles my affairs. He will be joining us. Will that be a problem?"

"Not at all."

Jack LoBianco sat in the third chair.

After a moment, Vongoli began. "Mrs. Lansdale, my father was Louis Vongoli. He grew up in Cicero. Years ago he had a run-in with your family. It forced him to relocate his family and change his name."

"Mr. Vongoli, I want to know about this note. The accusations you make are very serious and very dangerous," Anna Lansdale said. "I do not take this lightly; you have made a commitment that you will be held to. If there is any truth to what you suggest, I must know. To ignore it is out of the question."

"I anticipated that would be the case," said Vongoli.

"Then you must also expect that if these allegations are unfounded, Mr. Vongoli, you have put yourself in very serious jeopardy."

"Yes, I realize that also."

"So you are either convinced or suicidal," LoBianco said, speaking out for the first time.

"I'm convinced, Mrs. Lansdale," Vongoli said.

"You have taken a great risk coming here with this," the woman said, clutching the note.

"Will you hear me out?"

"First, I would like to know why you are taking such a risk," said Anna Lansdale. "I want to know what you expect to gain from this."

"I want my father's name back," said Vongoli.

An hour later, Jack LoBianco escorted Joseph Vongoli to the front door.

"You've upset her. I won't forget it," said LoBianco.

"It was unavoidable, and I'm sorry," said Vongoli. "I believe that your aunt had the right to know, and I needed her help. If I had gone another way, she would have heard it eventually and would have had no control over the consequences. I'll call you tomorrow with the final details."

"I think you are out of your fucking mind," LoBianco said. "My aunt may be an old woman, but she is still very powerful. You know our family. You know there is no place you'll be able to hide if this blows up in your face."

"May I ask you something?" Vongoli said.

"What?"

"Is it fear of your aunt that has discouraged you from expressing your own suspicions about your cousin Max?"

"If I thought I could convince her, there would be nothing to fear," said LoBianco.

"I'm gambling that I can convince her."

"I hope for her sake and for your sake that you know what you're doing," said LoBianco at the door.

"Keep hoping," said Vongoli as he turned and walked down the driveway.

Max Lansdale returned to his office suite at two with twenty thousand dollars in cash for his appointment at the Ghost Bar at three.

He walked past Darlene without a word and disappeared into his private office.

According to what Joey Russo had learned from Battle, the man who called himself Tucker varied the drop points for payments, always choosing public places, restaurants or taverns. Lansdale would arrive at the designated drop carrying a gift-wrapped box, sit at the bar, place the box on the bar, and wait to be contacted. A bartender or waitperson would deliver a note with instructions on where to leave the box. Lansdale had never seen the assassin. He only knew the man by the name Tucker.

Lansdale took a box and wrapping paper from his office closet.

He put the cash into the box and wrapped it.

He set the box on his desk and waited.

Down in the garage, a light tapping at the car window momentarily startled Eddie Hand. Eddie looked up to see a man standing beside the passenger door, smiling. He rolled down the window.

"Sorry to sneak up on you like that, Eddie," the man said. "I'm Joey Russo."

Joey offered his hand; Eddie reached out of the window and accepted it warmly.

"Good to meet you," Eddie said. "Hop in."

Joey walked around to the passenger side and climbed into the car.

"There's a shopping bag on the backseat," said Eddie. "It belonged to Tucker; Lieutenant Boyle thought you could use it."

"Nice touch, and just like Ray," said Joey. "How is Darlene doing?"

"Aside from being extremely bored, she's doing fine. Here's the phone number of the booth in the bagel shop," Eddie said, handing Russo a slip of paper.

"After I meet Lansdale at the bar, I'll go back to my hotel," Russo said. "I'm at the Allegro on State. Room 618. I'll call the phone booth from the hotel room. I would like you and Darlene to meet me there at my room when she is through at Lansdale's office for the day."

"We'll be there," said Eddie. "It should be shortly after five."

"Good," said Joey. "I'd better get over to the bar to wait for Lansdale."

Thursday afternoon. San Francisco.

Jake Diamond was trying to decide what to pack for his trip to Chicago.

The telephone rang.

"Yes?"

"Jake, it's Sonny."

"How was New York City?"

"Mostly business, but it all seemed to go well," said Sonny. "I *was* able to get in a little shopping and go out to dinner with Connie's brother, Louie."

"Now there's a good old-fashioned name," said Jake.

"It was Joey's father's name," said Sonny. "As I'm sure you know, it's customary to name the first son after his grandfather."

"I know the custom very well," said Jake. "I thank my brother every time I speak to him for being born first and saving me from being called Abraham."

"Joey called," said Sonny. "He said you need to phone Lansdale at his office at three thirty, Chicago time."

Jake looked at his wristwatch and did the math. "Good, I have some time to rehearse," Diamond said. "Any changes from the original script?"

"None."

"Okay. Three thirty Chicago time."

"Joey asked me to take you out to the airport," Sonny said. "Darlene will pick you up on the other end."

"Great. How about four?"

"I'll be there," said Sonny.

Twenty-six

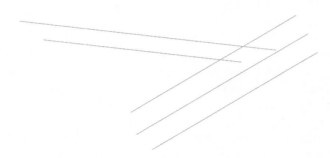

Joey Russo stood on Randolph Street, a few doors down from the Ghost Bar. He looked like a character in an early-seventies Scorsese film, thirty years older. Three-quarter-length leather jacket, dark long-sleeved turtleneck, black polyester dress slacks, wingtip shoes, and a porkpie hat. He wore dark glasses and held a rope-handled shopping bag.

Russo watched Lansdale go into the tavern, waited a few minutes, and followed. He spotted Lansdale on a stool, a gift-wrapped box and a drink sitting on the bar in front of him. Joey sat at the adjacent bar stool and placed the bag on the floor between them.

"Put the box into the bag, Lansdale," Joey said, "and don't look at me."

"What about the documents, Tucker?" Lansdale asked as he slipped the box into the shopping bag.

"Be at the phone booth at four," Russo said.

He stood, took the bag, and walked out to the street. Lansdale watched him leave, studying every characteristic.

Max Lansdale swore under his breath, took a minute to drain his scotch, and went back to his office. He entered the suite, passed Darlene without a word, went back to his desk, and paced, trying to come up with a solution to the fix he was in.

He had no intention of handing Jake Diamond a nickel. His plans for Diamond were crystal clear. It was the two hundred thousand dollars owed to Ventura that had him in a cold sweat. Given more time, he could surely work it out. He might be able to come up with half of the cash for Vito by the next day, but for Ventura and his New York partners half would not cut it. He thought about asking Ventura for more time, of laying the blame completely on Carl Hamilton and the Chicago end, but he feared he would lose Ventura's confidence nevertheless. He thought about calling Hamilton for an advance, but Carl Hamilton was a businessman and would not consider it good business.

There was one last way out, one option that Lansdale wished to avoid if at all possible. As the thought crept into his mind, Darlene rang his desk.

"Telephone call, Mr. Lansdale," Darlene said. "A Mr. Jake Diamond, calling from California."

"Put it through," said Lansdale.

Darlene transferred the call. She resisted the strong temptation to eavesdrop. She would wait and listen to the tape being recorded in Eddie's car down in the garage.

"Jake, good to hear from you," said Lansdale.

"I'm sure it is, Max," said Jake. "I'm going to make this short. I'll be in Chicago tomorrow. I will call you for a meeting."

"Will you have the documents?"

"I'll want to see the money first, Max. One hundred thousand dollars," said Diamond. "When I see the cash, I will take you to the documents."

"That's a lot of cash for a few pieces of paper."

"I have to share the money with Dr. Kearney's son," Jake said, "and these few pieces of paper could put you away for a very long time, Max. I'll call back tomorrow. If I even get a whiff of Ralph Battle anywhere near, all bets are off."

The line went dead.

Lansdale looked at his wristwatch. Fifteen minutes until four. He rushed down to the bagel shop to catch the phone call from Tucker.

At four, Joey Russo dialed the phone booth from his hotel room. Lansdale picked up on the first ring.

"What happened to the documents?"

"The little shit was all set to ambush you, Lansdale. Kearney was planning to take the money and leave you either knocked senseless or dead. He never had any papers."

"You're certain?"

"When I got the drop on him, I pressed the barrel of my gun against his forehead and asked him for the papers. He swore that he had given them to someone named Diamond. Under the circumstances, I don't think he was holding out. He insisted up until the moment I pulled the trigger."

"Fuck."

"I didn't charge you, Lansdale. And after all, I did have to waste time talking to the little worm."

"I need you again," said Lansdale.

"Who, where, when."

"This guy Diamond, sometime tomorrow. I'll have to get back to you."

"Call the machine; I'll call the booth an hour later."

"What if we don't have an hour? Could I leave the details on the answering machine?"

"You're asking a lot, Lansdale. It'll cost you more. If I need to rush off somewhere, make sure that you have twenty-five grand in cash handy."

"No problem," said Lansdale.

"Okay, I'll wait to hear from you."

The caller disconnected.

Lansdale slammed down the receiver in the phone booth and went back across to his office.

As Lansdale rode the elevator, he calculated what he would need. Three hundred thousand. Two hundred thousand for Ventura and a hundred to at least *show* to Jake Diamond. He could pay Tucker from Diamond's cash once Diamond was out of the way. He could raise one hundred on his own; he would have to borrow the rest. He could liquidate assets and have all of the money needed to pay back the loan by early the next week. As unhappy as he was about the prospect, he had no choice but to call his cousin, Jack.

He walked past Darlene and back to his desk. He rang his cousin's office. The receptionist put the call through to Jack LoBianco.

"Max?"

"Jack, I need a favor."

"What kind of favor, Max?"

"A loan. Just until early next week."

"How much?"

"Two hundred thousand."

"Did you say two hundred thousand?"

"Yes."

"What the fuck for?"

"I need to get it to Vito Ventura in New York."

"What the hell are you doing, getting involved with Ventura? The guy is bad news, Max."

Lansdale was not about to tell his cousin about the business he had been doing with Vito Ventura since Simon Lansdale died eight years earlier.

"He's very bad news, Jack, and I'm into him for two hundred grand. Gambling debts that Vito is suddenly not willing to wait for. Ventura made it very clear that he wouldn't give me the few days that I'll need to raise the cash; he said he would send someone to visit me. I don't have to tell you what kind of visit he has in mind."

"How the fuck did you get into him that deep?"

"Obviously I have a gambling problem, Jack. Are you going to help me out or lecture me?"

"When do you need the money?"

"Early tomorrow," said Lansdale.

"I don't know, Max."

"Jesus, Jack, we're family. Who am I supposed to turn to? Please, let me give you the information on how to wire the money to Ventura. Do I have to beg you, Jack?"

"Give me the information, Max."

Lansdale did.

"And you'll send the money?" said Lansdale.

"Only this one time."

"Thanks, Jack. I'll make it good."

"You disappoint me, Max."

"Please, don't say anything about this to my mother. It will cause her unnecessary grief, Jack," said Lansdale. "I promise you it won't happen again, I'll get help for my problem. Could you keep this between the two of us? For her sake, if not mine?"

"You disappoint me, Max," Jack LoBianco said again, and hung up.

Max Lansdale expelled a deep sigh of relief. He had bought time.

Once he was done with Jake Diamond, Max would put all of his energies into hunting down Badalamenti, getting his money back and getting answers. Since speaking to Ventura, the question had been eating away at Lansdale. If Sonny did not work for Vito, how had Badalamenti known that Max would be carrying all that cash? Lansdale figured it had to be Paul Sacco from the casino in Connecticut who brought Badalamenti in and marked Lansdale. And when Max tracked down Badalamenti and had proof, he would be able to square it with Ventura and have Paul Sacco thrown to the dogs in New York.

Down in his car in the garage, Eddie Hand called Joey Russo at the hotel.

"Yes?"

"It's Eddie. I don't know if it's important, Joey, but Lansdale just called Jack LoBianco for a loan. Two hundred thousand dollars to be wired to Vito Ventura in New York."

"That should surprise Ventura," said Russo. "We've got Lansdale scrambling to save his hide. Thanks for letting me know."

"Sure," said Eddie. "We'll see you over there when Darlene leaves the office."

"Good," said Joey.

Jack LoBianco called Vito Ventura in New York.

"Jack, I was just about to leave for dinner," Ventura said. "What can I do for you?"

"I understand that my cousin owes you money, Vito; he asked me if I would take care of it. I would prefer not to get involved; I'm calling to ask you to give him a few days to take care of it himself."

"No problem, Jack," Ventura said. "Tell Max to take his time."

"Thank you, Vito."

"Glad to help, Jack," said Ventura.

Ventura placed the receiver down.

What the hell was that all about? Ventura wondered.

Ventura decided that he didn't really care, since he already had his cash back and Lansdale was history.

Jack LoBianco started to reach for his phone to call Max Lansdale with the news. But then he thought about his aunt and the visitor to Lansdale's mother's house earlier that day.

LoBianco decided not to make the call.

Twenty minutes later, LoBianco received a phone call from Joseph Vongoli, who told LoBianco when and where to bring Mrs. Lansdale the following day.

"I hope that you're sure about this," said LoBianco. "There's no backing out now."

"There's a story of a paratrooper who was preparing to jump from a plane with four of his comrades," said Vongoli. "He turned to one of the others and asked: 'What happens if my chute doesn't open?'"

"And?"

"As they jumped, the other man said: 'Then you'll be the first to reach the ground.'"

"I did a little brushing up on local history. Your father was well thought of by the old-timers in Cicero," said LoBianco. "There was high praise for Louie Clams."

"I don't recall much about Illinois," said Vongoli. "I was very young when he moved the family to California."

"They remembered you also, always there hanging on to your father's coattails. They called you Joe Clams."

"It was a long time ago."

"I was told you were the only child," said LoBianco.

"I had a sister, she was much younger," said Vongoli. "Carla was born some years after we left Cicero."

"I know about your sister," said LoBianco. "I heard the story from my aunt. She never believed that Randolph was involved in your sister's death, and it won't be easy to convince her that Max had anything to do with it."

"I understand," said Vongoli. "What mother would easily believe such things about her child?"

"On the other hand, my aunt still believes that it was Harrison Chandler who murdered her son Randolph, and that you were there that day."

"It's been the going theory for some time."

"I'll escort my aunt to your meeting place tomorrow, and then it will be out of my hands," said Jack LoBianco. "The ultimate course of action will be entirely up to her."

"I understand."

"Between you and me, I never cared much for my cousin Max," said LoBianco before ending the call.

Darlene and Eddie arrived at Joey Russo's hotel room at half past five, carrying the surveillance equipment up from Eddie's car. Russo had taken two adjoining rooms at the Allegro, 618 and 620. The rooms were connected by a doorway, with a door on each side that locked from inside each room.

When Joey let them in, the doors between the two rooms were opened.

"We'll set up the equipment in 620," Joey said. "I want to be able to hear a pin drop in here."

"No problem," said Eddie, "this equipment will pick up a whisper."

"How about video?" asked Joey.

"If I set up both cameras," said Eddie, "we should be able to cover this entire room. I brought a small monitor; we can use the television in the other room to monitor the second camera."

"Great, let's get it set up, Eddie," said Russo. "When do you need to leave for the airport, Darlene?"

"Jake's flight arrives in an hour; I should probably get going soon."

Eddie handed Darlene his car keys, then began to help Joey Russo carry equipment into the next room.

Darlene watched the two men work for a while and then she left for the airport.

Jack LoBianco stopped in to see his aunt, to let her know that he had heard from Joseph Vongoli and to make the arrangements for picking her up the following day.

"Jack?" Anna Lansdale asked. "Are you prepared to deal with this man, Vongoli, if necessary? We cannot allow him to continue making false accusations against the family."

"He will be dealt with, and swiftly," said LoBianco. "You have my word."

"Good."

"Can I ask you a question, Aunt Anna?"

"Yes?"

"Have you ever known Max to have a gambling problem?"

"Oh, no, not Max," said the woman. "Your uncle Simon liked to play the horses, and Randolph enjoyed card games, but not Max. Every summer we visit Simon's brother in Lake Tahoe, and Max won't even touch a slot machine."

"Even in recent years?"

"We were out there in August; Max spent all of his time on the lake. Why do you ask?"

"It's nothing," said LoBianco. "Aunt Anna, with all respect, what will we do if there is any truth to Vongoli's allegations?"

"Max is my son, Jack, my youngest child," said Anna Lansdale. "I could not bear to outlive him. I've outlived one of my children already and it is a terrible thing. I can't bring myself to believe Vongoli, as convinced as he seems to be. Remember, he lost a sister. Such a loss may cloud his judgment. If Max is guilty of all that Vongoli suggests, I will see that Max is punished severely. But I would not wish to see my son die while I am still alive."

"I understand," said LoBianco.

"Would you do an old woman a favor, Jack?"

LoBianco looked at his aunt. He could not remember ever seeing her appear so fragile.

"Of course," said LoBianco. "Anything."

"Would you take me to my church?" said Anna Lansdale. "I would like to pray."

Darlene tapped lightly on the door of room 618.

"It's open," called Joey Russo from inside.

Darlene and Jake entered the room. Eddie Hand could hear them and see them on the two monitors as he finished adjusting the equipment in the adjoining room.

"Jake, how are you feeling?" asked Joey as they came in.

"Thankful that my wait in the wings is nearly over," said Diamond. "Thankful that it's warmed up considerably since I was first out here two months ago."

"It's going to heat up a lot more tomorrow afternoon, Jake," said Russo. "Are you ready?"

"As ready as I'm ever going to be, Joey."

"Good. Let's get something to eat and go over it one more time," said Joey.

Eddie Hand walked in through the connecting doorway. "Done," he said.

Darlene looked around the room. "Are the microphones and cameras already set up in here?" she asked.

"Don't you see them?" asked Eddie.

Darlene looked around again, more closely. "No."

"Good," said Eddie Hand. "Did I hear someone mention food?"

Twenty-seven

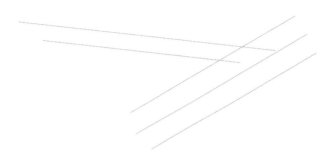

Max LANSDALE WAS AT THE BANK when the doors opened on Friday morning. He went directly to his safe-deposit box.

After removing twenty thousand to pay Tucker the day before, Lansdale had less than eighty thousand dollars in cash remaining in the safe box. Diamond would not be able to tell the difference and would never have the opportunity to count it. Lansdale put all of the money into a leather briefcase exactly like the one that he had carried from the casino in Connecticut.

As Lansdale walked to his office, he thought about the meeting with Jake Diamond. Diamond's future was very clear to Lansdale; the man had no future after today.

Lansdale was not terribly worried about the documents that Jake Diamond claimed to hold. He was confident that the documents could not convict him in a court of law. It was the dubious word of a former Chicago medical examiner who had, after all, admitted to falsifying official medical findings. It was Kearney's word against his own, and Max Lansdale felt he had enough friends and connections to avoid prosecution. It was all of the attention that the case would draw while it was being dragged through the legal system and the media that really worried Lansdale.

And above all, he dreaded the effect that an investigation and such allegations could have on his mother.

So Lansdale would do all he could to get his hands on the documents. But one way or the other, Jake Diamond was a dead man.

Lansdale walked into the office, ignored Darlene, and went back to his desk to wait for the call from Diamond.

Diamond woke to the sound of his hotel-room telephone. Jake had slept in room 618; Joey Russo had retired to room 620 next door, with the surveillance monitors.

"Good morning," Diamond said into the phone.

"Jake," said Joey, "I'm here in the hotel dining room. Come down and I'll buy you breakfast."

Twenty minutes later, Jake joined Joey at a table near a window looking out onto Randolph Street.

"Trouble sleeping, Jake?" Joey asked.

"The kneecap still keeps me awake from time to time," said Jake. "Why? Could you hear me moaning from the next room?"

"I turned on the television looking for Letterman, and there you were tossing and turning on the TV screen."

"Isn't that against the law?" asked Jake.

"Not since the Homeland Security Act. Are you going to be okay?"

"Absolutely."

A waitress brought a coffeepot, topped up Joey's cup, filled Jake's, and took their order.

"When you call Lansdale," Joey said, "tell him to meet you here at the hotel lounge. If he's half as smart as he thinks he is, he'll try to find out if you're staying here at the hotel. Otherwise, I'll suggest it myself."

"Okay."

"Set the meeting time for three fifteen, have him show you the money, and then take him straight up to your room."

"Got it."

"You have to get him to talk about his father and his brother. Whatever it takes, short of any blatant threat or coercion," said Joey. "Remember what we talked about last night. Appeal to his vanity, let Lansdale know how gutless you believe he is and get him bragging about how he handled his family problems on his own without hired help."

"Don't worry, Joey," said Jake. "I know how to push Lansdale's buttons."

"And you'll have to get him to talk before he loses patience and decides that it's time to call me in," said Joey. "I'd hate to have to whack you to protect my cover."

"I'll keep that in mind," said Jake. "And then you'll tell me why we don't just turn him over to the police?"

"You'll know this afternoon, Jake," promised Russo as the waitress delivered their food.

An hour later, Jake phoned Lansdale's office.

Darlene took the call and sent it back to Lansdale's desk.

"Jake, how was your trip?"

"Meet me at the cocktail lounge of the Allegro Hotel at three fifteen. Don't forget the cash," Jake said, and hung up.

Lansdale dialed the number of the man known as Tucker. The answering machine picked up and Lansdale simply stated his name. Then he called the Allegro Hotel and learned that Jake Diamond was checked into room 618.

Down in the parking garage, Eddie Hand phoned Joey Russo at the hotel. "Lansdale knows that Jake is staying there at the Allegro," said Eddie. "He'll be expecting a call from Tucker at the bagel shop in fifty minutes."

Lansdale picked up the receiver in the phone booth on the first ring and spoke. "Diamond wants a meet at three fifteen at the bar in the Allegro Hotel. He's checked into room 618."

"Stay near the phone. I'll call back in ten minutes."

Lansdale replaced the receiver, went over to the counter, and bought a coffee, then stood back near the phone booth sipping it; when the phone rang, he grabbed it.

"Yes?"

"I was able to reserve the adjoining room, 620. It's connected to Diamond's room. He'll probably take you up there to make the exchange. As soon as you are done with him, unlock the connecting door and call me in. Then take what you need and get out; I'll handle the rest. And don't forget to leave my cash."

Before Lansdale could comment on the plan, the line went dead.

"All set, Jake," Joey Russo said, hanging up on Max Lansdale. "Quarter past three, down in the lounge."

"I can hardly wait," said Diamond.

The hotel lounge was nearly empty when Lansdale came in, carrying the briefcase. He spotted Diamond at a table against the wall. He walked over, sat opposite Diamond, and placed the briefcase on the table between them.

"Open it," Jake said.

Lansdale undid the latches, opened the case, and turned it to face Diamond. The case was filled with cash.

"Can I buy you a drink, Jake?" Lansdale asked.

"Just follow me," Jake said, rising from his seat and moving out to the hotel lobby.

Lansdale silently followed Jake onto an elevator, up to the sixth floor, down the hall, and into room 618. He placed the briefcase on the bed.

"Let's have the documents, Diamond," he said. "I'm already tired of looking at you."

"You'll have to suffer a while longer, Max," Jake said. "There are a few things I need cleared up before we're done here."

"Oh?"

"Did Ralph Battle set the bomb in my place?"

"No, but I really couldn't tell you who did. Ralph never killed anyone, though he came very close to killing me," said Lansdale. "In any event, you won't have to deal with Ralph Battle again. Ever."

"Battle told me that he killed your father and your brother," Jake said. "Ralph swore that you begged him to do what you didn't have the stomach to do yourself."

"If Battle said that, he lied to you, Diamond. God knows why and I really couldn't care less," said Lansdale. "What's the point? Give me the documents, take your money, and let's get this over with."

"The point is that you are a worm, Lansdale. A spineless maggot who couldn't even work up the nerve to silence an old man without help," said Jake. "Did you have the guts to watch at least, or did you turn away like a coward when your paid assassin smothered your own father until the old man gave up the fight?"

"The old man gave it up more than twenty years before that

night. My father had accumulated wealth and power that was considerable in its time, through his connections with corrupt businessmen and politicians. And that should have been his gift to his sons. But when my mother's uncle Sam was shot to death, my father chickened out. He always claimed that he did it for us, to protect us. All he did was see to it that we inherited a dime-a-dozen law firm. By the time my father semiretired and left us to do all the grunt work, we may as well have changed our telephone number to 1-800-WHIPLASH.

"My father held the pursestrings to all of the money that remained after putting us both through law school, and after his uncontrollable gambling, his moronic financial investments, his extravagant spending, and the large payoff required to get free of his former colleagues. My father left us with little to guarantee our future security. Until the day he died, he paid us as if it were our weekly allowance.

"When I was approached with the proposition from New York, to move cash from casinos, I saw it as a way out of the hell that our father had left us in. Something for us. I brought the proposal to my brother, and Randolph was as spineless as the old man had become. I knew I couldn't bring it to my father without Randolph's support. I tried to come up with a way to handle it without their knowledge. I made binding promises and commitments in order to work it out. What I didn't count on was my brother running to my father like a fucking eight-year-old tattletale.

"My mother was out of town on the day that my father called me, wanting to speak. I couldn't get there until late. I found him already in his bed. He told me that my brother had blown the whistle on me. He warned me that if I even fantasized about doing business with the New York people, he would know about it and deal harshly. He spoke to me as if I were a fucking child, threatened to have me watched, swore that he would disown me. I assured him I wouldn't follow up. I bent over to kiss him good night and suddenly I was pressing a pillow over his face and I held it there until he couldn't make threats anymore. I hadn't planned it. I can't remember grabbing the pillow. I never felt remorse. My father was a tyrant and I never felt like a man until he was dead and buried. As I walked out of the house that night, I was already working out a plan to make sure that my fucking informant brother would never bring it back on me."

"So you hired Harrison Chandler to throw suspicion on your brother, and you ultimately put a bullet in Randolph's head," Jake said. "Jesus, Max, don't you think you've read a little too much Shakespeare?"

"Hand over the documents, Diamond," Max Lansdale said, "and perhaps you will live to tell the tragic tale to your grandchildren."

"What are you going to do, kill me with a pillow?"

"I had something more colorful in mind," Lansdale said as he went over to the connecting doorway.

He unlocked the door, opened it, and called through to the adjoining room.

"Come on in," he said.

The door from the other room swung open and Lansdale looked up to find his mother standing in the doorway, and Jack LoBianco just behind her.

Lansdale turned white. He was about to say something, but the hard look in his mother's eyes rendered him speechless.

"Jack," Anna Lansdale said to her nephew.

"Yes?"

"Take your cousin down to the lobby. I will join you there," she said. "I need a few moments to speak with Mr. Vongoli."

With that, Anna Lansdale moved back into the adjoining room.

Max Lansdale had not said a word.

"Let's go, Max," said LoBianco.

LoBianco took Lansdale by the elbow and began leading him to the door.

"You might want to take that briefcase," Jake Diamond said.

"What's in it?" asked LoBianco.

"A lot of cash."

"Why mention it?"

"I don't want to hear about it again later," Jake said. "Did I hear your aunt mention the name Vongoli?"

"Yes, Joseph Vongoli. Joe Clams," said Jack LoBianco, taking the briefcase. "Do you know him?"

"I know of him," Jake said.

If Diamond and Lansdale ever had something in common, it was the look of astonishment on both their faces.

LoBianco led Lansdale out of the hotel room.

Jake called Eddie Hand.

"All done there?" asked Eddie.

"I'm not quite sure, but you may as well head down and start collecting the equipment."

"We're on our way," said Eddie.

Jake Diamond sat down on the bed and waited.

A few minutes later, Anna Lansdale returned to the room. Jake rose.

"Mr. Diamond," she said. "I wanted to tell you that I'm sorry about the death of your friend."

"So am I," Jake said. "Thank you for saying so. May I escort you down to the lobby?"

"I can manage," the woman said, moving to the door. "Mr. Vongoli would like to speak with you now."

Anna Lansdale left the hotel room.

Jake Diamond walked through the connecting doorway to meet Joe Clams.

Twenty-eight

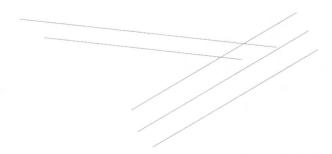

W<small>HEN</small> <small>I</small> <small>CAME</small> <small>THROUGH</small> <small>THE</small> <small>DOORWAY</small> into 620, I found Joey Russo sitting in one of the two chairs at the small table in the corner of the hotel room. Joey was as well dressed as I had ever seen him. On the table in front of him were a newly opened bottle of George Dickel and two glasses. He began to pour and invited me to take the other seat.

"Why keep it from me?" I asked as I sat.

"It has been a secret for nearly fifty years, Jake. Only my family has known who we are, and Sonny of course. Please don't take it personally. I took a big risk with Anna Lansdale and her nephew, and I didn't want to put any of you in jeopardy if it didn't work out. Anna Lansdale was a Giancana. She was the only person who could take the Vongoli name permanently off the Giancana vendetta list," said Joey. "By the way, you did a terrific job in there."

"Thank you," I said.

"I didn't know about your trouble with Lansdale until after the explosion. I had no idea that you were trying to find Harry Chandler and Joe Clams," Joey said, "or I would have returned early to help you out. By the time I did get back, you didn't seem very interested in Joseph Vongoli any longer. I felt that it would be best to keep it that way until this was over. Particularly after I learned that it was Max Lansdale who had my sister Carla killed."

"And now?" I asked.

"Now, Anna Lansdale and LoBianco have assured me that we can reclaim our family name without repercussions."

"What will happen to Max Lansdale?"

"As long as his mother is alive, his life will be a living nightmare," said Joey. "When she passes, I think Jack LoBianco will quickly send Max Lansdale to join his brother and his parents."

"Well, here's to the Vongoli family," I said, raising my glass. "Though it will be difficult getting accustomed to the new name."

"I'm sure it will be trickier for my children—Russo is the only name they've ever used. But they have hoped for this day all their lives, for me and for the memory of their grandfather. I think you'll all manage to adjust."

"Could I call you Joe Clams?" I asked.

"Do you consider me a close friend, Jake?"

"Yes, I do."

"Then you can call me *Joey* Clams if it suits you."

We both took a long drink. We heard the door open in the next room.

"Anyone here?" Darlene called.

"In here," called Joey Clams. "Bring a couple of glasses in with you."

Darlene and Eddie came through the connecting door, holding empty glasses.

Joey Vongoli poured George Dickel all around.

"Drink up," said Joey, "and let's get this equipment collected and out of here."

"And then we can go home?" asked Darlene.

"Yes," said Joey. "Then we can go home."

For the next four weeks I tried to keep busy and out of trouble.

I worked at settling into the new house. It began feeling more like home as I proceeded to accumulate the piles and clutter that I was accustomed to. My mother helped with family photographs, which I randomly spread throughout the rooms.

I was able to keep both the Toyota and the Chevrolet Impala convertible in the long driveway, freeing up Joey's valuable garage space. It was a lot more convenient, but I found myself missing the casual visits with Joey and Sonny that came with picking up the Chevy.

To help with the nesting process I invited Tom Romano and Ira Fennessy to the house for both Thursday-night card games in April, forgoing the normal rotation.

The house still felt too big to me.

Empty.

Darlene visited often, usually bringing Tug McGraw along. Darlene's boundless energy and the dog's constant exploration did a lot to fill the emptiness.

I found myself visiting my mother more often, and took Darlene and McGraw over to Pleasant Hill for Easter dinner with Mom and Aunt Rosalie.

At the office, we tried to keep Diamond Investigation active. We managed to satisfy four clients and take care of the monthly bills.

I was sleeping much better, the knee not keeping me awake as often. I took fifteen minutes every morning to work the leg as the physical therapist had ordered.

I had tried many times to visit Sally's grave but always lost courage. I decided I would go to her burial site when I was at the cemetery for the dedication of the new headstones that Joey had placed for his family.

We stood gathered on a hill at the Mount Tamalpais Cemetery in San Rafael, overlooking the Pacific.

The morning sky on the first Sunday in May was cloudless. Mount Tam loomed nearby; the Sausalito Marina and the Golden Gate were clearly visible to the south.

The three new headstones sat side by side. The names of Louis Vongoli, Maria Rosario Vongoli, and Carla Vongoli were proudly displayed.

Joey stood with his arm around Angela, their three children at their side. Sonny stood holding his young daughter, Louie Clams's great-granddaughter.

Other family and friends stood by silently.

A priest from Joey's parish in the city had made the twenty-mile trip to San Rafael to read from the Bible.

When the dedication was complete, I walked over to Joey.

"Are you coming over to the house, Jake?" he asked.

"I'll see how I feel. I'm going to walk down the hill to visit Sally's grave."

"Need company?"

"No, thanks."

"Thank you for being here today," Joey said.

"Where else would I be, Joey?" I said. "I'll try to make it over to your place later."

"Please do, there's a lot of food."

I walked down the hill and found the marker.

It was impossible to imagine that someone who had been so full of life was resting there.

I put out my empty hand, the hand that Sally would often hold tightly to keep me safe from myself. I felt a chill run up my arm. My fingers had begun to curl into a fist, and then I felt another hand slip into mine.

"Hey, pal," Darlene said. "Are you all right?"

I turned to face Darlene and felt the warmth of her palm. I gently tightened my grip.

"I think I will be, Darlene. Hang in there with me."

"I'm not going anywhere, Jake," she said. "Well, maybe to Joey's. Are you up for it?"

"Sure," I said. "I heard there's a lot of food."

We turned and walked away, hand in hand.